I0671823

A Fort in the Storm

By Mike Rossetti

This is a work of fiction. All of the characters, organizations and events portrayed in this novel are products of the author's imagination or are used fictitiously.

A Fort in the Storm Copyright © 2017 by Mike Rossetti
Cover artwork by Robert Campbell, Campbell Creative Group

All Rights Reserved

This book or any portion thereof may not be reproduced or used in any manner whatsoever without the express written permission of the author/publisher, except for the use of brief quotations in a book review.

For more information, email rossettimike1@gmail.com or visit www.mikerossettibooks.com.

ISBN: 978-0-692-84424-3v

To my wife, Pam, for all the support through the years. And to all the incredible staff and volunteers at Advocates for Children who do so much to help so many children.

Chapter One

Moonlight peeked through the clouds for only the briefest moment as Adam Durkin made his way down the tree-shrouded trail he navigated so many times in the past few years. Dirt soiled his tanned, tear-stained face, his dark hair matted against his forehead from sweat and the heavy, humid air that typically preceded a July thunderstorm in central Indiana.

While he had been on this trail countless times before, it never was like this – at night, in his pajamas and his bare feet, running from the fear steadily building in his mind for the past year. He was quickly finding it different in the dark. The steps weren't so sure, the holes and depressions that dotted the trail much deeper than he remembered, and he already fell twice and cut his right foot on either a branch or a sharp stone. He wasn't sure which, but he could feel the warm, sticky sensation of blood between his toes.

Still he made his way on, moving as quickly as he could without losing his sense of direction, while at the same time trying to keep track of whether anyone was following him. From his experience on the trail, he knew in relatively short time he'd come to the stream that ran through the woods that bordered the back of his family's property. From there, he could make his way north along the stream until he came to State Road 46, where just a few miles west the small neighboring town of Cullison had a Country Mart convenience store from which he could call for help.

Adam rounded the turn in the path where, to his left, he spent most of his time during the summer. There he built his fort, his haven where he could get away on those days where dad got a little too deep into the bottles of whiskey that became all too much a part of his daily life. On this night, though, Adam knew he couldn't stop here. It was too close, and the consequences of being found could be too great. The creek wasn't much further ahead when he heard the bellowing voice pierce the relative quiet of the woods.

"Adam, get your ass back here!" Close, it sounded. Too close, making Adam intensify what was already a relatively unsafe pace. "I tolds you I didn't mean it. I tolds you I was sorry."

The last few sentences passed through Adam's consciousness without a thought, for they were words he heard too many times recently, often enough they were becoming hollow and meaningless. He did, however, notice the way his father slurred the word "told." The more jumbled the words, the further dad was into the bottle, which – in Adam's mind – meant greater danger. This was the first time dad had hit him. Sure, he was spanked a few times growing up, but this was a slap across the face, and the emotional hurt it caused ran much deeper than any physical pain possibly could.

Adam almost face-planted when he hit the creek a moment later, but he gained his balance just in time to turn to his left and work his way quickly along the creek bed. The trail he took from his house continued past the creek, and Adam hoped his father would continue his search in that direction and not along the water line upon which he now moved even more quietly. If that happened, Adam would take to the thick woods that bordered the stream and look for a place to hide.

Behind him, it couldn't have been more than 50 yards or so, he heard a splash followed by, "Goddammit!" His father had made the creek. Instinctively, Adam paused and listened, as the decision his dad was about to make would determine the course he would take next. Not more than five seconds passed, and Adam could hear footsteps, not in the water or the muddy soil that bordered the creek, but on a hard surface and moving away from him over his right shoulder. Dad had stayed on the path.

Taking a sigh of relief, but realizing he was not yet out of the woods – figuratively or literally – Adam continued along the creek bed at a quicker pace. Less concerned now about making noise as he was about gaining distance before his father realized the trail had run cold, Adam paid no mind to the fact his feet ached and the cut he sustained minutes ago, was now throbbing.

Some rustling in the bushes ahead startled him briefly before he realized it was just a raccoon foraging, and just a few minutes later, 10-year-old Adam Durkin left the woods and found the busy two-lane road he sought. Turning west, he kept up his pace as he headed toward Cullison.

Chapter Two

It was 5:30 on a Tuesday afternoon as Micah Sanders fidgeted in his seat in the gallery of Courtroom B of the Lands County Courthouse. He couldn't stand to wear a tie, much less the dark blue suit he currently donned, but the occasion seemed to call for it based upon the role he was about to assume. He glanced nervously at the growing sweat stains under his arms as the judge entered from behind the bench. Micah jumped out of his seat along with his classmates, obviously following the "all rise" protocol from popular courtroom television shows and movies.

Judge Cynthia Stone smiled at the small group in front of her and motioned with her hand to take their seats.

"While I appreciate the show of respect," she said, "I stand here in awe of the service each of you has chosen to perform."

As the group of six women and two men, including Micah, took their seats, Judge Stone stood in front of the bench with a smile on her face.

"Tonight, we gather to induct eight new CASAs – Court Appointed Special Advocates, if you will – into one of, if not *the* most important volunteer roles I know of. Each of you has gone through more than 30 hours of training and all of you have done so on your own time with the full understanding of the responsibilities of which you are undertaking.

"As CASAs, you will stand up for the rights of – and more importantly – what is in the best interests of our area's most vulnerable citizens. You will step into these cases at the

Court's behest, you will work directly with the children and parents involved, as well as the Department of Child Services, and you will gain an understanding of each case that will allow you to be an impartial party able to make a recommendation to the Court. You should know the Court pays these recommendations from CASAs the utmost respect and, in many cases, the recommendation becomes the final decision."

Judge Stone paused momentarily as she gathered some notes from the bench behind her, and Micah surveyed his seven fellow volunteers. Each understood everything the judge was saying, as their trainer had prepared them well through their ten three-hour sessions over the previous six weeks. They all knew their new volunteer roles would ask them to serve as advocates to children who were the victims of abuse and neglect, to work through the politics and bureaucracy that sometimes get in the way of the best outcomes, and to do everything within their power to make sure each child assigned to them found a safe and loving permanent home as quickly as possible. Since there was a significant waiting list in all three of the counties their agency represented, each of them knew they would be assigned a case within days – a week at most – of the swearing-in ceremony currently taking place.

The judge turned back to the group and said, "Do each of you understand the importance of the role you are undertaking?" The new Advocates nodded in unison. "In that case, would Karen Anderson join me and the officers from Advocates for Children at the front of the room?"

As Karen Anderson made her way to the front and raised her right hand to swear she would uphold the policies she learned in training and would always work to serve the best interest of each child she would represent, Micah sighed contentedly, knowing he was undertaking a difficult assignment, but one that would make a real difference. When it came his turn – sixth of the eight volunteers sworn in during the ceremony – any doubt he had made the right choice had left him, and he was truly excited for what was to come next.

Chapter Three

The morning after the swearing in ceremony, Micah sat in his newspaper office at 8:15, a steaming cup of strong, black coffee gripped in his right hand as he flipped through the paper he and his editorial team produced every day. His daily routine always started early which, for the editor-in-chief at a daily newspaper, meant a long day. By the time the day's content was complete and stories were edited and ready for layout on the page, it wasn't unusual for Micah to be in the office until six or seven at night. He assembled a strong copy desk team that had his full confidence in page layout and delivery to the press crew, but up until that point each day, Micah was, admittedly, a bit of a micro-manager.

After the ceremony the evening before, Micah made his way down First Street from the courthouse to his favorite Italian restaurant, where he met a few of his fellow new CASAs for a light dinner. They split a couple bottles of wine to complement their plates of pasta and finished off the evening with a limoncello. Not one to drink much, especially during the week, Micah felt just a bit sluggish this morning as he read through the day's news.

As was typical in his small town of Williams, Indiana, not much happened the day before, at least not much that would qualify as "news" in larger cities. This was one of the reasons Micah chose this job, and the small, family-owned media company that currently employed him, over potential offers in bigger cities with larger paychecks. As someone with more than 20 years in the newspaper industry, including stints in New York, Chicago and Mobile, the editor job in Williams was a big change in his career trajectory, but one he and his wife felt was needed at the time.

The offer came about as the result of a friendship that began at a newspaper conference in Chicago seven years before Micah would ever see the small Indiana town for the first time. At the time, Micah was the junior city desk editor for the Chicago Tribune when he was selected by his superiors to attend the Inland Press Association's annual editorial conference. It was quite an honor, as most attendees were senior editors, publishers and owners of some of the best newspapers on the East Coast, the Midwest and in the South.

Thirty-two at that time, Micah's career remained on an upward trend over his 10 years in the industry, going from intern to beat reporter to senior reporter in New York prior to making the move to Chicago in 2001. The experiences he gained during that time turned him from an inward, quiet young man to the confident, outgoing person that walked into the Grand Ballroom at the Intercontinental Hotel on Michigan Avenue on the sultry August day where he first met John Hartfield.

The first time walking into a room at a national conference can be a bit intimidating. Hundreds, if not a thousand, men and women from all over the country, many who participate in these kinds of events multiple times per year, gather to listen to industry experts talk about trends, success stories, upcoming challenges, and innovations in a business in existence in the United States since Ben Franklin's time.

For Micah, the experience was exhilarating. He smiled as he took in the buzz throughout the room and strode directly up the center aisle to take an open seat toward the front. Next to him sat a man who stood out from many of the others in that he was not wearing a suit but a pair of khaki pants, white golf shirt and a blue sport coat. As he introduced himself, Micah estimated him to be in his late forties.

John Hartfield was different from most of the "higher-ups" Micah met in his time in the newspaper business. In New York and Chicago, ownership consisted of shareholders and top executive teams that spent less time in the office than they did jetting around to meetings, business trips, and frequent exotic vacations. Over the course of the day during breaks between sessions, Micah learned Hartfield was in his office in Williams most days overseeing a small group of newspapers in south central Indiana. To Micah, he came off as very unassuming, down-to-earth and easy to talk to. Still, as he described the towns his newspapers served, Micah couldn't help but think there couldn't be much news to cover, and it seemed a far cry from the virtual smorgasbord of stories he had to choose from in Chicago.

During the three-day conference, the two had dinner together during several of the optional group excursions and talked about the newspaper business over drinks at the bar. Micah learned a lot in the short time he was at the conference, and when it ended, he and Hartfield agreed to keep in touch.

Over the next few years, Hartfield and Micah exchanged emails and phone calls occasionally and saw each other most years at the annual Inland Press conference at which they met. The longer they knew each other, the less they talked about work, focusing more on family, personal lives and goals. As the friendship developed, Micah looked at Hartfield as a mentor as well.

In late 2005 on a Friday afternoon, Micah received a call in his office from Hartfield. He started the conversation asking about Micah's family and their plans for the holidays, and then asked Micah if he had a few minutes to talk. When he said he did, Hartfield told Micah to close his office door and proceeded to offer him a job as editor of one of his newspapers in Pearson, Indiana. Micah was a bit floored by the offer at the time. While the idea of heading up his own team was extremely appealing, he really enjoyed what he was doing in Chicago and his wife Kayla absolutely loved their suburb community of Northbrook. When he talked to Kayla that evening, the two agreed the timing just wasn't right, and Micah told Hartfield as much when he called him back Monday morning. To Hartfield's credit, he was disappointed but promised to keep in touch should anything else come open down the road.

Three months later, in March of 2006, Micah received another offer and, on this one, neither he nor Kayla could find a reason to pass it up. This one had come through a search firm that found Micah and wanted to gauge his interest on an opening in the Southeastern United States for a large newspaper company looking for an associate editor, basically second in command on the editorial side. The headhunter wouldn't tell Micah where the position was, or give any other details, until Micah expressed formal interest through submission of a resume. At the time, Micah was second-guessing his decision to pass up the offer in Indiana, and was beginning to have the nagging feeling he had hit his ceiling in Chicago. So, he sent on the resume and learned the position was in Mobile, Alabama for the Courier newspaper. The paper was a holding of Stills Publications, a group that owned newspapers throughout Alabama, Mississippi, Michigan, New Jersey and several other states.

One day after Micah sent the resume to the email address the search firm provided, he received a call from the editor of the Courier, and the two had a two-hour phone conversation that ended with an offer to fly Micah and Kayla from Chicago to Mobile for a formal interview the following week.

After the three-day visit to Mobile, which included the interviews, dinner with the editor and his wife, as well as the publisher and her husband, Micah was told the visit went extremely well and to expect an offer early the following week. During the time there, he and Kayla took the opportunity to visit the city of Mobile as well as the surrounding areas, just to see if it was somewhere they could be happy. When the offer came the following Monday, and amounted to 40 percent more than Micah made in Chicago, the decision was easy and the couple was bound for Alabama.

The first person Micah called after giving his two-week notice was Hartfield. Micah dialed and hung up twice before allowing the call to go through, as he anticipated Hartfield might be upset with him for accepting another job months after he hadn't been willing to listen to what his friend offered. However, when Micah told Hartfield the news, John couldn't have been happier for him, saying Stills was a great company and that he was going to gain valuable experience working in a different city and a vastly different region of the country.

In 2008, as the country settled into a crippling recession, newspapers – especially those in larger cities – began to feel the pinch from all sides. As younger audiences started gathering news and information from online sources, readership and subscriptions took a nosedive. As local companies contracted and stopped hiring, employment advertising – long a staple of newspaper classifieds – dropped by 20 to 30 percent. And as people cut back their spending and shopping habits, the large department, electronics and furniture stores that ran weekly inserts in the Sunday newspaper began to cut back on advertising like never seen before in the industry. For newspapers that hadn't prepared for this day, which consisted of most of them, the decline in revenue and profit came like a punch to the gut. Such was the case in Mobile, where Stills hadn't put much stock into the trending digital services movement, and layoffs, furloughs and other cost-cutting measures began rapidly.

At first the cuts left Micah relatively safe, although his team lost a photographer and a copy editor right away. As conditions worsened, though, everyone in the company took a five percent pay cut in exchange for furlough time and, in late 2009 the company announced more cuts coming after the holidays.

On a grey Friday afternoon in February – snow flurries were falling, something that hadn't happened in 10 years in lower Alabama – Micah sat in the publisher's office and learned his position would be cut effective March 1. Based on his short service with the company, he would be offered a month's severance pay. When Micah went home that day and shared the news with Kayla, she broke down and cried. The only other time he saw that was the day her father died three years previous.

The next morning, while Micah and Kayla sipped coffee in front of the fireplace in the beautiful country club community home they bought less than two years ago and could no longer afford, the phone rang. It was John Hartfield. Micah practically fell out of his chair when he told him there was another job he wanted to discuss.

Chapter Four

When Adam Durkin left the woods and turned west on State Road 46, the moon was completely obscured by the clouds that had now turned a dark black. Thunder cracked in the distance and the first few big drops of the impending storm actually felt good as they rinsed Adam's grimy face. The steady traffic that travels the road during daytime hours dwindled considerably in those moments before midnight, and for the first five minutes of his walk along the road, not a single car passed in either direction.

Finally, headlights broke the darkness before him and Adam inched closer to the road, being careful the driver could see him, but also not wanting to venture too close just in case he didn't. The regular headlamps of the car intensified to the high beams, and Adam knew he was spotted. The car, moving too fast to stop ahead of him, slowed down and pulled to the shoulder about 100 feet past the position Adam took alongside the road. As he moved toward the car and the person that stopped to help him, Adam saw the driver side door open and a man exit the vehicle, turn on a flashlight and begin moving toward him. Behind the glow of the flashlight, Adam couldn't see more than a shadow, but he kept moving toward the car and said, "Can you help me?"

The man hadn't yet said a word but continued moving toward him, the flashlight beam shining brightly in his eyes. No more than 30 feet away now, then 20, and then 10 and the beam grew brighter.

"Can you lower the light so I can see?" Adam asked, the uneasiness in his voice now completely apparent. The light, now just six feet away, turned from Adam's face to that of his rescuer.

"Uncle Jack?" The words barely made it out of his mouth before he saw the beam of the flashlight arc through the air toward his head, and then his world went black.

****

When Adam came out of the deep slumber, his head aching horribly on the left side and the metallic taste of blood still fresh in his mouth, it took him a moment to understand where he was. As he tried to lift his right hand to wipe his mouth and clear his eyes, he realized he was strapped to a wooden kitchen chair, each arm bound by a thick leather belt. As the fog cleared and he looked around, he realized he was in a cabin, and he remembered uttering his uncle's name right before he hit him in the head with the flashlight. What time it was, or how long he had been there, Adam had no idea. He smelled something else in the room, and when he looked down at his lap, he saw he wet his pants. Up until this point, he held it together, but now he started to cry.

After just a few seconds of tears, Adam heard heavy footsteps just behind him and, before he could turn his head, felt a hard slap greet the part of his face still smarting from the blow he took alongside the road.

"Quit your crying, you big pussy," Uncle Jack said from behind him. As Adam tried to pull it together to deter any further abuse, his uncle moved around to the front of him and lowered his face directly in front of Adam's.

"Look at you, all dirty, wet, and you even pissed your pants like a little baby! Your momma – my sister - would be so ashamed at you right now, if she wasn't buried in the ground a few miles from here."

At the mention of his mother, Adam found some resolve and immediately cut off any more tears or whimpering. Ever since his mom died of cancer two years earlier, Adam's life was a mess. In school, he went from a solid B student to failing most of his classes. Baseball, which he at one point loved more than anything, became unimportant to him, so much so that he told his dad the previous spring he wasn't going to play anymore. By that time, dad didn't care much, as most of his free time was spent sitting in the small living room of their cabin drinking Jim Beam. Adam tasted the stuff once to see what the big deal was, but he found it disgusting and, when he saw what it did to his dad, swore he'd never touch it again.

Uncle Jack was another thing altogether, though. He met him only a handful of times before, and most of those times were in the couple of years after his mom passed away. While she was alive, his mother had little use for her brother, calling him a loser or a bum several times when she thought Adam couldn't hear her. From what Adam knew of him, Jack had been horrible to mom when they were kids, and that continued into their adulthood. He overheard his mother several times saying she didn't want Jack in their lives at all, especially Adam's.

"Your daddy called me when you went missing," Uncle Jack said. "Told me you ran out the back door while he was watching TV, but I think he did something to you, didn't he?"

Adam shook his head, but Uncle Jack went on. "Did he hit you, like I did?" Adam paused, but again shook his head. "Did he touch you, maybe here?" Uncle Jack moved his hand toward the wet spot on the front of Adam's pajamas, pulling it back just before making contact.

"Or was he just busy being the big, stupid, shitty drunk he's become since my bitch of a sister went and got herself sick and died?"

Adam could hold it back no longer, and the tears once again started flowing. Uncle Jack raised his hand as if he was going to strike again, and Adam closed his eyes and braced for what was to come. When nothing happened for a moment or two, he opened them and saw his uncle left the room. Surveying the room around him, he saw just a dusty old sofa, a small television and an end table with a small clock on it that read 3:30. Since it was dark outside, Adam knew it was still the middle of the night and wondered if his father was still out looking for him. Suddenly, the thought of seeing his dad instead of his uncle was a big improvement.

The rest of the house was quiet now and Adam wondered where his uncle had gone. The clock on the end table moved from 3:30 to just past four when Adam gave in to the growing heaviness of his eyes and he dozed off, still strapped to the kitchen chair. When he awoke, it was just past seven and the morning glow of the rising sun peeked through the windows into the cabin. From the door off the living room, Adam heard his uncle snoring and figured he probably passed out after he grew bored torturing his nephew. For a moment, Adam thought about calling out his name and asking him to release him from his bonds, but he figured that would only bring more punches or slaps. He decided to stay quiet and found himself dozing again until he awoke to the straps on his arms being released. Glancing upward, he saw his uncle hovering over him, releasing the second of the two straps that held him. The clock on the end table read 7:30.

"You're going to go into the bathroom and clean yourself up, at least wash your face and get the blood off ya," Uncle Jack said. "Then I'm going to take you back to your loser dad, tell him I found you early this morning after looking all night. You're not going to say a word about anything that happened here, right?"

Adam understood exactly what his uncle meant, and he nodded affirmatively.

"If you do say anything, I won't just kill you. I'll start with your daddy and make you watch. Then I'll do things to you you would never forget, if I wasn't going to kill you too when I'm finished."

At this point, Adam was ready to do anything he needed to get out of there, so he nodded again and his uncle moved out of his way so he could go into the bathroom. The sink was rimmed with mold and the toilet looked like it was never cleaned, but Adam had to pee so badly he barely noticed. When he finished, he ran the water until it warmed up, took a dirty bar of soap from next to the sink between his hands and began washing the dirt and blood from his face. When he figured he was presentable enough, he left the bathroom and found his uncle waiting by the front door with his car keys in hand.

"Sit in the back so I don't have to look at you," was all Uncle Jack said as they exited the house, got in the car and drove the few miles back to Adam's house. When they got there, Uncle Jack stopped the car just long enough for

Adam to get out of the back seat and run into the house. When he looked back from inside his front door, his uncle's car was already gone.

The inside of the house was quiet, except for the faint sound of snoring coming from behind his dad's closed door. On the kitchen table, a half-eaten microwave burrito sat on a paper plate and in the kitchen sink, as was the nightly custom, an empty bottle of Beam was turned on its side. Dad always made sure every drop was gone before he would dispose of the bottle. As he routinely did, Adam took the bottle from the sink, cleaned up the kitchen table and took the trash out to the can they kept in the garage until the weekly pick-up. After he wiped down the sink, the kitchen counters and the table, Adam went into the bathroom and started the shower. As he let the water cascade over his exhausted and soiled body, he wondered if his father, upon waking, would even know he was gone through the night. He doubted it.

Chapter Five

Emma Abigail Sanders was born May 4, 2011 at Williams Regional Hospital. The winter was an extremely cold one, and Kayla's first pregnancy had been a difficult one. At 38, she was by no means too old to have a baby, but she was on the higher end of the spectrum and, seeing how it was her first, there were a couple instances where the Sanders and their doctors worried whether she could carry to term. Still she made it, and at 6 pounds, 12 ounces, Emma was absolutely perfect.

At the time, Micah was at The Sentinel a little more than a year and was starting to become engrained into the community. He joined the board of directors for several non-profit agencies and was intensely involved with the Williams Chamber of Commerce. Kayla spent her days early in the pregnancy volunteering at a local school as an aide, spending time reading to kindergartners and helping them with their school work. As the pregnancy moved into the third trimester, she found herself spending more time at home, not wanting to take the chance of being out on the roads in the cold and ice of late February and early March. Still she made a couple of friends through the volunteer effort.

After just a year in Williams, Micah and Kayla considered themselves content. Emma's arrival just made everything complete. Like all new parents, it took a little while to adjust to the unpredictable schedule of having a newborn in the house. Late-night wake up calls for feedings, diaper changes or fits of crying became the norm, and Micah did his best to keep up his routine at work, but more and more he found himself getting in a little later and having to leave earlier for various reasons. Other than Kayla, work was always Micah's focus, and the entrance of a new dependent in his life brought about a change he hadn't completely expected. Suddenly he realized he needed to depend upon his employees at work more than ever, to trust them more and let them make their mistakes without him catching them first. These mistakes happened – plenty of times – and each time Micah learned to move on just a little bit faster and to let them affect him just a little bit less.

Kayla saw a big change at home as well. Micah became much more attentive, not just to Emma, but to her as well. She always accepted his drive and his passion for his work and understood it was a big part of what made him the man with whom she had fallen in love. But with Emma's arrival, Kayla saw someone who suddenly valued sitting at the breakfast table just a little while longer, or getting home just a little earlier for some extra time on the carpet playing with her and Emma.

When Emma crawled for the first time, Micah was there, and when she took her first steps in the middle of the afternoon one day, Micah was home in minutes. On the evening of Emma's first birthday party, with wrapping paper and gifts still strewn about the living room floor and the birthday cake – torn apart by Emma's little hands – still on the kitchen table, Micah and Kayla poured glasses of wine after putting Emma to bed.

"What do you think of having another baby?" Micah asked as they cuddled into the couch. It was something he was thinking about for a couple of months, imagining how great it would be for Emma to have a sibling close in age with whom she could grow to be best friends. By the same token, he knew how difficult the pregnancy had been for Kayla, which is why he held off on bringing up the subject previously.

Kayla hesitated for a moment, her gaze fastened to the TV program muted before them. From the side, Micah thought he saw tears building in her eyes. Micah pulled her a little bit closer and kissed her cheek. Neither of them spoke another word for the next 10 minutes, but instead sipped their wine and stared silently at the gifts and paper on the floor.

"I love you sweetie," Micah finally said as they finished their wine. "Let's go to bed – we'll clean this mess up in the morning."

****

As Micah and Kayla got used to a toddler who moved past the crawling stage to walking between furniture pieces to finally plodding along on her own, they also settled into the pace of life with a child in their new community. In addition to the organizations for which Micah served as a board member, the Sanders joined the town's country club in June 2012. There they enjoyed time at the pool on weekends, and even occasionally in the evening until it would close around 7. Micah took up golf, even taking a few lessons, and by the end of the summer he was played regularly on Saturday mornings in the club's men's league.

For Kayla, tennis was a chance to take off some of the lingering baby weight that stuck with her and, as something she did competitively in high school and recreationally up until a few years ago, it didn't take her long to get back to playing fairly well. Summer became the Sanders' favorite time of year, as it is for most people in the north, as the long days allowed for plenty of outside time, even on weeknights when Micah could get out of the office before 6 or 6:30.

Regularly, Micah, Kayla and Emma drove to Goddard State Park, hiking the many trails that wound through the woods, playing with Emma on the playground or just sitting at a picnic table enjoying the fresh air. The area became home to them and they considered themselves truly blessed at how well the move to Indiana turned out.

At work, Micah built a solid staff and raised the level of the newspaper's editorial department to one that it hadn't achieved before. Earlier that year the paper received the Blue Ribbon, the state press association's highest honor for newspaper excellence, and recognizing Micah's staff as the best all-around in the state. Being a smaller community that relied on its local newspaper for community events and happenings, circulation leveled off following some of the initial declines just after 2010. In addition, the company invested in its websites and e-editions, and online readership was robust and growing steadily. While ad revenues weren't as strong as they were in newspapers' glory days, things held steady enough the company was not laying off employees or resorting to the extreme measures taken by many of its counterparts in the industry.

The summer of 2012 passed extremely quickly, as they usually do, and Micah and Kayla were preparing for Emma's second Christmas around the time a press release from the Lands County CASA organization appeared in Micah's email inbox. He read numerous press releases from the agency before, but hadn't paid much attention to them, as he received dozens of similar items from various groups each week. He always passed them along to his team for inclusion in the paper's community and volunteer opportunity news section. On occasion, the releases would lend themselves to a feature story of some kind, which Micah would typically read and approve.

For some reason on that Friday afternoon, though, Micah clicked on the release and opened it, rather than just sending it on to his news desk.

FOR IMMEDIATE RELEASE
Lands County CASA looks to attract volunteers as waiting list grows

(December 7, 2012) Lands County CASA Executive Director Marianne Cawley announced today that, despite recent successes in both volunteer recruitment and fundraising, the agency has not been able to keep up with the growing demand for Court Appointed Special Advocates, or CASAs.

Cawley attributed the growing waiting list to the rampant abuse of drugs like methamphetamine and, more recently, inexpensive street heroin that has become so prevalent in the county.

"Our staff and volunteers have done, and continue to do, an amazing job for the clients we serve," Cawley said. "The issue is that for every volunteer we're able to recruit, three new cases come to us."

If the agency is unable to attract more volunteers quickly, it will need to look for other ways to address the growing waiting list, Cawley said. This could include hiring additional staff, which of course pulls resources from another sector of the agency and requires additional grant money or fundraising. The other option is for the courts to hire lawyers to serve as guardians ad litem which, while better than nothing, are much more expensive and don't devote as much time to each individual case.

"Every study shows the most effective way to speed up the placement process and ensure each child receives the safe, loving environment he or she deserves is through the appointment of a CASA," Cawley said. "Guardians ad litem work well but they're expensive. Hiring additional staff allows us to quickly address a lot of cases, but there isn't that individual attention."

The agency is looking for anyone that has even a remote interest to call 812-555-0943 for more information. Cawley said CASAs come from all walks of life and, while the commitment is a big one and requires a fair amount of time, many of the meetings can be worked around a person's schedule.

"Certainly, there will be times where the CASA needs to be there at a set time," she said, "but we have CASAs who are full-time professionals and handle just one case at a time. Others are self-employed or retirees that can handle multiple or more time-consuming cases."

For more information on Lands County CASA, and the work the agency does, visit www.landcscountycasa.org.

When he finished the release, Micah sent it ahead to the news desk, but also made a mental note to look further into the organization when he had some time. His term on one of the boards on which he sat would end soon, and he looked forward to taking on a new challenge. It occurred to him this could be a perfect fit.

Chapter Six

On a very warm first Sunday in August, Adam Durkin camped in his fort in the woods, looking forward to the start of school the next day. Despite his struggles since mom passed away, Adam actually liked school, at least more than he liked being at home. Things settled down a bit the past couple weeks since Uncle Jack brought him home the night he ran away. Dad hadn't noticed he was gone or, if he did, he didn't say anything about it. Adam spent as much time outside as possible in the days since.

Before mom "left," as his father routinely said, things around the Durkin house were good. The small family lived on 11 acres a few miles west of Williams in a cabin home built in the 1950s.

Roger Durkin, Adam's father, was a native of Charleston, South Carolina and graduated from the University of South Carolina with a degree in Health & Human Performance. At USC, he pitched for the school's baseball team until he tore his rotator cuff, once during his freshman season and again just after a return from 14 months of rehab. The second tear ended his baseball career as a player, but he stayed involved with the team as a student assistant.

After college Roger earned his teaching certification and worked as a high school physical education teacher while coaching the varsity baseball team. There, he excelled both as teacher and coach, and by the age of 25 he was well-liked by his students, their parents and the administrators at the school.

Roger was at the center of a core of young faculty members who all started around the same time. There were seven of them between the ages of 24 and 27 – four women and three men – and all but one was single. Facing together all the challenges of being young, inexperienced teachers, they became very close as a group, routinely going out for drinks after work on Fridays and occasionally during the week as well. During one of the Friday excursions to the Double Deuce, a favorite country music spot for the group, Roger first met Annabelle Clement. A tall brunette with amazing curves and a killer smile, the two made eye contact across the bar on a crowded Friday evening in February 2002.

Roger was never shy around women, and at 6 feet, 3 inches with a chiseled physique, he hadn't a reason to be apprehensive, but something about Annabelle gave him pause. It took him close to an hour of occasional glances, first from him, then from her, eyes meeting and then quickly looking away, before Roger finally excused himself from his group of friends and walked over to the table where Annabelle sat with a couple of her friends.

As he reached her table, his mind had scrolled through some of his more successful pick-up lines from over the years, all of which he dismissed in favor of a simple, "hi." Annabelle's smile immediately lit him up as she answered with a basic, "hello." Roger offered to buy her a drink, and the two stepped away to a table in the corner of the bar, furthest away from the band belting out Lonestar's *I'm Already There.*

The two talked non-stop, and both were surprised when the bartender announced last call at 1:45 a.m. They laughed as they looked around the bar and noticed both groups of friends had left, and only about a dozen of the hundred plus people there when they met four hours earlier remained. The band had broken down and left nearly two hours ago but, that too, went unnoticed.

They decided to walk down the street to the all-night coffee shop for a bite to eat and a cup of coffee, and when Roger finally walked Annabelle – now Annie to him – back to her downtown apartment, he knew more about her than any woman he ever met.

Annie grew up in the small town of Williams, Indiana. After high school she attended Purdue, where she earned her degree in Mechanical Engineering. She was offered a job by a large manufacturer before she even graduated and went to work for their marine plant in Charleston. She was 24 and on the job in Charleston for a little less than two years, but was already promoted once and she anticipated another on the way in the coming months.

She was an accomplished volleyball player in high school and at Purdue, and obviously kept up the impressive muscle tone since her playing days ended two years ago. What Roger liked best, though, was the confidence Annie projected, and that smile – every time she flashed it – just about knocked him off his chair.

The first night ended with a quick, innocent kiss and an exchange of phone numbers. Roger completely ignored protocol and dialed her up early the next afternoon to see if she was available for dinner that night. Annie quickly accepted. While he didn't have a lot of money, Roger was frugal through the first few years of his teaching career and saved a good portion of what he took home from each paycheck. He made a reservation at one of the nicest restaurants in downtown Charleston, and the two shared a much quieter and peaceful evening than the night before.

It was obvious to both something special was forming between them. Neither believed in love at first sight, but this was as close as it got, and when the second date ended just after midnight, a much more passionate kiss on Annie's doorstep had Roger believing he may be invited in. Instead, when she pulled away after a seemingly endless kiss, Annie smiled and told Roger she thought they should slow things down just a little bit. Since they had known each other less than 36 hours, this was certainly a reasonable request and Roger agreed without issue. Well, except for the burning desire he could tell they both felt to rip off each other's clothes.

The next afternoon they agreed to get together at a downtown sports bar to watch the South Carolina basketball game against Georgia. Drinking ice cold beer and wolfing down a plate of nachos and chicken wings, they rooted the Gamecocks on to a win but decided to end the date immediately afterwards so they could both get ready for the busy work week ahead.

That week went by more slowly than any either of them ever experienced. They talked on the phone every night but one, and planned to get together for a morning run on Saturday. Both were avid runners and they decided they would set out from Annie's apartment downtown to run through the historic district and along the Ashley River. Afterwards they would clean up and grab some breakfast.

Saturday brought clear, sunny skies and a seasonable temperature of 54 degrees at 8 a.m. when Roger knocked on

Annie's front door. She answered in short, tight running shorts and a compression top, every curve outlined in perfect goddess fashion. They set out at a good pace and ended up doing six miles together in about 55 minutes, Roger pushing Annie at times and vice versa. When they finished, Annie set Roger up in her guest bathroom and they agreed to head to breakfast after they both showered and dressed.

A couple minutes into his shower as he was rinsing off the soap, the curtain pulled slowly open and Annie slipped into the shower with him, a coy smile on her face. He pulled her close and kissed her, first on the lips, then on the neck, working his way down to her left nipple. Annie moaned with pleasure and, pulling him closer, the two made love for the first time. Going out to breakfast never happened that morning. After drying off, the couple had a cup of coffee and a granola bar before heading to Annie's bedroom for a slower, but no less passionate interlude, followed by another two hours napping in each other's arms.

They spent the entire day together, including an evening with a pizza and a movie on Annie's couch. Roger spent the night and on Sunday morning over a breakfast of bacon and eggs, he looked at the beautiful young woman across from him and realized he had never felt this way about anyone. He didn't know at the time that Annie was thinking exactly the same thing. They talked that morning about trying to get together during the week, but Spring baseball practice was beginning and Roger's days that typically started at 6:45 a.m. wouldn't be ending until seven in the evening on practice days and nine or ten when the team had a game. Reluctantly they agreed they would have to be content meeting only on the weekends.

That agreement held for the next three weekends until, during a Sunday afternoon watching first round NCAA basketball tournament games, Roger asked Annie to move in with him.

"I know we've only been going out for a little more than a month," he said, "but this seeing each other only two days a week just sucks." Annie looked a bit apprehensive at first, but after a few seconds she smiled and told him she had never felt for anyone what she did for him and she couldn't stand not seeing each other on the weekdays either.

"Let's go for it," she said, and they agreed they would move her things over to his place the next weekend.

In May of that year, Roger asked Annie to be his wife and, six months later on Thanksgiving weekend, they married in her hometown in Indiana. Family and friends were at first concerned about how quickly the relationship progressed, but after any of them spent just a couple of hours with the two of them, any doubts quickly faded. The wedding was beautiful and the reception a huge hit, with many people commenting it was one of the best they ever attended. The party raged until just after midnight, when the drunken revelers could dance no more and the band packed up their gear and headed home.

The couple honeymooned in St. Thomas, content to while away the days on the beach, lounging by the pool, browsing in the shops or having a drink along Front Street. Watching a sunset from their hotel room balcony one evening, they talked about children, something they did informally after their engagement, and decided they wanted to wait a couple of years before Annie went off her birth control medication.

In May 2003, as Roger was finishing off another baseball season and counting down to the end of the school year, and as the couple was getting ready to celebrate their six-month anniversary, Annie came home from work on a Wednesday afternoon and announced she was offered another promotion. This one, however, required a move from Charleston back to Williams, but it also involved a 30 percent pay increase, not to mention it was a huge step in Annie's career. At 25, she was elevated into her company's leadership development program, used to identify and train employees the company views as potential corporate directors. As much as Roger loved Charleston and South Carolina, he knew the opportunity was too good to pass up.

The couple made the drive to Williams the following weekend and, staying with Annie's parents, took a few days to look at homes for sale in the area. Roger stopped in to the county's school headquarters and inquired about jobs, finding out one of the high schools in town had several teaching openings. While there, he filled out an application and attached his resume.

As he was leaving the school building, his cell phone rang and Annie gave him an address of a home she wanted him to see. It was about a twenty-minute drive across town, and Annie told him to meet her out front. She arranged for the listing agent to meet them there as well and, a half hour later, the three cars parked in front of a cabin home on a scenic wooded lot. The property was eleven total acres, much of it small hills and trees, but with a two-acre stocked pond and a three-bedroom, two-and-a-half bath cabin. The home was in great condition and being sold by an older couple looking to downsize.

Watching Annie, Roger knew she was already in love with the place, but listed at $359,000, he wondered if they could afford it, especially since they would be first-time homeowners. After touring the house and walking around the property, they asked the agent to give them a day or two to talk things over.

Back at his in-laws' place later that afternoon, Roger sat on the back deck facing the swimming pool. It still had the cover that protected it through winter, but just a few weeks from now it would be open and used heavily for the next few months. Annie walked out with a couple glasses of iced tea and sat down beside him.

"My father wants to help us get the house," she said. "I think if we make an offer somewhere between three-forty and three-four-five, the sellers would probably accept. With my salary and assuming the school hires you, the bank would likely loan us somewhere around $300,000. If we borrow $20,000 from dad, we wouldn't have to drain our savings to make the down payment."

Roger thought for a moment, but having never borrowed money from anyone – not even his parents for college – he hated the idea of accepting the offer. "Or we could just look for a place in the two-fifty to three hundred range," he finally said.

Annie's shoulders sagged, the disappointment apparent on her face, but deep down she knew where he was coming from. "Let's sleep on it and we'll talk more about it tomorrow."

The next morning, reading his in-laws' copy of the Saturday newspaper, Roger perused an article about the local real estate market essentially stating that home sales in the county were at their strongest point ever, and Realtors couldn't get enough listings to keep up with demand. He was already leaning toward taking up his father-in-law on the offer and buying Annie's dream house, but this article to Roger made up his mind. When Annie came down the stairs after her shower, he smiled and said, "Let's make an offer."

With the Realtor's help, they made an offer that afternoon of $340,000. The sellers countered at $350,000 and by Monday afternoon, they had a contract at $345,000. As they were passing through the mountains of North Carolina on their way back to Charleston to finish out the school year and prepare for their move, Roger's phone rang. It was the Lands County School Corporation, and the principal at the high school wanted to arrange an interview in the second week of June. The school year in Charleston would end the first week, and they set a date for the second Thursday of the month.

Annie planned to start work in Williams on June 1, so Roger would take care of the final arrangements in Charleston, finish out the school year and drive the U-haul up on the Monday of the second week of June. In the last week of May, they secured the final loan from the bank, so inspections were set to begin on the home that week as well. A tentative closing date of July 1 was set on what would become their new home.

The move went smoothly, and since neither of them owned many possessions, there really wasn't much to take with them. Roger was hired to teach freshman and sophomore P.E. the following school year, and the couple spent the month of June in Annie's old room of her parents' house. Everything went according to plan with inspections on the new property, and other than a couple minor things that needed taken care of, the place was in great shape. The closing happened as scheduled on July 1, and the next day Annie's parents helped the couple move their relatively few possessions from the small storage unit they rented over to the new house.

That summer went by quickly. Annie, in her new position, had to travel about six weeks out of the year, and her first trip with the company – over to England for a week – was coming up around the same time Roger would be starting the school year in his new job.

"When I get back from the U.K.," Annie said one evening as she and Roger were sitting on the back deck overlooking the pond on a beautiful July evening, "what do you say I go off the birth control and we see what happens?"

Roger practically jumped over the table to hug her. Although he hadn't said anything out loud, he wanted kids from the day he met Annie, and the thought of having his own little baseball or softball player running around this beautiful new property was on his mind all summer.

In late September 2003, Annie's home pregnancy test showed positive, and two days later a doctor confirmed it.

Chapter Seven

In the newspaper business, especially for someone who works on the news side, it is common to become desensitized to violence, crime and many of the other unthinkable things one person can do to another. In bigger cities, such as the ones Micah covered prior to moving to Williams, those types of stories were part of the daily fabric, each one seemingly worse than its predecessor. Luckily, in the small town in which he currently resided Micah only saw this ugliest side of human nature on an occasional basis. Murders were extremely rare, violent crime happened only a few times per year and, for the most part, people felt safe in just about any pocket of the city. On May 1, 2014, however, just days before Emma's third birthday, Micah and his team were forced to cover the ghastliest crime of his career, and possibly the worst crime to ever take place in his small, conservative Indiana community.

It was around 6 p.m. and the newsroom was preparing to lay out the next day's edition. Micah grabbed his jacket and was getting ready to head out the door for the evening when a call came over the department's police scanner. Patrols responded to a call over on Washburn Street, where neighbors called in a domestic dispute in progress. Three gunshots were fired, and all available units were enroute.

Micah called across the room to his city editor, Tom Davis, and told him to grab his gear and head to the scene. At the last minute, Micah decided to ride along as well.

When they arrived at the crime scene, police had already secured the area around the house. Eight squad cars parked at the scene, as well as two ambulances, and a crowd of neighbors gathered to see if they could catch a glimpse of what was going on. Cops went in and out of the house, and as he watched, Chief Detective Caroline Riche entered the front door. In the driveway, a young officer sat on the hood of a squad car, his face in his hands and another cop, apparently his partner, leaned over him. Micah leapt to the conclusion these were the first officers on the scene, who had walked in on something they hadn't experienced before.

On the outside of the perimeter, Micah noticed Public Information Officer Jonah Stiles and made his way over to him after telling Davis to begin interviewing anyone who saw or heard anything. As he approached, Stiles looked towards him and held up a hand.

"Nothing at this time, Micah," he said. "You know I can't give you anything yet."

Micah and Stiles became acquainted over the past couple of years since Stiles had been appointed to his post. They served together on the board of directors for one of the area's non-profits, and worked together on several fundraisers and outreach programs. Obviously, they met on a professional level as well, not just for crimes and investigations, but also on many of the programs the city conducted each year. They considered each other friends, but Micah noticed the tone that evening was not what he was used to from Stiles.

"Understandable," Micah said, "I'll catch up with you in a bit."

From there, Micah began working the crowd and happened upon the woman who lived next door to the crime scene. She told him that around 5:45 she heard yelling and a couple of screams come from the house next door. "It happens about once a week over there," she said, "so I don't pay much attention to it since I never seen someone hurt." The shouting didn't last long, and things quieted down for about five or ten minutes after that.

The neighbor told Micah, as far as she knows, the couple who lived there when she moved into her place three years ago split up a few months earlier. The mother, at least she assumed it was the mother, lived in the house with her four kids – three boys and a girl, all between the ages of three and nine.

"The father, or whoever he is, comes around just about every day, and I seen him going into the house pretty late at night on a regular basis," she continued. "But that's not my business, so I don't pay much attention." It was obvious she did, in fact, pay a lot of attention.

"So anyways, them kids they was running in and out of the house like they usually do, the littlest one was just in diapers, like he usually is. I saw the man come out and grab the little one and yell at the girl to get her ass back inside.

"I was just minding my business, washing my dishes in the sink and gettin' ready to make supper, and I saw her run back inside before the man slammed the door shut. A couple minutes later, three gunshots, and I called the cops."

Micah, making notes on the reporter's tablet he always carried with him, looked the woman over. "You said the couple has four children that you know of, but you only mentioned the baby and the girl. Did you see the other two boys?"

The neighbor thought for a moment, and replied she had not seen the other two for the past couple of days.

"Those four kids are usually outside playing as much as they can be," she said, "and with the weather finally starting to warm up these last couple days, they would always be out in the yard."

Micah got the woman's name, wrote down her address and thanked her for the information. By now, several of the officers started canvassing the crowd to determine if anyone had seen anything. When Stiles saw Micah had been talking to the neighbor, he made his way back over to him.

"Find anything out?" Stiles asked.

"Just background information on the family that lives here," Micah said, "and of course she heard the gunshots, but she also saw at least two of the kids outside right before the gunfire began, and she spotted a male adult in the house at the time."

Micah could tell from the look on Stiles' face this wasn't an ordinary call, and the gunshots that had now been confirmed hadn't just been into the ceiling or floor.

"C'mon, Jonah," Micah said, "what the hell happened in there?"

Stiles looked away briefly, and when he turned back, he wiped a tear from his eye. He had to catch himself twice as he started to speak.

"All I can say right now is we have five down, three dead and the other two not far off," he finally managed. "But I need you to keep this down to that for now. We're still looking for the gun and the shooter, and we don't need any vigilantes joining us on the hunt."

Micah nodded, although he knew he had the right to report on anything he had seen or heard during any of the conversations that night. But, as he was getting ready to move away to find out what Davis had learned, Stiles grabbed his arm.

"Micah, listen," Stiles said, choking up again. "I know you need to do your job, but this one's different." Another tear escaped his eye. "We're going to find this piece of shit tonight, and I'm going to have a long night ahead of me preparing what to tell you guys tomorrow. After that I'm going to need to talk to someone – as a friend, not as a reporter."

Micah nodded, understanding he would probably end up getting a lot more detail than he wanted – or could use in a news story. "I'll catch you when you're ready," he said, and walked off to find his city editor. Just as he was turning away, a gunshot sounded well behind the house in the woods on the back of the property.

Over Stiles' radio, Micah heard, "Suspect is down. Repeat, suspect is down."

The story on the newspaper's website a few hours later reported only on a multiple homicide in Williams. It listed the address of the crime, the number of victims and the name of the family on the deed. The suspect had escaped from the scene briefly, but had been shot and was in critical condition in a secured ward at the hospital. More details to follow.

****

Those details emerged over the next few days, and as occurs with most crime stories, many of the gaps filled in. By the afternoon after the shootings, the names of the children, their mother and the suspect, father to the two youngest

44

children, were released and included in the news article. The two kids still alive when officers responded hadn't even made it to the hospital before they too succumbed to their injuries.

Two days later, the suspect's condition was upgraded to stable, and he was scheduled to be arraigned within the week. On a Friday afternoon at 2 p.m., two days after the shootings and the day before Emma's birthday, the phone rang in Micah's office, the caller ID showing Stiles' cell number. Micah picked up, and before he said hello, Stiles said, "I need a drink. A fucking lot of drinks. Can you meet me?"

"Now?" Micah asked, noting it was still a few hours before the proverbial happy hour.

Now, indeed, was Stiles' response, and they arranged to meet in 15 minutes at their favorite bar downtown.

When Micah walked in, right on time, Stiles sat in a booth in the back corner of the bar near the emergency exit. The door was propped open, and as Micah approached, Stiles raised a cigarette in a shaky hand toward his lips. Smoking was illegal in all indoor establishments in Williams since the beginning of 2012, but apparently the owner, Jimmy, made an exception in this case. Besides, the place was empty except for the two of them, and after Micah entered he noticed Jimmy change the "open" sign to "closed" and lock the front door. He then brought Micah a rocks glass filled with ice, and Stiles filled the glass from the bottle of Makers Mark already on the table.

"I took the liberty of ordering for us," Stiles said, uttering an odd chuckle unlike any Micah heard before. "Want one?" he asked, sliding the pack of cigarettes toward

Micah, who simply shook his hand and slid them back across at his friend.

They sat in silence for a few minutes, and Micah had time to consider the fact he actually missed the smell of cigarette smoke in a bar. The burn of the bourbon going down his throat felt good, and Micah waited for his friend to initiate the conversation. After all, he thought, I am here for him.

Stiles finished off his first glass of bourbon with a big last swig and, taking the bottle, poured another one. Slamming the bottle back to the table, causing his glass to splash over the rim a bit, he looked across the table at Micah.

"Worst thing I've ever seen," he said, practically in a whisper. Then, a little louder, "Worst thing I've ever fucking seen in 27 years of this shit."

After a short pause and another pull from his cigarette, Stiles started into the story slowly, reiterating this was all off the record and they were only talking as friends. He hadn't been first on the scene; that "honor" had fallen to the young officers Micah noticed that evening. They did a pretty good job overall of securing the house and not disturbing the evidence, Stiles said, and he arrived about 10 minutes later. By that time, the detectives were there and the investigation was underway.

As Stiles started to describe what they found when they went into the house, Micah noticed his glass was empty, but before he could reach for the bottle, Stiles grabbed it and filled both of their glasses.

The place could only be described as a bloodbath, Stiles said. Just inside the doorway, they found the girl. Only five years old, she apparently went inside after her father called her and before he hit her three times in the head with a blunt object. The cops guessed the object was the butt of the nine-millimeter handgun from which he fired the shots. They determined the three blows to the head were enough to kill her, but he shot her in the back of the head as well, after she fell onto the old rug just inside the doorway.

"We're guessing the mother was next to go, almost immediately," Stiles continued, pausing only long enough for an occasional sip of bourbon or another puff of cigarette. "The son of a bitch had apparently tied her to a kitchen chair he had moved into the living room, giving her a front row view of him killing their daughter. She was probably screaming her head off when he shot her in the face."

According to Stiles, the father then turned to the baby sitting on the floor, and fired one last shot between his eyes, before taking off into the woods where he was eventually shot and arrested.

By now, Stiles and Micah were more than halfway through the 750ml bottle of Makers, but if the alcohol was having any effect, it was hardly noticeable against the horror story Stiles shared. As badly as Micah wanted to vomit and get out of there, he sat quietly while his friend continued.

"And as bad as all of that was," Stiles said, "when we searched the house we found a locked door to the closet in the master bedroom. It wasn't your basic door lock like you'd find on most bedroom doors – it was a deadbolt, and it had been locked from the outside with a key. The smell that was coming from inside that door, however, left no doubt as to what we would find when we got in there."

Once the technicians unlocked the door, they discovered the bodies of the two older boys. One was seven and the oldest nine, and based on the level of decomposition, both were dead for around four days.

"We're thinking he was forcing the mother to stay in the house, to sleep in her fucking bed, while her two dead sons were rotting away in the closet." Stiles picked his glass up, then put it down and lowered his face into his hands, taking a few minutes to pull himself back together.

"So anyways, this dickhead isn't talking. We tried to interview him once his condition improved, but he hasn't said a word yet. Not a single word."

Stiles said the department did some digging, though, and found out the family had a history of domestic disturbance calls to the police, including a couple of times where the father was accused of hitting either the mother or one of the kids. In both cases, the mother refused to press charges, and the guy was back at the house within hours of being detained.

The Department of Child Services even investigated the family a couple of times after the calls started popping up on their radar, but in two separate instances, the case worker determined there was adequate supervision for the children and she saw no issues requiring further action on their behalf.

When Stiles finished his story, he looked drained and decided it best to call a cab to get him home. Micah would have offered to drive him, but he knew he probably shouldn't be driving yet, either. After Stiles gave him a quick hug and fell into the cab, Micah took a slow walk back to his office, closing his door behind him. As he activated his computer and looked through a couple stories for the weekend issues his thoughts kept returning to the details of the story his friend told him that afternoon. Mostly, though, he kept thinking about how different this whole situation would have been had DCS come to a different conclusion on the viability of guardianship of the two parents involved in this case.

Finished with his work for the day, Micah launched the browser connection on his computer and brought up the website for the Department of Child Services. Greeting him on the front page of the site was the photo of a little girl on top of a playground slide with the words, "Keeping Her Safe…It's Our Mission" beside her. The next slide on the rotating screen touted the Child Abuse Hotline. Glancing down the page, he noticed a link for Child Abuse and Neglect Reports by month. The most recent report filed on the site was for March 2014, and he clicked on the link to bring up the statistics.

Statewide in Indiana in March 2014, there were 273 substantiated cases of sexual abuse (to go along with 1,271 unsubstantiated cases), 239 cases of physical abuse (2,466 unsubstantiated) and 1,765 cases of neglect (8,501 unsubstantiated). Scrolling down the alphabetical listing to Lands, the statistics were of course on a much smaller scale, but still disturbing. Micah started making some notes on the pad beside his computer.

-Consider why so many unsubstantiated cases compared to number substantiated
-What constitutes "neglect"
-What has the trend been in the past 12 months? 24 months? Etc.

Micah's cell phone buzzed as he finished up the notes. Looking at the screen he saw it was Kayla, and more than an hour had passed since he returned to his office. It was almost 6 p.m. and he was supposed to pick Kayla and Emma up at 6:15 to go out and grab some pizza – Emma's favorite. Tomorrow would be a small birthday party at their house with Kayla's parents and a few of Emma's friends from day care, but tonight was just for the three of them.

Picking up the phone, Micah said, "I'm leaving now – be there in 10 minutes." Standing up from behind his desk, he was glad to note the effects of the bourbon, at least for the most part, had worn off.

Chapter Eight

The first six years of Adam's life consisted of the moments and memories that – in a perfect world – every child deserves. His mom and dad were as happy as any two people could be. The small family loved spending time outside, hiking in the woods, out on the paddle boat on their small pond, or maybe having a picnic dinner on the back deck. In winter when bitter cold would limit outdoor time, they huddled up on the floor in front of their fireplace and play games or watch movies together.

Annie still traveled about six weeks of the year for work, but she also earned four weeks of vacation, so when Roger was out of school for the summer, the family would pack up the car with all their camping gear and head off each year in a different direction. When Adam was three, they went up to Maine, New Hampshire and the rest of New England. The next year they headed west to Colorado for 10 days. At age five, Adam got to experience Disney World for the first time, the family setting up camp at Fort Wilderness for a week. The summer after his sixth birthday, Adam took his first ride on an airplane, as the family flew to San Francisco to spend two weeks in California, Oregon and Washington. They rented a 27-foot motor home and spent the entire time traversing the beauty of the Pacific Coast Highway, exploring the towns and cities along the way.

Adam was enamored with the magnificence of the PCH. He spent the hours on the road with his face pressed to the window, looking down the sheer cliffs that dropped hundreds of feet to the raging ocean. When the family pulled the RV into one of the parking lots for the public beaches along the way, Adam especially loved guessing the height of the waves. He was amazed at how much bigger the waves in the Pacific were from what he witnessed in the Atlantic, and he was in awe of the way they crashed down upon the huge boulders in the water, splashing in every direction around them. Every time he turned from the water and looked at his parents, they were holding hands, hugging, or just looking back at him and smiling. So many of his friends at school had parents who were divorced – he was old enough to understand what that meant now – and he was so glad he wasn't one of those kids who had to spend one weekend with dad and the next with mom. He could tell a lot of the kids at school were jealous when they'd come back to a new school year and share what they did that summer. Only a few told of vacations even remotely similar to Adam's, and he knew he was a pretty lucky boy. And then, on a beautiful October day in 2010, his life started to change.

During the fall months when it wasn't baseball season, Roger usually picked Adam up from the afterschool program when he finished his tasks at the end of each day. Typically that was somewhere between 4 and 4:30. During baseball season in the spring, Adam stayed at after-school until Annie picked him up around 5:30 or 6. Regardless of the time of year, Adam enjoyed the afterschool program, where he got some time to play with his friends, but also the chance to get his homework done so he wouldn't have to do it in the evening when he was home. So, when both of his parents showed up together at 3 p.m. on that Tuesday as school was letting out, Adam wondered if something was wrong.

"Hey buddy," his mom said, greeting him with a smile. "I got out of work a little early and wanted to come pick you up today." She grabbed his backpack from him and helped him into the backseat of the car. "Your dad's going to run out and pick up some pizza and a movie in a little while, and we're going to pretend it's a Friday."

Adam beamed a smile, thinking it was pretty cool they would turn a school night into what was usually their Friday routine. They had a great time watching *How to Train Your Dragon* in 3D on their new television with the special glasses, and Adam's only disappointment when he went to bed at nine was he had to get up for school the next morning. Ten minutes after Roger and Annie kissed Adam good night and closed his door, he needed to go to the bathroom and made his way down the hallway from his bedroom. On his way back to bed, Adam heard his parents talking quietly in the living room, but in between the conversation he could tell his mother was crying. They whispered quietly, but Adam heard something about them going to see the doctor that day.

When he walked out into the living room, Annie choked back the tears as Adam said, "Mom, what's wrong?" She didn't answer right away, but pulled him close to her, the tears from her face soaking into the shoulder of his pajamas.

"Nothing sweetie," she said. "Everything is going to be fine."

As she tucked him back into bed, she smiled and promised they would talk more about it the next day, but it was nothing he needed to worry about. "Just a little scare," was how she put it.

****

As it turned out, that "little scare" was invasive ductal carcinoma, the most common type of breast cancer. A week earlier, while she was getting dressed, Annie felt a lump in her left underarm and, since her mother was treated for breast cancer years before, she made a doctor's appointment immediately. An MRI confirmed the lump and a biopsy confirmed the cancer. She got the news around lunchtime the day she picked up Adam from school, telling her supervisor at work she wasn't feeling well and needed to go home.

A few days after their movie night, Annie and Roger sat in an oncologist's office and learned her cancer was in stage 3C and was inoperable. Her first thought was this meant it was untreatable, but the doctor went on to tell her this simply meant surgery alone would not be enough to remove the cancer, hence the "inoperable" part. In addition to cancer in her breast, it had spread to other lymph nodes and possibly to some other organs. Further testing would be required to gauge the extent of the spreading, but the doctor recommended radiation and chemotherapy treatments begin immediately.

"Doctor, am I going to die from this?" Annie asked, just coming out of the haze clouding her mind from the doctor's first sentences after using the word inoperable.

The look on his face did nothing to ease her mind, and when he told her the five-year survival rate for her stage of cancer was around 70 percent, she immediately counted herself in the 30 percent that would not make it through those five years. Even though, based on the history of her mother fighting the disease Annie knew she had a strong chance of facing it herself someday, for someone who had always been so healthy, and almost never sick, the prognosis sent her reeling.

As they drove away from the doctor's office that day, Roger and Annie had a tough time saying anything at first. He drove with his eyes straight forward while Annie stared out the passenger window. When they pulled up to a stoplight, Roger looked over and saw tears streaming down his wife's face.

He reached over and grabbed her hand in his and said, "Baby, we'll beat this." Choking back his own tears, Roger worked hard to make himself believe it, at least enough to convince Annie.

When they returned home, they collapsed on the couch and, wrapped tightly in Roger's arms, Annie let forth the sobs she had been holding back. Roger called Annie's father and told him they were tied up with a doctor's appointment, asking him to pick up Adam from school. They hadn't yet shared the news with Annie's parents, but Roger knew that would need to happen later that evening. They'd also need to talk to Adam and give at least enough information to understand all the effects that Annie's treatments would have on him and their family in the coming months. But for now, Roger just sat there on the couch, in a state of disbelief himself, holding his crying wife and doing his best to just be there for her. He knew there was nothing in the world he could say to make things better, so for now his love was all he had to give.

****

The chemo treatments started the next week, and the side effects that typically go with the therapy hit Annie like a locomotive. Nausea and diarrhea became her way of life. When she could bring herself to eat something, she could rarely keep it down. Roger offered as much support as possible, taking days off when Annie was feeling especially bad, but watching his beautiful, strong wife erode before his eyes was tearing him apart. Annie's parents were a huge help, coming over whenever needed, but also knowing to give the couple the space they needed to deal with what they were facing. Annie's dad had some health problems of his own, and they all worried he was on his way to a heart attack or a stroke.

After the first round of treatment, the doctor felt like they had some success in shrinking the cancer cells, but he knew it was going to take several more rounds of treatment – along with the radiation – for them to have any chance of saying the cancer was in remission. Then, in late 2011 in the early stages of Annie's third round of chemotherapy, a PET scan showed the cancer had progressed into her bones and her lungs. For the first time, the doctor used the word "terminal" and discussions changed from hope and treatment to quality of life and keeping Annie comfortable until the end. The doctor told them, in all likelihood, Annie had anywhere from six months to a year to live.

After absorbing the initial blow of the news, and once they arrived back at their house, Annie looked at Roger and smiled.

"You know what?" she said. "I'm okay with this."

Roger just looked at her, still in shock himself from the sucker punch they had sustained just a half hour earlier.

"After slugging it out for the past year, going through all these treatments and feeling rotten the whole time, I'm just glad it's going to be over," she said, taking a seat at the kitchen table. "I think, deep down, I knew from the start I wasn't going to make it through this."

Roger sat down with her at the table, and put his face in his hands.

Annie reached over and touched his chin, raising his head so he was facing her. Tears glistened on his cheeks as she started to speak again.

"We're going to cry today, and we're going to have my parents over for dinner so we can tell them and Adam what's going on. And tonight, we can all cry, and yell, and curse and be as pissed off as we want. And then, starting tomorrow, we're going to live - all of us. We're going to live every day. We're going to smile and laugh and play and dance and sing and do all the wonderful, happy things we've always done."

In that moment, Roger saw the strong, vital woman he loved since the day he met her, rather than the drugged, sick person the cancer treatments turned Annie into during the past year. And, to his surprise, he smiled.

So, that evening, they did exactly what Annie said. Before Annie's parents arrived, they picked Adam up from school, brought him home and broke the news to him. He started crying immediately and clung to Annie like he'd never let her go. Like they did for each other so many times during the past year, they just held on and cried together. When Annie's parents arrived around six, they opened a bottle of wine and broke the news to them as well. Annie's dad slammed his fist on the table, but walked around and hugged his daughter before stepping out the back door. A proud man his whole life, he didn't want his family to see him cry. Annie's mom had the same reaction as Adam and they just held each other. An hour later, the whole family was seated at the table, picking at the lasagna and garlic bread Roger picked up from the family's favorite Italian place in town.

Annie shared the wish she told Roger about earlier in the day that they were all allowed to do whatever they needed to do that evening to get out the anger and the sadness, or whatever emotion they needed to express. After that, she wanted them all to enjoy whatever time remained and to treat that time like the gift that she knew it was.

Christmas came a few weeks later, and it was a happy one, filled with love and laughter, and carried out as if nothing was wrong. The day after Christmas, the entire family, including Annie's parents, got on a plane and flew to St. Thomas. Annie wanted the family to see the beautiful island on which they spent their honeymoon, to lie on the beach under the gorgeous sunshine and to eat in some of the amazing seafood restaurants they enjoyed nine years earlier. It was an incredible week and, on the evening before they were to fly home, they all decided to stay three more days. Annie's dad rented a house on the neighboring island of St. John, where the family snorkeled, swam, cooked and just enjoyed each other in the idyllic surroundings.

When they finally returned home, winter settled in to Indiana. Eight inches of snow greeted them the day after they got back from the islands, along with a polar vortex that dropped the daily high temperatures into the single digits. Roger worked most days, staying home only when Annie was having a "bad day," which wasn't that often at that point. Adam was back in school and, for the most part, was keeping his grades up and looking forward to the spring baseball season. He and Annie talked often about getting back out on the baseball field, and she admitted she could not wait to watch him move up into the eight- to 10-year-old age group.

"That's when you really start to learn some of the game's strategy," was what Roger told them, and he started working with Adam on improving his swing in the basement as February rolled into March.

Tryouts and practice began toward the end of March, and the cancer was taking its toll on Annie. Her energy levels were sporadic at best, and the doctor recommended the family have a nurse come in to administer her pain medication and to help with some of the things that needed done. They took this advice, and having the nurse there was a big help to all of them.

On days when she was feeling well enough, Annie rode with Roger to Adam's practices, and when they started playing games, she was there as often as she felt up to it. During those first few games, the weather was still cool, and Annie sat in a lawn chair with blankets atop her body. She was starting to lose weight rapidly, and 55 degrees felt like 20 to her.

By April, Annie was confined to her bed, no longer having the energy to get up without assistance, and the doctors recommended the family consult a Hospice agency which, again, they did.

On the third of May, just before 10 at night, Roger sat beside Annie's bed listening to the soft rasp she emitted with each exhale. She was going in and out of consciousness, and the doctor when he had stopped by earlier told him Annie would likely pass at any minute. Adam laid on the bed with her as long as he could, but he fell asleep about a half hour earlier, and Roger held him to Annie's lips to give him a kiss on the cheek before he carried him over to the chair in the corner of the room.

With her son sleeping in the corner, and her husband sitting on the bed beside her, Annie opened her eyes wide and managed as close to a smile as she could get at that point.

"Listen, sweetie," she said. "I think I'm going now."

Roger grabbed her hand just a bit tighter, the tears that were welling in his eyes now spilling out. "No, baby. Please."

She nodded her head weakly. "It's time. And I'm good. I have been so blessed to have you and that sweet boy over there." She paused to catch her breath. "I want you to find someone else to love him and to love you."

Roger shook his head emphatically. "No, never."

Annie pulled his hand to her chest. "You have filled this heart of mine since the day I met you, and when it's time, you need to do that for someone else as well. You have too much love to give to keep it welled up inside of you."

"But, there's no way," he replied. "I can't ever imagine being with anyone other than you. Not ever again."

Annie smiled one last time. "Don't promise me now, but when the time comes and things are right, be open to it. I will always love you." With that, Annie closed her eyes for the last time, and Roger let his head fall to her lap as he sobbed quietly into the thick stack of blankets that covered her frail body.

"God, I love you," he said over and over until he thought there were no tears left, at least for that night.

Chapter Nine

After Micah and Kayla put Emma to bed following a great dinner at their favorite pizza place, they poured a glass of wine and sat down to wrap the last few birthday gifts for the party the next day. Micah hadn't said anything to Kayla yet about the meeting with Stiles earlier in the day, and he certainly didn't want to subject her to the gory details, but it was weighing on him and he felt he needed to let some of it go if he was going to have any chance to get some sleep that night.

"I guess what bothers me the most," he said after filling her in on the basic details of the case, "is DCS actually investigated this guy on a couple of occasions, and in each case found no action was warranted."

Kayla took a sip of her wine. "I read all the time those case workers are overloaded with work, have to manage too many cases, aren't paid enough and are generally frustrated with the system themselves. I'm sure, like a lot of social workers, they feel like they have to choose their battles and work on the cases that need the most attention."

"It just pisses me off someone should have seen something like this coming," Micah said. "Multiple complaints of domestic violence, even if the lady was too frightened to press charges, should have led someone to the conclusion those kids were in danger."

Kayla agreed with Micah, of course, but she definitely saw the grey areas of problems more than her husband did.

Micah poured the rest of the bottle into their glasses and stood up looking out at the streetlight in front of their house. "I just think of that sweet little girl sleeping in the next room, and I can't imagine ever having the urge to do anything but protect her. These people that hurt and kill their children and their spouses, where do you think they turn down the path that leads them there?"

Kayla shrugged her shoulders. "I suppose for a lot of them it started with the way they were treated growing up. People who are subjected to violent and abusive behavior when they're kids are much more likely to become abusers themselves as adults. But, I don't know. I think about the world that Emma is going to grow up in and it scares me to death. Somewhere along the line core values, respect for others and general good-naturedness just became far too scarce in our society."

Micah walked back from the window and sat down on the couch. "I'm going to bring this up at our content meeting on Monday and propose we work on a series about DCS and its processes for evaluating cases, look deeper into the role the police departments play in bringing these cases to them, and uncover exactly how much bureaucratic red tape ties the hands of these case workers who are supposed to be looking out for the kids' best interests."

"You're talking about a massive undertaking," Kayla replied. "And you know, it's been done many times before, I'm sure. You could just find that you're beating your head against a wall and getting nowhere."

"I'm not going to be able to just let this go, though," he said. "For Emma's sake, and for all those kids out there whose parents will never stand up for them, somebody has to do something."

Kayla smiled and took Micah's hand as he continued. "I've been thinking about this the last couple days, and I believe everything I've done in my career so far has led me here to this place, to this story. Newspapers were originally created to keep an eye on government agencies and to ensure they were always working for the betterment of the people they serve. Somewhere along the line some people in the business moved away from that mission and got too caught up in feature stories and personality profiles, but that is still the core of our mission."

"Then I think you need to go for it," Kayla finally said. "If anybody can make a difference, you can, at least on the local level." Giving him a kiss on the cheek, she stood up, grabbed their wine glasses and took them to the kitchen. "I'm going to go in and get ready for bed. See you in there?"

"In a bit," Micah said, grabbing the note pad he had left on the table earlier. "I'm going to make some notes for the Monday meeting while I'm on this line of thinking."

She smiled at him, thinking she hadn't seen Micah like this in quite a while. "Just don't stay up too late," she told him, knowing all too well he wouldn't be coming to bed for several hours.

When Micah finished scribbling notes on the pad, he looked at the clock and saw it was almost two a.m. Nearly two and a half hours passed since Kayla went to bed, but he had outlined the entire news feature series he would present to the editors and reporters on Monday, and it took him another half hour to calm down enough to turn in himself.

Emma's birthday party was a smashing success, and Micah and Kayla completely forgot about the previous evening's conversation as they watched their daughter smile and laugh as she played with her three friends while the adults finished their birthday cake and drank coffee. The party's theme was Disney's *Frozen*, like just about every other little girl's party in 2014.

Emma was dressed in her Ana dress, by far that year's favorite gift. Of the other three girls at the party, there were two other Anas and one Elsa. As they chased each other around the yard on a beautiful Saturday afternoon, the kids' parents, Micah and Kayla, and Kayla's parents just enjoyed watching them, talking about upcoming summer vacation plans and thinking ahead a couple of years to when they would be starting school. For the most part, though, they all just watched the girls and admired the fact they could live in their little fantasy worlds without all the cares and worries that would surface soon enough.

As Micah watched, he was careful not to let his mind venture too far into the "abyss" as he called it whenever he was into a serious story, but he made a mental note to devote part of his series to the innocence of youth. The girls' laughter and occasional excited screams got him thinking about the journey that someone goes through in life.

You start out in the womb, nurtured in the most safe, protective cocoon possible before bursting out into an infinite world that you will slowly, yet all too quickly, must explore. As a baby, you are cuddled close to mom's breast, and as you grow to become a toddler taking those first few steps, there is always a hand there to guide you, to protect you, and to keep you from falling.

When you get your first bike, those guiding hands take the form of training wheels, where you'll build your confidence before finally insisting that your parents take them off. And when you fall for the first time, it hurts like hell, but you soon realize the hurt goes away and you learn from it and get better because of it.

And then it's off to school, where you start to learn for the first time that people are different and we all come from different places and do things in unique ways. As the world starts to get bigger for you, it becomes obvious the protective "coating" that encasing you through the first few years of your life is starting to wear off. Then the first bully comes along and knocks you down, and in a way, you're a little disappointed your parents didn't tell you not everyone in the world is nice. But at the time, you don't realize the last thing a parent wants to do is to make you predisposed to cynicism. No, you'll learn that soon enough on your own.

As a teenager, you start to buy into that cynicism. Everyone is against you, especially your parents, and you find yourself taking one of two roads – either you protect yourself within your circle of friends and rely on them to support you and help you through some of the most difficult years of your life, or you retreat within yourself and spend most time doing whatever keeps you from having to face the world around you. For some, it is video games, for others books, writing or watching TV.

For those who go on to college, there is an incubation period before adulthood, one that changes your views on just about everything. While you learn how to fend for yourself for the first time, you also have the safety net provided by the structure of school and, for most students, the fact your family, at least in some form, is still within reach. During this time, political opinions are shaped, thought processes mature greatly and the lens in which you view the world distorts, changes, and then changes again. You begin to understand just how different everything and everybody is, and that cynicism continues to grow.

After college, you head out into a world where you're expected to pay the bills, address issues on your own and now, when you fall, the results can be much more painful and the effects much longer lasting. And over time, you build up another protective barrier for yourself – one that allows you to keep out the ugliness of the world as much as possible and to focus on the good things in life, the things that make you happy and help you recover from those times when something invades your shield.

"Micah, are you still with us?" Kayla was saying, pulling him out of his fugue. Micah realized everyone at the table was looking at him and laughing.

"Sorry," he said, "I was just watching the kids play and it got me thinking about something."

A few minutes later, they were all wrapped up in their various conversations again, and a half hour later, the party started to break up when one of the couples told their daughter it was time to leave. The kids who were so full of energy just an hour ago were now in different states ranging from crying from exhaustion to sleeping on the couch, as Emma was doing. Nap time had come, which meant the adult party was over as well.

****

Monday afternoon at two, Micah sat at the head of the conference room table and looked out at his editors and senior reporters. He loved this weekly meeting because, in most cases, everyone was refreshed from the weekend and looking forward to presenting their ideas for upcoming stories. On most weeks, Micah went around the table and allowed his employees to present their ideas, while his editorial assistant jotted the ideas down on a white board. He followed the same protocol on that Monday as well, but when the last reporter finished with her ideas, instead of reading through the suggestions and developing an outline, Micah added his own idea to the mix.

"On the heels of the homicides last week," he began, "I think it's really important for our community that its newspaper makes every effort to get to the root of *why* this happened. When we're working our way through journalism school, we're all taught to address the who, what, when, where, why and how. When I look at this story, we've addressed every one of these except the 'why.' It is my belief, in this case, that is the most important question we need to answer for our readers, our community, and for anyone else that might be following this story."

From there, Micah laid out the plan he put together on Friday evening and, as he built to the end, he saw the excitement in the eyes of everyone in the room. His staff ranged from a veteran who had spent his entire 34-year career at The Sentinel, to a couple of journeymen who had worked for multiple newspapers in different cities, to a couple of young copy editors right out of school who, in the past week, were getting their first taste of a real true-life crime story. For the younger folks, this would be the biggest story – by far – any of them had worked on, but even for the career writers, this would at least rank in their top five.

By the time they finished talking about the series and putting together the content lineup for the week, it was after five o'clock. The group determined the series would consist of at least five feature stories and would play itself out in the Sunday edition over the next five weeks or more. The first Sunday would be an introduction to the case and the series, and would be researched by the entire staff. It was decided unanimously that Micah should write the first feature. After that, the staff would collaborate on each Sunday's feature.

When Micah headed back to his desk, he began looking through the numerous emails that had flooded his inbox over the past three hours. The one that caught his eye, however, was from Lands County CASA, announcing the start of a new training class the following week and the need to pick up a few more volunteers to round out the class.

Micah talked to Kayla a couple of times about the organization and told her, at some point, he was going to think about volunteering with them in some capacity. With everything that happened in the past week, and with the idea the training could offer him another perspective in the DCS series they would begin working on, Micah used his mouse and moved the cursor on his screen to the "reply" button. Immediately, the reply screen appeared on his monitor, and he typed "I am interested in learning more about your organization, and possibly participating in the upcoming training class. Please let me know when would be a convenient time to discuss."

Micah thought for just a second, and then hit "send."

Chapter Ten

Adam took the loss of his mother extremely hard. When Roger told him about it the morning after Annie passed away – Adam slept through the ambulance coming to pick her up and take her away – he broke down and cried all the next day. Sure, he knew it was coming. Both of his parents, his mother especially, had several conversations with him about the day to come when she would no longer be with him. His mom told him repeatedly she needed him to be strong and help his dad with a lot of the things around the house she did before she got sick. So, in his own way, Adam had prepared himself. But that first day she was no longer there, no longer with him, all he could do was lie on his bed and cry. And when the tears dried up and he thought he couldn't cry anymore, he'd clean himself up and get ready to go downstairs to check on dad, and then the tears would start again.

Through that first day, and into the second without mom, Adam could hardly bring himself to get out of bed even to go to the bathroom. Dad would stop by every so often just to check up on him, and they would just lie on the bed without saying a word. Once or twice during the first day, dad tried to talk to him about how great his mom was and how she wanted them to go on living and to move past things, but each time he tried to get out more than a couple sentences, dad choked up and just hugged Adam for a few moments before leaving the room.

The funeral took place a couple days later. Adam wore the sport coat mom & dad bought him for his cousin's first communion earlier that year. People came up to him, hugged him and tried to say something they thought would help him, but Adam barely heard any of it. Adam couldn't even remember anything the priest said during the service, and when they lowered his mom's casket into the big hole they dug, he closed his eyes the entire time.

The next couple of days weren't much better. It rained for three days straight after the funeral, so he and dad were pretty much stuck in the house. Roger took leave for the remainder of the school year so he could be there for Adam and deal with things himself. He tried several times to come in to talk to his son, but all the conversations just ended with the two of them breaking down.

The following weekend arrived, and the sun finally broke through the clouds. Adam woke up from a restless sleep around 8 that Saturday, and the sun shined through the window for the first time since the day of the funeral. As he wiped the sleep from his eyes, dad entered his room with a smile on his face. It was the first time he had seen his dad smile since his mom passed away, and he did his best to smile back at him.

"Come on, buddy," dad said, pulling the covers off his son. "We're going to get out of this house for a while today."

Adam did as instructed, taking his first shower in a couple of days and getting himself dressed. It was a beautiful day for mid-May – sunny and 74 degrees by the time they left the house around 10 – and dad packed a cooler and loaded the car up with their boots and walking sticks for a hike in the state park down the road.

About halfway to the park, dad looked over at Adam and said, "I've done enough crying for now. How about you?" Adam nodded, but couldn't put into words his thought that he might never finish crying.

Dad parked the car at their favorite place at Mirror Lake at 10:30, and they started out on the two-mile hike around the lake. Hiking this spot was always one of mom's favorite things, and she weighed on both their minds as they started down the trail. Adam took the lead, as he knew this trail well, and they spent the first 30 minutes hiking in silence, looking around at the trees just coming into full foliage after the cold winter. All around them, birds sang, squirrels playfully chased each other up and down trees, and families took full advantage of the nice day as the park filled up fast.

Instinctively, halfway around the lake, Adam walked over to the picnic table that was the setting for many lunches and dinners for his family, and even some breakfasts when they got an early start or camped in the campground a mile up the trail. He sat down as dad pulled a couple of sandwiches from the cooler and handed one to him.

Taking a bite from his sandwich, which tasted really good as he hadn't eaten much the past couple of days, Adam said, "I miss her real bad."

"Me too, buddy. Me too."

They ate the rest of the meal in silence, staring out over the lake as the sun cast diamond-like glitters across the water's surface. Mallard ducks swam across their periphery, and they watched the way their bodies moved effortlessly across the water's surface. Neither of them said what they both thought, that as nice as this was, it just wasn't the same without Annie. At that moment, Adam realized nothing would ever be the same.

****

Through that first summer, dad tried his hardest. He continued to coach Adam's baseball team until the season ended, and game days were the same as they always were. All games – wins and losses – were followed by a trip for ice cream, sometimes with the entire team. In addition, they still went out on the occasional hike, tried to have their Friday movie nights as often as possible, and even talked about taking a father and son vacation. They thought of the idea of maybe going to Canada to go fishing, or just head to the mountains of North Carolina or Tennessee, but in the end, they both knew their hearts wouldn't be in it without Annie, so the idea was nothing more than talk.

Nights were the worst for both. Dad did a good job of being strong during the day while Adam was awake. He was back to making a joke or being goofy like he used to, trying his hardest to make Adam laugh, but both knew the effort was good but the result ineffective. At night, after he was supposed to be asleep, Adam sometimes moved quietly down the hall and, through the closed door, he heard his dad crying softly or mumbling to himself. He couldn't make out everything he said, but on occasion heard things like, "Why did you leave me?" and "What am I supposed to do now?" To these questions, there was never an answer, and on those nights Adam headed back to his bedroom and cried himself to sleep.

Adam thought it was August 2012 that the first bottle of Jim Beam turned up. At first, dad never let him see him drink it, and the empty bottle wouldn't be there very often – maybe just once every couple of weeks. As fall turned to winter and the cold brought on the loneliness and isolation that accompany it, Jim Beam's appearance became more frequent, and dad sometimes had a small glass of the brown stuff either with dinner or immediately afterwards. At the time, Roger was back to teaching at the high school, although he decided to step down as baseball coach, saying his heart just wasn't in it and he needed to be home for Adam after school.

Still, things weren't bad through winter and spring of 2013, and Adam never saw his dad drunk, although those occasional small glasses of whiskey at dinner turned into a larger glass pretty much every night. Conversation between the two of them cut down dramatically as well, usually limited to "How was school today?" or "Did you learn anything new today?" Most of Adam's answers consisted of a couple words, and after that, dad wouldn't ask anything else.

On a Friday afternoon in June that year, Adam came into the house after playing out in his fort. He spent more and more time out there, playing made up games where he was always someone other than himself. When he walked into the house to ask about dinner, a man he recognized but couldn't quite place sat on the couch across from his dad's chair.

The two men looked up at him as he entered, and his dad said, "Do you remember your Uncle Jack?" A bottle of Beam was on the table between them, and each of them had a tall glass filled with ice and whiskey in their hands.

Adam met his uncle only one time before, and that was mostly by accident when Jack came to the house one day when he and his parents were having dinner. He stumbled loudly into the house and Annie rushed from the dinner table, grabbed him by the arm and led him back out the front door. Through the screen door, Adam could hear his mom say, "I told you never to come here. What do you want?" At that time, dad went over and closed the front door, and the rest of the conversation remained private. Adam asked his dad about the man at the time, and dad told him it was his uncle, but he and mom did not get along very well.

"What's up, kid?" Uncle Jack said, looking Adam up and down in a way that made him feel a little uncomfortable.

"Nothing," was all Adam could come up with. "I just came in to see what was for dinner."

"Well, your daddy and I was just talking," Uncle Jack said. "We should be finished pretty soon."

His dad confirmed they would be done soon and, when they were, he would order a pizza for the two of them. "Movie tonight?" Adam asked, watching his uncle out of the corner of his eye.

"Sure, buddy," dad said. "Just go to your room and give us a few more minutes."

Fifteen minutes passed before Adam heard the screen door bang shut. He cracked his door, looked down the hall and saw his father seated in the room by himself. When Adam walked out into the living room, his father picked up the bottle of Beam and took it to the kitchen where he replaced it in the upper cabinet in which it resided.

"Why was Uncle Jack here?"

His dad looked toward the front door as if he expected Jack to walk back inside before he said, "He just wanted to talk to me about something. I don't think he'll be back again for a while."

And he wasn't. In fact, Adam didn't see his uncle again until August, late in the afternoon following his first day of fourth grade. After the bus dropped him off in front of his house, since dad wasn't home yet, Adam took the new copy of Sports Illustrated out to his fort with him. He was a big Cardinals fan and they were in the midst of another pennant race. Sports Illustrated always did a great job covering baseball, and he loved to read through each new issue as soon as it arrived in the mail.

Evening approached when he finished up the last article of the magazine, and Adam decided to call it a day and head in to see what was for dinner. When he got back to the house, his father's car sat in its usual place on the side. Behind it was the SUV he remembered his uncle driving when he saw him earlier in the summer. Adam hesitated momentarily, and then headed toward the back door. He entered as quietly as he could, hoping to sneak off to his room without being noticed, but from the living room he heard, "I think he just came in. Put it away."

"Hey Adam, come on out here," his dad called from the living room. Slowly, he made his way down the hall and found his dad and uncle sitting in their usual spots. The bottle of Beam was present again, and both of them slurred their words as they told him to sit down.

"Whatcha do out in them woods all the time?" Jack asked him. Adam looked at his dad, whose head leaned back on the couch, eyes shut.

"Nothing much," Adam said. "Just play."

"Bys yourself?" The words were thick coming from Uncle Jack's mouth, and Adam didn't like the way he looked at him. His father looked like he was about to fall asleep.

"Most of the time," Adam said.

"Well, a kid your age should have some friends around. Don't you got any friends?"

Adam shook his head at first, but then said, "At school. None of them live around here."

"Well, you better get yourself some dinner," Jack said. "I don't think your daddy is feeling too good this fine day." Uncle Jack smiled, and Adam averted his eyes as quickly as he could. He didn't like the way his uncle's teeth looked, all uneven and stained.

Waiting to see if his uncle said or did anything else, Adam finally turned and went into the kitchen. In the freezer, he located one of the pre-packaged meals he liked, opened the box and slid it into the microwave. While he waited for it to cook, he alternated looking out the kitchen window and back at the living room to make sure he was still alone. When the timer beeped, he pulled the meal out of the microwave, grabbed a fork and knife along with a bottle of water from the fridge, and headed back into his room, where he locked the door.

As he finished the last couple bites of his turkey dinner, the knob on his bedroom door rattled, stopped and rattled again. From outside, "Why's this locked?" It was Uncle Jack.

Adam stayed quiet for a minute, hoping his uncle would just give up and leave. "Open it up, kid. Your daddy's sleeping and I gotta leave. I need to tell you something before I go."

Reluctantly, Adam made his way from his desk over to the door, unlocked it and looked up as his uncle opened the door. Uncle Jack swayed briefly before putting his hand on the door jamb to steady himself.

In his thick, syrupy voice he said, "I gave your daddy some medicine a little while ago. You know he hasn't been doing very well since your mama left."

Adam nodded his head but didn't say anything. He wondered what kind of "medicine" his uncle could possibly give his dad.

"Anyways," Jack continued. "If he ain't awake in an hour or so, you need to try to wake him up. If he doesn't wake up then, you better call 911 and get an ambulance out here."

Adam felt the panic welling up inside of him, but his instincts told him he needed to just stay quiet to get Uncle Jack to leave without doing anything to him.

"I'm reals sorry about your momma," Uncle Jack said. "She and I didn't get along well, but she was my sister." He swayed in the doorway before saying, "Give me a hug."

Before Adam could retreat, his uncle wrapped him in his arms, the smell of body odor and old whiskey nearly gagging him. He felt his uncle's hands on his back, the right one working its way down to his butt, where it squeezed lightly and lingered just a little too long.

Finally, his uncle let him go, before turning and heading back toward the front of the house. As he left, he looked over at dad and said, "Remember, one hour, then call for help."

When the front screen door closed and Adam heard Uncle Jack's car start up, he ran to the couch and tried to rouse his dad, who startled for a second, turned his head and started snoring again. At least he's still breathing, Adam thought. On his second try a few minutes later he was able to wake dad and asked him if he wanted anything to eat. Dad shook his head no, but at least kept his eyes open, focused on something up on the ceiling. Adam just sat there with him for what seemed like an eternity and, after a while, his dad stood up slowly and told him it was time for both of them to go to bed.

As Roger was turning in to his bedroom, Adam called from the living room, "Dad?"

He stopped, rubbed at his eyes and looked back at his son. "What, buddy?"

In that moment, Adam wanted to ask his dad what made him fall asleep, tell him just how scared he was and talk to him about the uncomfortable way his uncle made him feel, especially when he touched his backside, but instead all he could manage was, "Nothing. I'll see you in the morning."

"Night buddy," his dad said, closing the bedroom door, through which Adam could hear his father collapse onto his bed.

As he walked into his own bedroom, Adam realized he still smelled his uncle's lingering odor on him, and he peeled off his clothes, threw them into the hall so they weren't in his bedroom with him and walked to the bathroom to take a shower. He closed his eyes as the hot water washed over his body and tried unsuccessfully to forget the way his uncle's hug felt. As had become a nearly nightly custom, he started crying, missing his mom, hating what was happening to his dad, and hating even more that Uncle Jack started coming around, even if it was infrequently. Finishing the shower, he toweled off, put on his pajamas and got in bed, hoping sleep would come quickly. It didn't.

Chapter Eleven

Micah worked on the finishing touches on part one of the DCS series scheduled to begin that Sunday when his cell phone vibrated on the desk next to him. The number was not one he had programmed into his contacts, but it was local so he picked it up. "This is Micah Sanders."

"Mr. Sanders, good afternoon," the caller said. "My name is Marianne Cawley and I am the Executive Director for Lands County CASA."

Remembering the email he sent a couple days earlier, Micah expected to hear back from someone with the organization.

"Ms. Cawley, thank you for calling."

"I have to say, we were pleasantly surprised to get your inquiry," she said, "and I wanted to be in touch with you sooner, but I've been out of town at our state conference the past couple of days."

Micah acknowledged he received her out of office notification after he sent his email. "I've been giving this some thought the past couple of months, and I would like to learn more about what is involved with becoming a CASA. I'm not sure my schedule will allow it at this point, but I'd like to hear more about it."

After chatting for a few more minutes, the two arranged to meet for lunch on Friday at noon, and Micah entered the appointment in his calendar on his phone. Turning back to his monitor, he continued writing the final few paragraphs of his Sunday feature.

The first installment of the series came together nicely. On Tuesday, Micah spent several hours at the Department of Child Services offices, interviewing the director and a senior case worker. Both were a little guarded at first, obviously worried the newspaper's story would be unflattering to the agency. Micah spent a fair amount of time reassuring each of them he would be as fair as possible, and he had the feeling going in that, within DCS there were a lot of good people whose hands were tied by bureaucracy and legal red tape. During both interviews, it was apparent that was the case. After finishing the final sentence of the story, Micah's eyes drifted back to the top of the page to review what he had written.

A Time for Action
Could intervention by DCS have prevented the Henley murders?
By Micah Sanders & staff
Part One of an Ongoing Series

By now, anyone who reads this paper, and just about everyone else in and around Williams, knows the story. On and before May 1 in his small home on Washburn Street, Curtis Henley allegedly killed his wife, Karri, his sons Curtis Jr., Will and David, and his daughter Haylee. The arraignment is in the books, with Henley entering a not guilty plea, and a trial date of November 17 has been set.

Throughout Williams, theories as to why such a thing could happen or how a person could do such a thing are as rampant and varied as the people who present them. From speculation about drug and alcohol use to the idea "the guy is just nuts," most people have formed a preliminary opinion to the point that jury selection in this case will be, to say the least, challenging.

In cases such as these, regardless of the circumstances surrounding the "why" and the "how," one cannot help but wonder what could have been done in the weeks, months and years leading up to the act that could have changed the outcome and prevented the tragedy. It is human nature to look back, to second guess, and to speculate on how different things could have been if someone had stepped in and done something, or just taken a path opposite the one chosen.

That someone, in this case, is the Department of Child Services and, over the coming weeks, *The Sentinel* will offer an in-depth look at this state-funded agency, discuss the processes used to determine courses of action, and examine the outcomes brought about in those cases.

Let me state upfront this is not meant to be an indictment on the DCS or the people who work there. In our initial interviews this week, it was apparent there are some very dedicated people within the agency and they have chosen a vocation that, without a doubt, puts them in a lot of difficult positions where the right answer is rarely the easy one.

Records show the Henley household was investigated twice by DCS, the first time about a year and a half before the shootings, and the second time just more than eight months prior. In both cases, interviews were conducted, the children were interviewed and examined, and the conclusion was that, while the household was not necessarily ideal, DCS action was not warranted at either point.

The goal of this series is to examine this particular case, ensure the proper procedures were followed and, if they were, take a look at whether the procedures, mandated for the most part by state law, are adequate to ensure the welfare of children and families in similar circumstances.

The world we live in today is faced with challenges our grandparents and even our parents could not have envisioned. Elements like drug and alcohol abuse exist on a much grander scale than they did a couple generations ago. Illegal guns are everywhere. What is worse is it has become obvious that moral turpitude in our society has declined, and things that used to be considered sacred and off-limits are no longer so.

As these societal "norms" have changed, the rules that govern them have struggled to keep up, as politicians have kept an eye toward violation of personal liberties – rightly so – to the point where we start to wonder if we're doing a better job protecting the criminals than we are the innocent.

After this introduction to the series, we will move next week to a discussion with DCS Director Sandra Bless. She, along with senior caseworker Craig Evans, met with *Sentinel* staffers this week, and both have agreed to more in-depth interviews in the coming weeks. During the series, we will also meet with state lawmakers, judges and, hopefully, members of the public who have had interactions with DCS.

If you or someone you know is interested in participating in an interview, we would love to talk to you and, of course, would be more than willing to treat discussions in a confidential manner. Those willing to talk with us can reach me directly at msanders@thesentinel.net or on my personal line at (812) 555-4200.

Lastly, as with anything in our newspaper, we invite public comment during this series. If it is determined that some of the processes and procedures used by DCS need to change, we can certainly help to drive the effort but it will be the public, as voters, that can most effectively influence our legislators.

We hope you find the upcoming series informative, and we look forward to creating a positive dialogue.

****

At precisely noon on Friday, Micah walked into the only Japanese restaurant in downtown Williams and recognized Marianne Cawley from photos he had seen of her in various stories that had run in the paper. She was seated at a table by the window, and when she saw Micah, who she recognized from his picture in each day's paper, she stood up and greeted him with a smile.

"Mr. Sanders," she said, "thank you so much for initiating this, and for meeting me."

"Please, Ms. Cawley, call me Micah."

"I will if you'll call me Mari," she said.

The two agreed to proceed on a first-name basis and after ordering a glass of ice water and an iced tea, engaged in small talk centering around Micah's involvement with other non-profits and his thoughts on his adopted city as well as Mari's time with the agency – 21 years – and how long she lived in Williams.

After ordering some lunch – sushi for both – they started in on a discussion about Lands County CASA and the requirements for becoming an advocate.

****

The process starts off with several requirements, including state and federal background checks, a child abuse registry check, as well as three personal references supporting the candidate's ability to handle the role of CASA. After that, an in-depth interview determines if the candidate has had any experience with abuse or neglect, ascertains his or her thoughts on corporal punishment, and determines if there are any other things in the person's background that may hamper the ability to make impartial recommendations to the court.

Once those hurdles are cleared, the trainee goes through 30 hours of training over a six-week period, using a training manual filled with case studies and applicable state law. Following the training sessions, the soon-to-be CASA signs a confidentiality agreement and goes through at least five hours of court observation, where he or she gets to see an entire case through from start to finish. After that, the swearing-in ceremony is held for the trainee, and that person becomes a CASA and is typically assigned a first case relatively quickly.

"Our waiting list just continues to grow, unfortunately," Mari said. "And while we've been able to outpace our volunteer numbers year after year, we just can't keep up with the increase in cases we're assigned each year."

"What got me thinking about this," Micah said, "in addition to your press releases and the amazing work your agency does, were the recent Henley shootings."

"Horrible," she replied. "Just horrible." Micah could see in her eyes the case was one that affected her deeply, as it did him, but in the short time he had spent with Mari he gathered that *every* case affected her.

"Forgive me for asking," Micah said, "but how do you do your job for as long as you have done it? How do you – day in and day out – look into the abyss containing the worst humanity has to offer and still keep your sanity?"

Mari looked out the window momentarily, took a drink of water, and then looked back at Micah. "A mentor of mine, very early in my career, gave me some good advice when I first took over this job in the early 90s. She told me I was going to see a lot of terrible things – things a 'normal' person couldn't ever comprehend. She also said there were going to be times where I would wonder how we could ever live in such a world – and I have wondered that so many times.

"The advice she gave, though, was when things would start to look their darkest and when I was getting to the point where I was convinced nothing I was doing was making a difference, I needed to focus on the outcomes and that more times than not – many more times in fact – we are putting these children in far better circumstances than they were in prior to our insertion into their cases."

Mari paused as if waiting for the next question to come. Micah thought for a moment on how to best phrase what he was about to ask, but Mari just encouraged him to ask it straight out. "I know what you want to ask next," she said. "You're going to say that the whole thing just seems rather hopeless, and that for each case we positively resolve, two more come up that need taking care of. Or something to that effect." She smiled.

"Something to that effect," Micah agreed.

"Micah, you have to understand, this agency like others that deal with domestic violence, hunger, homelessness – you name it – can only look at one case at a time. We aren't going to change the world overnight or stop bad things from happening, but we can make a profound difference in the lives of every child we take under our wing. We can change his world. And maybe, just maybe, if we can do that enough times, we can finally put an end to the cycle of violence."

Mari went on to explain that most abusers were once abused themselves and the most important role a CASA can play is to show the children involved that the behavior is not acceptable and they did not deserve what happened to them. "By doing so, we re-train these victims and we empower them to think differently so that when they are adults, the cycle does not begin anew."

Micah nodded as he looked at his watch. The time passed quickly and it was now after 1:30, quickly approaching a 2 p.m. meeting he needed to attend. He told

Mari he needed to head back to the office, but that she had given him a lot to think about.

"I'd like to have another conversation with my wife and give this a little more thought," he said, "but I am definitely intrigued with the work you do and I just feel like I need to do something to help."

"Well, you're already helping," she replied. "The coverage in the newspaper makes a world of difference. Every time an article runs we see an uptick in inquiries about volunteering, donating, or helping in some other way. But I would be lying if I said that I wasn't really hoping that you choose to sign on as a CASA volunteer."

Micah promised to discuss things with Kayla over the weekend and told Mari he would be in touch Monday or Tuesday with any additional questions that may arise. The two stood, shook hands and headed back to their respective offices.

Chapter Twelve

Adam's fifth-grade school year was nothing like the ones before it. Up until then, he took great pride in doing a good job in school, turning in all his work on time, and pleasing his parents and teachers. While he wasn't the most popular kid in school, he always had a couple of good friends he would play with at recess and occasionally outside of school.

Adam was coming off a long and lonely summer. Dad's drinking was much more intense during the early part of the summer. It seemed like he could hold it together for the most part during the school year since teaching and having to be at school kept him busy and distracted, but during the long days of summer with little to do, dad turned to the bottle early and kept things going through the afternoon and late into the night.

In addition, Uncle Jack started coming around more often. On one of the early visits, Adam walked in from playing outside and saw his uncle sticking a needle in his dad's arm. It was the kind of needle doctors used at their offices to give shots when people needed them, but he felt he probably shouldn't ask his dad and uncle what they were doing. Instead he went to his room and retreated into the make-believe world he created for himself that summer.

The first couple times Uncle Jack came to visit, Adam did his best to stay out in the woods as much as possible, but he came in around dinner time, and his uncle was usually still there. While in the house, Adam stayed locked in his room. During Uncle Jack's visits, dad pretty much stayed on the couch and dozed in and out of sleep, and while his dad was out, his uncle knocked on Adam's door and say, "What ya doing in there, kid?"

The first time, Adam just tried to ignore him, but his uncle started rapping more loudly on the door until Adam felt he had to open it. On that day, Uncle Jack stayed in the room with him for almost a full hour, and he made Adam show him his toys and what he liked to do when he was in the room. Adam's distrust of him was obvious from the start, and he asked the boy several times why he didn't like him, or if he was afraid of him. Adam lied and told him that he just didn't know him very well.

"Well, I'm going to be coming around here more often, cuz your daddy needs a friend. And maybe the two of us can get to know each other a little better."

During this visit to Adam's room, his uncle came across as a decent guy, taking an interest in what Adam liked and as the hour went by, Adam found himself liking him more than he thought he would. As they wrapped up the visit, they sat on the floor next to Adam's bed and flipped through the latest issue of Sports Illustrated. Uncle Jack sat to Adam's left as they went through the magazine. As his uncle reached over to turn the page, his right hand went past the magazine and brushed against Adam's private area, but then quickly moved away. Adam tried to dismiss it as simply as an accident before his mind went back to Uncle Jack squeezing his butt almost a year earlier.

Apparently, Uncle Jack could see his nephew's wheels turning, as he abruptly stood up and said he needed to go. "I enjoyed visiting with you and getting to know you, buddy," Adam's uncle said, opening the door. "Maybe next time you can show me that fort of yours."

Adam thought to himself he would never do any such thing, but he nodded to avoid any kind of confrontation. In his mind, he wondered if maybe, just maybe, his uncle brushing the front of his pants was just an accident. Lying in his bed that night after he confirmed his dad made it to bed, he realized he enjoyed visiting with Uncle Jack and he thought maybe he wasn't such a bad guy after all. With so little family in his life, he wanted to believe someone other than his dad cared about him and would be there for him if he needed it. With that thought, he fell asleep and slept through the night.

Uncle Jack never mentioned the fort again. Adam wondered if he would, but eventually allowed himself to believe his uncle realized the fort was his secret place, somewhere he had to get away if he ever needed it. During his visits, which came about once a week by the time July rolled around, his uncle was always friendly with him, especially early in the visits before he and dad started the heavy drinking. While he wasn't comfortable hugging Uncle Jack yet, Adam wasn't afraid of him anymore, and he didn't try to stay away from him. There hadn't been any more uncomfortable touches, and contact was pretty much limited to a hand on the shoulder or a pat on the head or back. In his mind, Adam began to let go of the two times he had been uncomfortable, telling him he must have made too big of a deal about those instances.

At the same time, Adam was becoming closer to Uncle Jack, dad seemed to be withdrawing more and more each day. He lost weight at a rapid pace, and Adam didn't like the way the skin around his face hung loosely around his jaw and neck. He always knew his dad as the strong, athletic type, and the physical changes he saw in the past year worried him. Whenever he tried to get his dad to eat something, he declined, and when Adam cooked something and put it in front of him, he picked at a few bites before leaving most of the food uneaten.

Adam thought, at least school would be starting up soon, and dad always seemed to do better when he had classes to focus on during the daytime. He tried to talk to his dad a couple times about his drinking, never quite sure a good way to bring it up, and each time those conversations ended with dad telling him he was fine, and he was just going through a tough time right now. Adam didn't know how to take the conversation to the next level, so he would usually just let his dad out of it at that point.

On a Sunday morning in mid-July, just a few days before the first time his father hit him, Adam sat on the couch watching television when Uncle Jack's car pulled into the driveway. Dad was still sleeping in his bedroom, and Adam was surprised at his uncle's visit, since he usually didn't come around so early in the day.

He walked in the open screen door without knocking and sat down on the chair across from Adam. "Your daddy still sleeping?" he asked.

Without looking away from the cartoon he was watching, Adam nodded.

"I'm going to go wake him up," Uncle Jack said. "I gotta talk to him about something."

Adam looked away from the TV long enough to watch his uncle enter his dad's room and shut the door behind him. He couldn't make out what they said on the other side of the door, but he heard two voices so he knew his dad had awakened.

Another ten minutes passed, and the show Adam was watching came to an end. He got up, took his empty cereal bowl to the sink and went into the bathroom to take a shower. As he finished rinsing the shampoo out of his hair, the bathroom door opened, the shower curtain pulled back, and his uncle stared at his wet body with a creepy smile on his face unlike any Adam saw from him before. Adam tried to cover himself with his hands, but he knew his uncle already saw him, and he didn't seem eager to pull the curtain back.

"Hey little buddy," he said, the smile still there. "I'm done talking to your daddy and just wanted to say goodbye before I left." His eyes went up and down Adam's body one more time, the smile continuing, and he said, "I'll see you soon."

With that, he pulled the curtain closed and promptly left the bathroom. Adam exhaled the breath he was holding in, and he sat down in the tub and cried into his hands as the hot water showered over him. He couldn't recall a time in his life when he was so afraid, and any doubt he ever had about the appropriateness of his uncle's touches left him for good.

His mind raced with questions as to whether he should say something to his father, but he kept coming back to the strange relationship his dad and uncle developed that summer, and in the back of his mind he was terrified his uncle would hurt him, his dad, or both if he were to say anything. After a few more minutes, he convinced himself that, since his uncle hadn't touched him – only looked – he'd keep it quiet for the time being.

When he got out of the shower, he quickly locked the door just in case Uncle Jack hadn't left, then toweled himself and slipped on his underwear. He listened at the door for a moment, and when he didn't hear any sounds, he cracked it so he could peer out into the hall and living room. When he saw no one, he cautiously opened the door, hurried to his room and locked the door behind him to get dressed. As he finished and went back out into the house, he realized dad was still in the bedroom and figured he had fallen back asleep after Uncle Jack left. The sun was climbing high in the sky and the thermometer outside their back door already read 84 degrees at 11 a.m. when Adam jumped the last three steps off his back deck and raced into the woods to the security of his fort.

****

Four days later, on Thursday, July 23, the day that Adam's life started to change again began like just about every other that summer. Dad was sleeping off the previous night's Beam. Adam got himself out of bed, had his breakfast, watched SportsCenter and put his clothes on to head out to the woods for the day. It was now four days since his uncle looked him over, and the memory still lingered vividly in his mind especially when he was in the bathroom, so he only showered once since Sunday.

Out in his fort, he assembled a collection of plastic army figurines, the small kind popular when his dad and even his grandfather were children, and he set up for what was to be an epic battle. All summer, the good guys – his guys – made progress on the enemy camp, causing retreat and ready to take them down for the final time. After a long battle – the plastic digital watch on his wrist read 12:47 – he felt hungry and headed back toward the house to make a peanut butter sandwich.

When he entered the house, everything was quiet, but a bowl on the counter that hadn't been there earlier let him know his father was up, or at least had been. He walked quietly down the hall and heard snoring coming from inside his dad's bedroom. Adam sighed, shrugged his shoulders, and went back to the kitchen to make his sandwich. As he passed through the living room, he noticed a needle – the kind he saw Uncle Jack use earlier in the summer – sitting on the table. He picked it up, saw there was residue in the vial, and set it back down quickly. This was the first time he saw a syringe since the night with his uncle, and Adam ran back down the hall and opened his father's door.

"Dad, are you okay?" he asked.

His father stirred, rolled onto his back and turned his head toward the door but didn't open his eyes. "Huh, what?" he slurred, almost indecipherable.

"Dad, I think you should get up," Adam pleaded, moving alongside his bed.

Dad cracked one eye and looked at his boy. He made a weak attempt at a smile and said, "I'll be okay, buddy. Just not feeling my best today. Need a little more sleep."

Adam debated internally for a moment, then turned and headed back toward the door. From behind him, he heard his father mumble, "Love you, buddy," followed immediately by a guttural snore.

The rest of the afternoon and into the early evening Adam spent in the woods, the Americans finally finishing off those villainous North Koreans. Adam saw on the news the North Koreans were threatening the USA earlier in the summer, and since then he made it his mission to do his part to put an end to their tyranny. Today, mission accomplished.

He closed the fort and headed back toward the house as the temperature was just beginning to drop, the first signs of evening encroaching on the heat of the summer day. From his position on the back deck, Adam saw the flicker of the television in the living room and found his dad in his usual spot resting on the couch, a glass in his hand and a large bottle of whiskey on the table in front of him.

"What you been doing?" he slurred, the words moving together without a pause in between any of them.

"Just playing out in the woods," Adam said. "I was going to grab some dinner."

"Good," dad said. "Make me some, too."

Adam was pleased his father asked for food. The weight loss had continued through the summer and every day seemed to bring less appetite for anything other than whiskey and whatever was in the syringe he found earlier in the day.

During the past year, Adam became more proficient in food preparation and graduated from frozen dinners every night to boiling water for spaghetti and cooking up some jarred sauce to throw over the top of it. Since dad was joining him for dinner, tonight would be pasta.

When it was ready, Adam laid out two nice plates and carried them to the kitchen table, which he set with a tablecloth and utensils, and called his dad into the kitchen. He poured them both glasses of ice water and set them at the table as well, and he was glad when his dad came to the table without his glass or bottle of whiskey.

Dad looked over the food approvingly, smiled at his son, took his seat and immediately dove into the plate of food. He ate more in the next five minutes than Adam saw him eat all summer, and when dad got up and fixed himself a second plate, Adam felt a brief glimmer of hope that things could someday return to normal.

They hadn't spoken to each other yet, but Adam was content to just let his father eat his spaghetti, and the sounds of pasta being slurped up made the lack of conversation oddly pleasant.

When they finished their dinner and cleaned up the kitchen – his dad fumbled the plates twice trying to put them back in the cabinet, but hadn't dropped them – dad kissed Adam on the top of the head and told him to come watch some television with him.

They turned on their favorite crime show, and during the first commercial, dad took a sip from his whiskey and looked at Adam.

"Look, buddy," he said, still slurring but not as bad as before dinner. "I know I haven't done very well this summer, and I know I got some fixin' to do. I messed up pretty bad with everything since momma left." Dad started to cry just a little bit.

Adam thought about saying something, but remained silent.

"Anyways," dad continued. "School starts back next week, and I'm going to get some help with my drinking. I need some help, buddy."

Adam nodded, and slid closer to his dad on the couch. He put his arm around his father and rested his head on his shoulder.

"Dad, I saw the needle on the table earlier today. What is that stuff Uncle Jack gave you?"

With his face turned downward, he couldn't see the change in his father's facial expression, but he felt his whole body tense as soon as Adam got the words out. His dad pushed Adam off him, sending him reeling and hitting the side of his head against the padded armrest of the couch.

"You weren't supposed to see that, goddammit!" Adam saw dad's arm swing toward him as if in slow motion, and he did all he could to shield himself from the blow, but the open hand slammed into his left ear, snapping his head to the side.

Before the force of the blow even set in, dad said, "Oh shit, I'm so sorry. I'm so sorry." He started crying, as Adam looked at him, the tears now flowing down the boy's face as well. Adam looked on in stunned silence as his dad fell into the chair, and without another thought, he jumped off the couch and ran through the back door, through the yard and into the woods. He remembered hearing the back door slamming behind him once, and then again when his father started his pursuit, but after that most of the night was a blur in his memory until he woke up in Uncle Jack's cabin hours later.

****

In the weeks following the night Adam ran away, only to be found by Uncle Jack, tied to the chair and threatened, things were quiet at Adam's house. His dad never said a word about what happened that night. He offered no apologies for the hard smack to the side of the head and said nothing about Adam's whereabouts through the evening or how he ended up back at the house when his father awoke the following morning.

One thing that started to change, though, was dad cut back his drinking considerably. In the two weeks leading up to the start of school, the empty bottle of Beam in the sink went from a nightly occurrence to around every third night. Once school started back, Adam didn't see his father drink at all. What Adam didn't know was Roger started going to AA meetings every day after school, and as August rolled into September, Adam noticed his dad starting to eat normally again, putting on some of the weight he lost, and even starting to work out again to regain some of the muscle form he lost during the past six months or so.

Sitting at the dinner table on Thursday night before Labor Day weekend, dad let Adam know he started the Alcoholics Anonymous meetings the first day of school and he hadn't had a drink since then. He said he was working hard the first three weeks of the school year to get himself back together, but one of the steps in his recovery was making amends to the people he hurt.

"I turned down a dark path, buddy," he said to Adam that evening. "Your mom was everything to me – everything to us – and when she died I held it together for you as much as I could. Well, at least until I couldn't hold it together anymore.

"The thing about drinking the way I was is it dulls the pain so you can't feel it so much anymore, but at the same time, it only allows you to escape while it has you in its grips. The nightmares are still always there, and when you wake up the next day, the only way to put down that pain again is to start drinking all over again."

Roger went on for nearly 30 minutes, basically unloading everything he was holding back for the past two years. He apologized to Adam for not being there for him and for forcing Adam to grow up too fast, but he especially apologized for all the times he hurt him, not just the one time he hit him, but for all the emotional pain he caused as well.

When he finished, they were both crying and hugging and telling each other how things were going to be different and how they were finally going to move on past losing a mother, a wife, and a best friend. Roger emptied the house of every bottle of booze weeks earlier and now, through a simple conversation with his son, he emptied their world of the pain and misery under which they lived the previous couple of years.

For the first time in a long time, Roger tucked Adam into bed that night. Before he did, they made plans to pack up the car Saturday morning and head down to Kentucky to spend a couple nights tent camping in a favorite campground they used many times before for short weekend getaways. Dad called it their chance to say goodbye to summer, and to welcome some great new memories they were about to make. Before they went, though, dad mentioned that after he got out of his meeting the next afternoon, he and Adam would grab a pizza and see a movie – anything Adam wanted – on Friday night.

When Adam laid his head down on his pillow, the nightmares and restless sleep of the past many months gave way to happy dreams of his parents, together again, and all the memories they made as a family. He awoke to a beautiful sunrise, got dressed and happily accepted his dad's offer of a ride to school rather than his usual bus ride. Excited about the big weekend ahead, that school day seemed to last forever, but when the final bell sounded at 3 p.m. he ran to the bus, hopped on and started talking to some friends he hadn't spent much time with in a while. Back at the house, he packed his bag for the next couple of days, and as he was packing up his last few items, dad arrived home.

They had a great time together that night, splitting a sausage pizza at their favorite place and watching Dolphin Tale 2, which Adam chose. They saw the first one a few years earlier before each of them lost the most important woman in his life, but neither of them mentioned how much they were thinking of Annie as they sat through the sequel. Instead, they smiled a lot, laughed at the right times, and remembered what it felt like to laugh. For both of them, that evening felt like Annie was back with them, at least for a while.

The camping trip had a similar feel to it the entire weekend. During the day, still pleasantly warm in early September, they hiked, went fishing, and even did some whitewater rafting on Sunday. At night, they cooked up some steaks and the fish they brought in case they didn't catch anything, which they didn't, and they sat by the campfire and talked. No ghost stories, Adam said. Without verbalizing it, both realized they lived their own personal ghost stories in the too recent past, so there was no reason to make them up around a fire.

When they packed the gear into the car on Monday afternoon, a lot of healing had taken place and the drive back to Williams was filled with a lot of laughs, talking and stories about some of their great vacations of the past. Dad promised more of those in the years to come, starting with the next summer. He also talked to Adam about getting back involved with baseball in the Spring, and since he wasn't coaching the high school team anymore, he thought he would sign up to coach Adam's team, if he decided he wanted to play. Adam admitted he missed playing the past year, and they made plans to throw the ball around before dinner once they got home that afternoon.

As they drove through Louisville, over the Ohio River and past the "Welcome to Indiana" sign, Adam felt content and happy, for the first time really since his mom died. He looked out the window and smiled before turning back and looking at his dad.

"Dad?"

"Yeah, buddy?"

"I'm really glad you're back," Adam said. "I miss mom every day. But I really have missed you."

Dad just nodded, smiled and wiped a single tear from his eye.

Chapter Thirteen

The day after the first installment of The Sentinel's DCS feature ran in the paper, Micah was back in the office early and the blinking light on his phone let him know he had voicemails. He wasn't surprised by this as, throughout the day Sunday as people finished reading his column, his inbox filled up with letters to the editor, most favoring the newspaper taking a hard look at the agency in light of the Henley murders. Almost unanimously, readers were outraged there was even a possibility something could have been done before Henley shot his wife and kids and, despite the fact Micah essentially pleaded with his readers not to jump to conclusions, it was obvious that a lot of minds were already made up that DCS was negligent.

None too happy about that was DCS Director Bless, whose voice was the first Micah heard as he started through the eleven voicemails in his box.

"Micah, this is Sandra Bless," she started, the tension and frustration obvious in her voice. "Our phones blew up all day yesterday, and when people couldn't reach our regular office numbers since it was Sunday, they started calling the hotline. They're ready to burn the place down."

Micah had the article in front of him as he listened to the rest of the voicemail, and he quickly realized his request for a "positive dialogue" in the last line of the article was not off to a good start. His eyes kept going to the subhead, and he wondered if the question of whether DCS intervention possibly preventing the murders was a fair one to ask up front. Part of him knew the subhead could be inflammatory when he wrote it, but he also knew it would draw a lot of reader interest and set the tone for the article and those to follow in the coming weeks.

When the voicemail finally ended, Sandra Bless asked for a return call but told Micah she was going to get instruction on Monday as to whether she or any of her employees would participate in the follow-up interviews. From Micah's vantage point, he knew the agency would weigh whether they helped their cause by participating in the story or just letting the reporters speculate, essentially allowing readers to fill in any gaps that might exist.

Micah listened to the remaining voicemails, eight of which were also about the story, and none from people initially planned as sources. Still, there were three people who said they previously interacted with DCS in some way, and all were willing to share their stories. Micah noted the names and numbers, before walking down the hall to get a cup of coffee.

Over the weekend, he and Kayla discussed his Friday meeting with Mari Cawley. In addition to all the information Mari presented during their lunch, she gave Micah a copy of the training manual used in the upcoming class. He and Kayla flipped through it and reviewed the contents, even spending some time reading a few of the case studies in the manual.

By the end of the weekend, Micah was about 90 percent sure he wanted to sign up for the class, but he felt he needed to have a discussion with his publisher and owner prior to committing. From everything Mari told him, he could work a fair amount of the responsibilities around his schedule, but he needed to be available for court hearings and the occasional emergency that may arise. His company was always open to employees volunteering their time and being involved in the community, but he still felt it good form to ask permission since some of the time could be during work hours.

A new CASA training session was starting in early to mid-July and, since Micah knew the sessions only took place several times a year, he felt if he was going to volunteer he needed to be a part of the next class. Things were so busy at work at the moment, and with his staff in the middle of the DCS story, he wasn't sure it was the best time to do it but deep down he felt it was a now or never situation.

When he met with his boss a couple hours later and got the go-ahead, Micah made the decision, picked up the phone and called Mari Cawley to tell her he was in. Mari told him she would send over the paperwork for the background checks later in the day, and once those were completed they would schedule the interview.

Chapter Fourteen

The week after the camping trip, Adam felt his motivation returning and his teachers could see a change in him, back to the boy he was before his mother passed away. He worked much harder in his classes, spent more time socializing with the other students outside of class, and no longer sat alone many days in the cafeteria. In addition, the unbridled smile that was so much a part of his personality until the last couple years returned, replacing the sullen look that took its place recently.

At home, dad seemed happy again and the two spent every evening together having dinner, finishing Adam's homework and then watching a little television before bed each night. On the weekend after Labor Day, they went camping again – this time just down the road in the state park and only for one night. Still, in early September, the weather was nearly perfect for camping – warm during the daylight hours, but cooling quickly in the evening and making the conditions perfect for a campfire. As far as Adam knew, dad hadn't taken a drink in several weeks, and he talked frequently during their dinners about how much the AA meetings helped him. He even told Adam he now had a sponsor he could call anytime he needed him, and the sponsor was someone who went through the same problems, so he understood what it was like.

By this time, Adam had seen enough bad come from drinking and drugs he convinced himself he would never get anywhere close to either. He was getting to the age where kids at school started talking about watching their parents drink – some even tried it themselves a couple times – and when these conversations would start, Adam just grew quiet and tried to slip away from the group.

He still hadn't figured out which drugs his father and uncle did during the summer. From his research on the Internet, he knew there were several injectable drugs, but since his dad's reaction the night he told him about seeing the needle, he had no desire to bring up the subject again. Besides, things were definitely getting better and he had just about convinced himself he could start to put those dark chapters of his life behind him.

Monday after the one-night camping trip was one of Adam's best days at school in a long time. He got 100 percent on the math test he and dad studied for on Sunday night, and during recess he scored 10 points in the basketball game the kids played. He never was very good at basketball, but that day every shot at the hoop went in.

During the game, he apparently caught the eye of Katie Stilton, without a doubt the prettiest girl in class, and she came over and talked to him as they walked back into the building. Adam liked the way Katie kept smiling at him and looking at him as they walked, and he found himself slowing down to make sure it took as long as possible to get back to their classroom. As they entered the classroom, she touched his lower arm, letting her hand slide down into his for the briefest of moments. The smile on Adam's face stayed with him through the rest of the day, and his attention during class was no longer on what his teacher said.

When the school bus dropped him off, Adam was still beaming as he ran up the winding driveway that led from the road back to his house. When he turned the corner where his house came into view, he stopped in his tracks when he saw the familiar SUV, his uncle leaning against it smoking a cigarette. Uncle Jack hadn't come back since the day he looked Adam over in the shower and Adam hadn't seen him since he picked him up the night he ran away. With dad doing so much better, Adam thought maybe they wouldn't see him around anymore.

For a couple of moments, Adam just stood there, approximately 100 yards separating him and the person he feared the most. Adam considered his options and was just about to turn and run back toward the road when another voice spoke up inside of him, one which told him he couldn't run forever. For one thing, his uncle had a car and if he tried to get away, it would be easy enough to track him down. Sure, he could run through the woods where Uncle Jack wouldn't be able to drive, and Adam knew there was no way Jack could outrun him. He also knew if he did that, he would probably get away for that day, but it wouldn't solve the problem because his uncle could come back any day he wanted.

Deep down, Adam knew the time had come for him to tell his dad everything about Uncle Jack and let his father deal with it. He decided to do that when his dad got home from work, but for now he needed to confront his fears and deal with Uncle Jack. Slowly, but confidently, putting aside the fear bubbling up in his gut, he started walking up the driveway toward his uncle's car.

Uncle Jack still hadn't said anything. He just watched Adam as he battled with his emotions and made his decision to approach, and as Adam got to within twenty yards of him, he still leaned on the car, regularly puffing from the burning butt in his hand.

"What are you doing here?" Adam said, doing his best to sound confident so as not to betray the growing fear he felt with every step.

Uncle Jack just stared at him, his eyes bloodshot and an uneven smile playing around the dying cigarette that now dangled from his lips. "Where's your daddy?" he finally asked.

Hearing his uncle's voice asking the question made Adam consider one more time he should just turn and get as far from the man as possible. Still, he convinced himself he needed to grow up and not be such a baby.

"He's…he's still at work, but he should be home any minute now," Adam finally replied.

"You and I both know that's not true," Uncle Jack said, the words as thick as Adam ever heard coming from him. "But both you and him have been ignoring me this past month or so. I've even tried calling him a couple of times, but he never calls me back."

Adam felt anger rising inside him, and it quickly replaced the fear he felt when he first saw his uncle. "That's probably because he's stopped drinking and doesn't want anything to do with you."

Before the words finished coming out of his mouth Adam knew he probably overstepped, and the change on his uncle's face from drunken indifference to absolute rage sent a shiver through Adam like he never felt before.

"You little shit," Jack said, steadying himself as he removed his ample backside from the car. "How dare you talk to me like that? After all I did for you and your daddy this summer!" He wasn't moving quickly, but his stumbling footsteps picked up pace as he started toward Adam, who moved his way around the car and inched toward the front door of the house, still battling between the fear of his uncle and the anger he felt.

"After all you did this summer?" Adam said, the anger winning for the moment. "Giving my dad too much whiskey and drugs and making him feel bad?" He couldn't believe the words coming out of his mouth, but at the same time he was determined to stand his ground and not let his uncle see his fear.

Still the words appeared to pierce his Uncle Jack in a way unimaginable, and he quickened his pace toward his nephew. The fear returned and Adam turned and ran toward the front door, but by the time he got there, his uncle caught up and turned him around.

The first blow hit Adam on the left cheek with a closed fist, and he immediately tasted blood in his mouth as he staggered to his right, further from the front door he so desperately wished to slip through. Any confidence that resided within him moments ago was now fully gone, and the fear rushed through him at what was to come. He had just enough time to realize it would be at least a couple hours before dad came home before another blow hit him on the other side of the head. As he was about to scream with the hope that someone would hear him, his uncle wrapped him up, covered his mouth with his huge hand, and carried him through the front door and into the cabin.

Uncle Jack threw Adam down onto the couch, and a moment later another punch to the head sent Adam into a daze. The last thing he remembered as he blacked out was the feeling of his pants coming off and the smell of his uncle as he moved in close to him. Then, his world went dark.

****

Roger finished up his daily routine – teaching classes all day, an hour or two grading papers or preparing lesson plans before heading off to his 4 p.m. Alcoholics Anonymous meeting – when he arrived home just a little before 6 p.m. As he pulled into his driveway, he thought about how much better he felt the last few days. The feeling of needing a drink every moment of the day lessened gradually to only thinking about it hourly, then only occasionally. Now, what was an incessant need so recently was just a nagging desire in the dark reaches of his mind and, with each passing day, he felt more and more in control.

What's more, he felt his strength returning. In the mirror, he saw the return of the strong, good-looking guy he was when he had Annie. He thought of her all the time, every moment of every day. But the memories that until recently only brought pain and needed to be numbed with alcohol and drugs now brought happiness, acceptance and thankfulness he experienced them in the first place.

At night, he dreamed of his wife and son, and instead of the ghostly hauntings that were his dreams during the past year, the visions came in sunlight, on mountains, in swimming pools and other happy places that made him awake refreshed instead of scared and exhausted.

What he noticed the most, however, was every day was just a little better than the last. He tortured himself for the first few weeks over what he put Adam through, and he couldn't believe he let himself go from being such a strong role model for his son to the loser he became during his alcohol and drug abuse. Since their camping trip over Labor Day weekend, he started to forgive himself and he could tell that Adam was as well.

As he stepped out of his car, he took a moment to enjoy the way the sunlight filtered through the tall oak, hickory and pine trees surrounding the cabin. There were still a couple hours of daylight left, and he thought he might pull out a couple of the steaks he bought over the weekend to throw on the grill.

When Roger entered the house, he called to Adam and when he didn't respond, he figured he was probably out in his fort behind the house. Walking through the living room, he noticed two of the couch cushions on the floor with the bottom cushions spread apart and a little out of whack. He wondered if Adam brought a friend home with him and the two had been wrestling in the living room. After checking Adam's bedroom to no avail, he opened the back door and listened for the sounds of kids playing. When he didn't hear anything other than the birds and small animals moving in the woods, he called out Adam's name but got no answer.

Now growing a little worried, he shut the door behind him and started out into the woods. The fort in which Adam liked to play was just a couple hundred yards behind the house, and he could always hear calls from the house. Roger's pace quickened to a jog as he continued calling Adam's name with no response.

When he came to the trail that led to Adam's fort about fifty feet off the main path, Roger worked his way back through the brush. The fort consisted of a bunch of logs

Roger, Annie and Adam gathered several years before, stacked in a rectangular shape about eight feet square and covered with long branches to make a thin thatched roof. For an adult to enter, he had to get down onto all fours and crawl through the small space a young boy could merely duck under. As Roger crawled in, his eyes immediately went to the far corner where Adam curled up, rocking himself back and forth and whimpering quietly. His son wore only his underpants, filthy as if he rolled around in the dirt, and the early stages of bruising formed around both eyes and on both cheeks.

For the briefest second, Roger stared in disbelief, a million thoughts running through his mind. Forcing himself from his brief fugue, he moved over and sat next to Adam. When he put his arm around him, Adam moved away quickly, apparently startled by the contact.

"Buddy," Roger said, "what happened?"

Adam just continued rocking slowly back and forth, his knees curled to his chest and his arms pulling them as close as possible. His face was filthy with dried blood and dirt parted by tears spilled earlier. At the moment, Adam wasn't crying, just murmuring quietly to himself, staring straight ahead and rocking.

Roger let a moment pass and tried to get his son to look at him, but Adam only closed his eyes as if he couldn't stand to look at anything. He tried a couple other times to get his son to speak, but Adam just kept whimpering inaudibly. Finally, on the third try, Roger got an arm around his son's shoulders, and Adam limply let his head fall to his dad's shoulder. They sat there for a few moments longer before

Roger decided he needed to get Adam to the house and get him some help.

He waited for Adam to object as he pulled him through the small opening of the fort, but when there was no resistance, he lifted his son and carried him through the woods and back toward the house. As they mounted the steps to the back door and entered, Adam pulled away from Roger's shoulder and looked him square in the eyes. His hands began flailing at Roger's chest and shoulders and he yelled out, "No! Uncle Jack, no!"

Roger pulled his son close and held him as tight as he could, and that was all Adam said as he laid his head back down on his shoulder and began crying uncontrollably. When he quit a few moments later, Roger took him in and laid him on his bed, grabbing his cell phone as he did so. He stepped just outside the door and watched his son as he dialed 911. Adam just stared up at the ceiling, but the words he yelled out echoed through Roger's mind as he called for the police and an ambulance.

****

As the paramedics worked on Adam, still unresponsive, a young police officer whispered with Roger in the corner of the room. Recounting his trip home from his AA meeting, looking for Adam throughout the house and continuing his search until finding his son in the woods, Roger detailed for the officer everything leading up to his 911 call.

"Mr. Durkin," the older of the two paramedics interrupted, "we need to take Adam to the hospital right away. It appears he was sexually assaulted."

Roger could feel the gazes of everyone in the room burning through him, but his mind immediately went back to Adam's shouts as they entered the house.

"Do you know of anyone who could have done this?" the police officer was asking.

Roger was just about to give up Jack, when another thought hit him.

"No," he said. "No idea."

****

At the hospital, doctors and nurses gathered around Adam, tended to the bruises, took blood, and talked quietly to the unresponsive 10-year-old boy on the bed before them. The lead doctor pulled Roger aside earlier and told him they were treating Adam for shock and running tests to make sure they didn't need to worry about sexually transmitted diseases. They wouldn't have the results back until the next day, but they said they collected a semen sample they hoped would identify the attacker.

Several police officers and doctors asked Roger if he had any thoughts on who might have intercepted Adam after he got off the bus, something they already confirmed with his bus driver. They asked if there were any neighbors, family members, or anyone else Roger suspected, and while Roger knew exactly who did this, he made up his mind he wanted to handle the situation before the police could get their hands on his brother-in-law. He was also pretty sure the officers and doctors had not yet ruled him out as a suspect, and he was sure they were already checking his alibi that he attended his AA meeting. By law, the doctors and cops were obligated to call the Department of Child Services, and Roger was told a case worker wanted to talk to him in the hospital's waiting room as soon as they finished working on Adam.

Around 10 that night, after the doctors assured Roger that Adam was resting comfortably, and after he had met with the DCS caseworker for nearly an hour, Roger excused himself and said he was going home to take a shower and pick up some clean clothes, then he would return to the hospital and wait for Adam to wake up in the morning.

On his way out of the hospital, he picked up his cell phone and called his in-laws, who moved out of Williams a year earlier to Gulf Shores, Alabama. After Annie's death, they tried to hang in there for Roger and Adam and, as much as they loved seeing their grandson, the pain they faced every day apparently was just too much for them. They made up their mind to retire to Gulf Shores, and saw Adam only once since they left. Still, Roger knew he needed their help in the coming days.

Despite the relatively late hour, although it was an hour earlier in Gulf Shores, Annie's dad picked up on the second ring. "Tom, this is Roger. I need your help."

Roger laid out for Annie's father most of the details, leaving out of the story the person he knew responsible. Roger wondered if Tom would suspect Jack, especially knowing all of the problems he caused over the years, but he highly doubted it. When they hung up the phone 10 minutes later, Tom promised he and Annie's mother would be in the car early the next morning and arrive in Williams by mid-afternoon. Roger thanked him and hung up the phone. He wondered if he left any suspicion with Tom as to what he intended to do, but he didn't really care as everything was about to start happening very fast.

Five minutes after hanging up on the phone conversation, Roger pulled his car into Jack's driveway, shutting off the headlights as he entered from the road. Like many people in this area of the county, Jack had a long driveway and the house was not visible from the road. Pulling his car into a break in the trees, Roger got out, quietly closed the car door and popped the trunk. Pulling out the tire iron, he carefully shut the trunk and started up the long driveway.

As the house came into view, light emitted from the single window in the main room at the front of the small cabin. The flickering light made it apparent the television was still on, but knowing the way Jack liked to drink and drug himself to sleep each night, Roger highly doubted he was paying much attention to any kind of show. Just a few feet from the house, Roger looked into the window and saw Jack was still awake, although barely. Jack stared at the television, but his eyes were merely slits and his face showed no signs of recognition or emotion. In front of him on the table sat a three-quarter empty bottle of vodka, a syringe and a lit candle.

Roger's grip on the tire iron tightened as he moved from the window and quickly covered the short distance to the front door. He wanted the element of surprise, although he highly doubted he needed it given Jack's condition, so he slowly turned the doorknob which, of course, was unlocked. He swung the door slowly, and peered around the edge. Despite the fact the door stood directly behind the television and right in line with Jack's vision, he showed no signs of noticing a visitor until Roger was fully inside the house and closed the door. His eyes went from Roger's face to the tire iron before moving back in the general direction of the television.

"Whadda you want?" Jack slurred.

Roger stared at him briefly, in disbelief both at the question and the fact Jack didn't look the least bit concerned. "What do you think I want, you fucking piece of shit?"

Jack emitted a ghastly laugh, rolling his head onto the back of the couch and nearly choking as he returned his eyes back to Roger. "You're here about the boy, aren't you?"

For a moment, Roger had forgotten the tire iron, which now felt like an extension of his arm. He also realized he had taken two steps inside the doorway and was now just several paces from his brother-in-law.

Jack sat just a little more upright now that Roger was just outside of arm's length, and he looked him directly in the eye.

"You know," Jack said again, his voice somehow becoming a little clearer. "I think deep down he wanted it. He was always looking at me, and those eyes were just begging me to touch him. I think he liked…"

Before he could finish the sentence, Roger took two more steps, raised the cold steel in his hand, and swung it in a downward motion. Jack moved his head just enough the first blow missed its mark and landed squarely on his shoulder. The crack of bone as his clavicle shattered registered a pain severe enough Jack felt it even through his alcohol- and drug-induced state. Just as he let out the first scream, Roger struck again, this time bringing the iron down on Jack's midsection, breaking several ribs.

Jack fell into a supine position on the couch, one hand reaching for his shoulder while the other grabbed at his chest. With each passing second, his breath shortened and Roger realized the second blow probably caused at least one rib to pierce a lung. At the same time, the thought came to him he was glad the first blow missed Jack's head because it might have killed him instantly.

Roger took a knee beside the couch, grabbed the sweaty, greasy patch of hair on the back of Jack's scalp, and twisted it so they were eye to eye. Tears streamed down Jack's face, and it occurred to Roger he was probably going into a state of shock like the one he put Adam in just hours earlier.

To make sure he got Jack's attention, Roger smacked him on the cheek and forced Jack to look at him. "You raped my son," he whispered, and then shouted, "You raped my son!"

Jack almost looked like he smiled, and Roger resisted the urge to end it right there.

"You brought everything bad into our lives after Annie died," Roger continued. Jack's breathing turned to short gasps as his lungs worked feverishly to stay inflated. "Annie knew how you were, and she kept you away from us. But I was stupid and let you in, and you do this."

Roger stood up, the tire iron still in his hand. He moved back toward the door.

"I came here to kill you, to send you to Hell where you can burn for eternity." Roger moved a step closer to the couch to make sure Jack could hear him. "You know what, though, that's too good for you. I want you to suffer the way Adam and I are going to suffer because of what you did."

121

He swung the tire iron again, connecting with the lower half of Jack's left leg, splintering the bones there, then did the same to Jack's right leg. As Jack howled in pain, Roger stood and moved back toward the door. As he did so, he tipped over the lit candle on the table, watching as a stack of papers next to it caught on fire. A moment later, the wooden table in front of the couch was also ablaze. As Jack opened the door, he looked once more into his brother-in-law's eyes. The flames just a couple feet in front of him danced in the reflection of Jack's eyes, and any hint of a smile gave way to a recognition that he was about to be caught in the blaze without any hope of moving.

"Maybe you'll burn here before you burn in hell," Roger said as he walked out and closed the door behind him, grabbing Jack's cell phone as he left. As he ran down the driveway, tire iron still in hand, he dialed 911 and reported his cabin was on fire and he was trapped inside. Without disconnecting the line, he threw the phone into the creek bordering Jack's property, then got into his car and calmly drove out onto the road. Several miles after he turned off Jack's road and onto the main highway, he saw the first approaching fire trucks and heard their sirens screaming as they approached. After pulling the car to the side of the road to let the engines safely pass, he continued back to his house to clean himself up, grab some fresh clothes and head back to the hospital.

Chapter Fifteen

The morning after his conversation with Mari Cawley, Micah filled out all the paperwork for his background checks with Lands County CASA and started in to the second part of the DCS series. Together he and his team conducted several more interviews over the past few days and prepared to dig into the first and second calls DCS received concerning issues at the Henley household. Micah again took the lead on writing part two, but he received much more input from his reporters and editors on this segment, as it would be considerably more involved.

They agreed they would run a short recap of the previous week's stories each Sunday just in case anyone missed any of the lead-ins to that week's feature. The editorial staff put that together as Micah read through what he keyed in for the weekend's story.

A Time for Action
Records show DCS visited Henley home at least twice leading up to murders
By Micah Sanders & Staff
Part Two of an Ongoing Series

On the evening of December 17, 2012, police responded to reports of a domestic disturbance at 414 Washburn St. to a home owned by Curtis and Karri Henley. The 911 call came from a neighbor who said she heard "screaming, cursing and things breaking" coming from the house next door. The woman, unidentified for this story, reported yelling coming from the house was not unusual, but she was concerned about the level of this particular escalation, especially since the couple had kids in the house.

When officers responded, reports say Karri Henley answered the door. She wore a pair of shorts and a tee shirt, her hair in disarray, and officers noticed several bruises on her arms and legs, although none of them looked fresh. They told her a neighbor reported what sounded like fighting coming from the house and they asked her the location of her husband. She said he had been there but left a few moments earlier to get cigarettes.

When asked if her husband hit her or any of the children, Karri Henley said he had never hit any of them. Officers asked her where she got the bruises and she said she was clumsy and regularly bumped into things. She then reluctantly agreed to allow the officers to look around the house and check on the children, who were playing in their bedrooms.

While one officer checked on the children, the other looked around the kitchen and the remainder of the home. The call report stated the "kitchen and bathroom appeared as if they have not been cleaned in some time. Scraps of food lay on the floor throughout the kitchen, mold build-up is evident on the countertops and in the refrigerator, and evidence of the presence of rodents is apparent. The bathtub is ringed with filth, and areas throughout the bathroom, in the shower and on the sink show extensive mold and mildew."

According to the report, the three children appeared safe, although all said they had not bathed that day. Other than that, they showed no signs of abuse and appeared to be well-fed.

Micah paused as he considered the direction the story would take from there. He and his team conducted several interviews over the past few days and discovered that Karri Henley told the officers that evening her neighbor was nosy and "needed to mind her own business," and she and her kids were fine. The officers told her they were concerned about the living conditions of the children and they would be making a report to DCS so they could investigate.

DCS Director Sandra Bless received the report from the officers the next morning and passed the case along to Senior Caseworker Craig Evans. Evans was escorted by an officer to the home the next day and found nothing of concern in the home, which apparently was cleaned up significantly since the evening in question. The kids were all bathed and groomed, and all appeared safe and happy in Evans' estimation. He made notes to conduct a surprise follow-up visit in the coming days, but no record of that visit existed.

When Micah asked Evans why the follow up had not occurred, Evans shrugged his shoulders and said it was not uncommon for DCS follow-up visits to fall through the cracks, especially if the initial visit failed to reveal any imminent danger to the children in question. Basically, Evans said, there are just far too many cases for far too few caseworkers and that priority must be given to the most serious situations.

Micah stated he could certainly understand that, and he made notes to look further into the DCS budget and the state allocations that made up its annual funding.

During interviews, Bless was much more guarded when discussing the situation than Evans. As director of the organization, she was in a much more sensitive political position than her underlings, and she was very careful about what she said – and did not say – during the interviews, especially considering the result of the Henley investigation. No doubt her career was on the line with this case, and Micah felt the further he dug into the story, the worse things would become for Director Bless.

DCS' second call to the Henley home came almost nine months later on August 9, 2013. Police investigated another reported domestic disturbance, this time when Karri Henley ran from the back door of the house screaming her husband was threatening to kill one of her children. Karri was several months pregnant at the time, and when she fled from the house she ran to a home adjoining the Henley's backyard, where a neighbor called the police. When officers responded, they handcuffed Curtis Henley and took him to the station for questioning. A butcher knife removed from the block on the kitchen counter was on the floor when officers arrived. The three children appeared unharmed, although all were crying when police responded to the call.

Karri Henley told officers her husband held their oldest son, Curtis Jr. by the hair and put the knife to his throat after the boy back-talked his father over permission to go on a school field trip. Karri said Curtis was drinking earlier in the day, and when his son didn't like the fact his dad told him he couldn't go on a school trip to the zoo because the family couldn't afford it, he started arguing with his father. As the argument escalated, Curtis went to the kitchen, grabbed the knife and yanked his son's head back by the hair, placing the knife within a couple inches of the boy's throat.

When police asked Curtis Jr. to tell them what happened, the boy – eight at the time – told them his father only yelled at him and that his mother sometimes made up stories to get his father in trouble. When they asked Curtis Jr. if he knew anything about the knife being on the floor, he told them that it was possible his mother had put it there as part of her "act," as he called it. A day later, Karri recanted her story and said she had made the whole thing up because she and Curtis were fighting and she wanted to "pay him back." When officers couldn't find any other evidence, they released Curtis and informed Karri of the penalties for filing a false police report, but in the end, they decided not to pursue charges against her.

Still, the report appeared on DCS' radar, and Craig Evans made another visit to the Henley household, this time interviewing separately each member of the household, including all the children. At the time, Evans was involved with more than 20 other cases, two of which involved sexual abuse of children, and while he suspected several members of the Henley household lied about what took place there, he found not enough evidence existed to warrant further action.

Micah found the further he got into the story, the more his frustration grew. It was becoming obvious there were no easy fixes to the challenges faced by law enforcement and government agencies like DCS. He wondered how many cases were taking place right at that moment similar to the early stages of the Henley case and, no matter how hard the cops or DCS worked, how many of them would end in a bad way. He knew the Henley murders were an extreme case, but how many of these cases of abuse cannot be substantiated only because the victims are too afraid to be forthcoming? And while most likely will not end in murder many will end with the victims growing up to become abusers themselves, only to continue the cycle and further the problem.

Needing a break, Micah stood and walked through the newsroom, passing his writers and editors busily working on the next day's paper. Again, his mind drifted to Emma, and he wondered what kind of world she was going to grow up in and, even worse, the kind of world in which she would raise her children. Micah shook his head and grabbed his coat, deciding he needed a diversion.

Chapter Sixteen

By the time Roger went home, showered, put on some fresh clothes and headed back to the hospital it was just after 1 a.m. The nurse on duty assured him Adam had not stirred while he was away and the doctor on call stopped by less than an hour earlier to check on him. So far, he appeared to be doing well, at least physically.

Roger pulled the visitors chair from the corner of the room to the side of his son's bed, being careful not to make any noise that would wake Adam. He knew for quite a while, sleep was the only respite from the terror Adam faced the previous day, and even in sleep the horrible nightmares would linger, waiting to attack without warning. Tears welled up as Roger looked at his boy, and he started thinking about the unfairness of life. Just when he and Adam turned the corner and finally prepared to move on from Annie's death, something had to happen – just like it always seemed to. At the same time, the reality of what Roger did to Jack settled in and, while he couldn't say he regretted the action, the realization he would pay for it hit home in a big way during his drive to the hospital.

He planned to wait until Adam woke up in the morning, see how his son felt and then decide whether to turn himself into the police. In retrospect, Roger wished he had just set fire to Jack's house without entering. Even better, he could have injected Jack with enough of the heroin he so loved that he fell asleep, after which Roger could have set the blaze and the cops likely would have ruled the blaze an accident brought about during Jack's drug use. But he also knew when he went to Jack's house in his rage, reason wasn't with him and he had every intention of beating his brother-in-law to death with the tire iron. After the first blow to the shoulder, the thought came to him that quick death was too good for Jack, and that is when he decided to make him suffer.

At this point, Roger had no idea whether Jack lived or died in the fire, and honestly, he didn't care, but either way the doctors would discover the broken bones and would not be able to dismiss it as something that Jack could have done to himself. Besides, if Jack did somehow make it through the injuries and the fire, it was likely he would remember who visited him, and that would be the end for Roger. Unless, of course, Jack was smart enough to realize this could also bring to light the fact he was guilty of raping a child.

The ideas swirled through Roger's mind as he sat at Adam's bedside, and the realization his actions now meant his son would have neither his mother nor father, at least for the foreseeable future, hit home. Roger laid his head on the bed beside his son, again careful not to wake him, terrified for the future his little boy now faced.

****

The clock on the wall in Adam's room read 7:05 when Roger realized someone was tapping him on his shoulder. He fell asleep in the chair with his head resting on Adam's bed, and when he jerked up from the restless few hours of sleep, his neck ached and he saw the nurse he talked to upon his return to the hospital.

Rubbing the sleep from his eyes and running his fingers through his hair, Roger asked, "Did he wake up at all during the night?"

The nurse shook her head. "He went through a lot yesterday. You need to understand that even when he awakens it could take some time before he's ready to talk."

They were whispering to each other. "Have you seen this sort of thing before?" Roger asked.

"Only once, to a six-year-old girl," she replied. "I hoped I would never have to see it again."

Roger thought about asking what happened with the girl, but decided against it, partly because he figured the nurse legally couldn't say anything about it, but more so because he feared what answer she might give if she did tell him.

"The doctor should be in soon, Mr. Durkin," the nurse said, and walked out of the room.

Roger stood up and stretched his tall frame, working especially on the neck and shoulder muscles that were in a very unnatural position now for several hours. He walked into the bathroom to relieve himself, washed his hands and splashed some water on his face. Looking into the mirror, he thought to himself about the enormous uncertainty the day ahead would bring and silently wondered what things would look like in the next 12 or 18 hours.

After drying off his face and combing his hair, Roger quietly opened the bathroom door and saw his son staring right at him. Bolting back to Adam's bedside, he forced a smile and said, "Hey, buddy, you're awake!"

Adam blinked his eyes and stared blankly at Roger, but said nothing. His face had taken on an ashen hue, replacing the light tan and slightly blushed cheeks that comprised his normal complexion. Roger just hoped somehow, someday, his son could move past everything that happened and would happen in the coming days. For now, though, he just stared at his son and ran his fingers through his hair, content to see Adam's brown eyes even if the light that normally lived there was not currently present.

The doctor walked in a moment later and smiled, glad to see Adam was at least awake. The boy just kept his eyes on Roger as if moving them away would force him to look at – and remember – everything that happened the previous day.

Dr. Berne moved to the side of the bed opposite Roger and tilted Adam's head so he looked in his direction. Adam looked at first as if he would resist, but after only a moment, allowed his eyes to look toward the doctor, who shined a small flashlight into Adam's pupils. The boy's eyes responded appropriately, and the doctor moved on to check reflexes in his legs. As he finished, he glanced at the blood pressure and heart rate monitor, logged a few things into the laptop he carried in with him, and motioned for Roger to meet him in the hall. As Roger stood up from his chair, Adam's hand rapidly grabbed at his father's wrist, a look of panic engulfing his son's face. The fingernails burrowed into Roger's skin, and he quickly sat back down.

"Buddy, it's okay," he said. "I'm going to be right there with the doctor." Adam's eyes continued for a moment to plead with his father not to leave, but he still said nothing. After a moment, his grip eased and his face returned to the impassive stare it held previously.

Roger stood again, and this time Adam just moved his gaze to a spot on the ceiling. Moving just outside the doorway, but making sure to stay within Adam's view if he looked that way, Roger joined the doctor in the hallway.

"Mr. Durkin, it looks like we're past the concern of shock," the doctor said quietly. Roger wondered if calm, emotionless speech was something medical students learned in school or if it just developed through experience and years on the job. "Also, the tests show no signs of STDs. Both of those are very good news."

Roger nodded in agreement.

"The biggest issue Adam will have going forward will be dealing with this psychologically. We've given him some medication to mitigate the pain of the rape, and that will fade in the coming days. But the memories and the psychological damage will take much longer to go away, and probably will require some extensive therapy."

Roger just nodded again. "We have a family friend that is a child psychologist, and I'll get Adam started with her as soon as I get home."

The doctor nodded, but didn't say anything for a moment. Finally, he looked at Roger and said, "I know the police asked you this multiple times last night, but do you have any idea who could have done this?"

Not expecting this question from the doctor, Roger looked down the long hallway while he thought about what to say next. After a short moment, he looked in Dr. Berne's eyes, shook his head and just said, "I really don't know."

"Well, we turned the semen sample over to the police for DNA testing," the doctor replied. "Hopefully they're able to come up with something from that. I'll be back to check on Adam in a bit."

Roger nodded and turned to head back into the room. Adam's eyes were closed, and his rhythmic breathing let Roger know his son was asleep.

****

Adam spent the next few hours going in and out of sleep. He still wasn't speaking and the only food Roger or the nurses could manage to get him to eat was a bit of Jell-O late in the morning.

A little after 2 p.m. with Adam back asleep, Annie's father, Tom, appeared in the doorway. Roger looked up at him and noticed him staring down at Adam. It had only been a little over a year since Roger last saw Tom, but his first impression was the man had aged 10 years at least. The stress of losing your little girl, Roger thought as he stood up, walked across the room and gave Tom a brief hug. As they pulled apart, Tom grasped Roger's shoulders and squeezed lightly, conveying the message he was there for him.

"Where's Jan?" Roger asked, wondering why Annie's mom wasn't standing there with them. Tom leaned his head toward the hallway, and the two men moved just a bit further out of Adam's range. Once there, Tom spoke for the first time.

"How's Adam?" Tom asked, ignoring Roger's question.

Roger told him what the doctor said that morning, and that they were still waiting for Adam to speak for the first time. When he finished, he inquired again on the location of Annie's mother.

"She's downstairs. We got a call early this morning, not long after we left Gulf Shores," Tom started. "It was from a doctor in this hospital." Roger had a feeling what was coming next.

"Our son, Jack – I don't know how well you know him, or if you know him at all – was brought in with extensive burns all over his body. Apparently, he was doing drugs – he's had a problem with them since he was a teenager – and somehow his house started on fire."

Roger worked as hard as he could to control the look on his face, hoping he looked surprised or interested, anything other than worried.

Tom continued. "We only saw him for a moment, and that was through a window, but the doctors say he has second- and third-degree burns over more than half of his body. They're only giving him a fifty-fifty chance of surviving, assuming he can make it through these first few days without catching any kind of infection."

Roger looked for any sign Tom was waiting for a response or looking for non-verbal "tell," but as far as he could say, the man was just relaying a story.

"I'm sorry to hear about Jack," Roger lied. "I only met him a couple of times. Annie said they didn't get along very well and that Jack had a lot of issues she didn't want to expose Adam to."

Tom nodded. "The guy has been a mess his entire adult life, and even a little bit before that. Anyways, I need to grab some coffee and take it down to Jan. We're both exhausted, but she was still talking to the doctors and I wanted to let you know we were here. We'll be up in a little while when we're finished down there."

The two shook hands and exchanged another quick hug. As far as Roger could tell, Tom already made up his mind Jack's fire was nothing more than an accident brought on by his drug use, but then again, he probably hadn't yet heard about the other injuries. In either case, Roger knew once all the cards were on the table, it wasn't a big leap to believe Roger tried to murder his brother-in-law when he found out what he did to his son.

His head spinning again, Roger went back into the room and took a seat beside Adam's bed, looking down at the innocent face sleeping peacefully as if nothing happened. God, he wished that were the case.

Chapter Seventeen

Throughout his CASA training sessions, Micah was impressed by the amount of information the coordinator could convey to the new volunteers, none of which had any kind of previous education in the law. And while the sessions only touched upon child protection laws and how the courts work, they spent much of their time talking about the interactions of families, needs of children and the ways in which a CASA is meant to interact with the children they represent.

Over the six weeks of training, Micah was surprised how much he and every other volunteer learned. While he was skeptical going into the training ordinary people could learn enough in six weeks to undertake the role they accepted, by the time they wrapped up the sessions and the five hours of court observation, all the volunteers were extremely eager to receive their first cases and to use the knowledge they now possessed.

At the same time, Micah and his team worked through the DCS feature on the Henley murders and, what was originally scheduled as a five- or six-week feature stretched on throughout the summer. The team found it extremely difficult to get the information they needed from both DCS and the state legislators from their area, so they made the determination to treat the story with on-going coverage, rather than a tight six-segment package. Readers were extremely interested in the story, and the letters to the editor turned into a back and forth debate over readers' opinions for the state's reaction.

DCS made the decision to basically stonewall the newspaper in its attempts to talk to anyone within the organization, so reporters focused more on the legislators that voted on the funding for the organization as well as the judges who sat on child protection cases. Both sets of people were only sporadically available, so the newspaper continued its dogged pursuit of sources and the story dragged on for a much longer period than originally intended.

For Micah, the series became a personal mission. The fact DCS made the decision to turn away from open discussion led him to believe their own internal investigations turned up information damaging to individuals within the organization. One thing he learned in his career is the less open publicly funded agencies become, the more they have to hide and the more important it was for the newspaper to serve its role of watchdog.

Micah always took great pride in the role newspapers played within their communities, and he found it sad so many younger people had no concept of the responsibility journalists have of keeping watch over what goes on in government and ensuring the best interests of the people are served. Of course, much of the blame fell upon the yellow journalism that pervaded the television airwaves, especially national news organizations that aligned themselves with one political party or another, not that they ever admitted to doing so. Unfortunately, in the minds of the millennial and younger generations, all "journalists" were the same, regardless of whether they adhered to the same ethical standards Micah and his colleagues learned in their training.

Yet, he still made it his mission, and he felt he did a good job training those in his newsroom to accept the same responsibility. So far, the work they turned out in the DCS series was exceptional, and Micah had the feeling his team was only weeks away from turning over the leaf that would flip the story upside down.

Sitting at his desk the day after graduation from his CASA training, he looked at the certificate he received the night before. Immediately, his thoughts shifted to the kids in the Henley case, and he asked himself what he would have done if that had been his case. Would he have been able to do anything that would have gotten those children out of that house before their father lost his mind, or would the system have tied his hands to the point where he just became another frustrated by-stander wondering what might have been?

Frustrated, he stood up from his desk and decided it was time to go home. The training and his work took up a lot of his time in the previous weeks, and he decided he owed Kayla an evening out. He dialed his next door neighbor whose teenage daughter sometimes babysat for them and was able to secure her services for a few hours that evening. Closing his office door, he decided to do his best to leave his work – and his worries – locked up in there at least for the night.

Chapter Eighteen

Roger returned from grabbing a bite to eat in the hospital's cafeteria to find both of his in-laws seated beside Adam's bed just after five p.m. Adam's eyes were still closed, and by all indications he was still sleeping. Jan looked up at Roger and offered a brief smile before returning her gaze back to her grandson. In the meantime, Tom stood up and made his way over to the door to talk to Roger.

"Did he wake up at all?" Roger asked.

"Very briefly," Tom said. "He opened his eyes, looked at us and then around the room, and then closed them again."

"How's Jack?"

Tom looked down at the floor, searching for the words he wanted. "He's in a medically induced coma. The doctors say they're going to keep him that way for at least two weeks. They say the pain from the burns would be too much for anyone to endure."

Roger almost offered his condolences, but simply nodded and looked back toward Adam's bed.

"Why don't you and Jan go downstairs and grab some dinner?" Roger said, ending the uncomfortable science. "I just ate, and I'll sit with Adam for a while."

Tom motioned for Jan to join him in the hallway, which she did, stopping briefly to give Roger a hug. The two were close until Annie's death, but looking at her now reminded Roger of how Annie would have looked later in life, and the pain he suppressed for the past few months stabbed sharply at his heart. As his in-laws made their way down the hall, Roger took his place at his son's bedside once again.

Looking at Adam's face, Roger couldn't help but think of Annie. In some ways, he wished so much she were there now so they could lean on each other, but in others he was thankful she didn't have to go through the pain of seeing her son in his current state. Everything happens for a reason, he thought, although for the life of him he could not think of a reason for his wife dying so young from cancer and his son facing the brutality of rape at the hands of a drunken, drugged-up loser. But then again, deep down he knew there was a reason for Adam's rape, and that was fully on him. He was the one that brought Jack into their lives. His need for any kind of companionship, the weakness that turned him into an alcoholic and recreational drug user, and the fact he turned a blind eye to what was going on in his son's life were the reasons Adam was raped. Roger knew no matter what he did going forward, he would always have to live with that.

Roger's self-flagellation ended when he felt a hand touch his. His eyes, which were staring up at the ceiling, moved down to see his son's hand on top of his on the bed. Adam's eyes were open, and for the briefest second Roger thought he saw a hint of compassion and understanding in them. It was if Adam sensed what his dad was thinking and going through, and he found his way out of his trance long enough to offer his father a look that said that he didn't blame him and he needed to stop blaming himself. The two stared at each other for a second, and Adam moved his lips as if he was trying to smile. Roger tried to convince himself it was more than just a reflex, but in the end, he could not be sure. A moment later, Adam closed his eyes again and this time, he slept through the night.

****

A fiery red light beaming against the wall opposite Adam's bed awoke Roger early the next morning. He stood from the chair he slept in through the night, stretched and made his way to the window. The sun was just beginning to peak over the horizon, casting a pink and orange reflection off the low-lying clouds to the east.

"Dad?" he heard from behind him. It took a second or two for him to realize it was the sound of Adam's voice. Turning quickly back toward the bed, he crossed the few steps between the window and the spot his son occupied for the past 40 hours. A single tear escaped Roger's eye as he looked down to see Adam looking up at him.

"Hi buddy. Man, it's great to hear your voice."

"I'm thirsty," Adam said, licking his lips. Roger grabbed the water pitcher from the table next to the bed, filled the cup and helped Adam sit up enough to drink from the straw. He drank down about half of the water, paused and then finished off the rest.

"How are you feeling?" Roger asked. He was a little bit afraid of the answer but also wanted to keep Adam talking.

"A little hungry," Adam said, but didn't offer any insight into his physical state.

Roger moved to the doorway and signaled for the nurse. As she approached, Roger told her Adam was awake and speaking. She moved to his bedside, smiled and

142

promised to get him some breakfast and to let the doctor know he was responsive.

A few minutes later, Adam sat upright in the bed eating some Jell-O and a piece of dry toast. Roger was content to just watch his son eat – slowly at first, but as his stomach accepted the food, he finished off the toast quickly and asked for another piece. When he finished, he told Roger he needed to go to the bathroom, and the nurse gave him permission to help him go. As he peed, for what seemed an eternity, he looked up at Roger and said, "Dad, what happened?"

Roger rehearsed through the previous day how he would answer such a question, but now that it was posed to him, he found himself searching for the right thing to say.

"What do you remember?"

Adam flushed the toilet and turned back toward the bed. Halfway there, he stopped and turned to his dad.

"I remember getting home from school and seeing Uncle Jack's car," he started slowly. "I told him he wasn't supposed to be there and he wasn't welcome at our house anymore. Then, I think he hit me."

"Is that all you remember?"

Adam took a few cautious steps and leaned against the side of the bed. He nodded and said, "The next thing I remember was waking up, looking around the hospital room and seeing you sitting there beside me. Then I think I fell back asleep."

Roger told him they were in the hospital for a day and a half after Adam suffered a pretty bad beating from his uncle. He left out any further details but could see the fear

143

building in Adam's eyes and through the stiffening of his body.

"Where's…where's Uncle Jack now?" Adam finally asked.

"He's not going to hurt you again," Roger said, taking a place on the bed and pulling Adam close to him to reinforce his son's security. "Never again. I promise."

Adam seemed to consider this for a moment, letting his dad hold him. After a few moments, he pulled away and looked up at Roger. "When can we go home?" Roger smiled, stood and told Adam he would go ask the doctor that very question.

****

Jan and Tom returned to the room just after nine and were delighted to see Adam awake and speaking again. The doctor left shortly before they arrived, and he determined Adam would be kept for observation for one more night and, if all went well, he could return home the next day. Adam was excited to see his grandparents, as he hadn't seen them in more than a year, and he loved hearing about their condo on the beach in Alabama. As lunchtime approached, they promised him he and Roger could come down to visit, possibly for Christmas vacation.

Throughout the day, Adam was animated and happy. He ate a small chicken breast and some fruit for lunch, and the four spent the afternoon playing card games and watching a couple of television shows. Roger watched for any signs of trauma in Adam, and though he knew they would come eventually, he was happy to see his son enjoying himself and smiling again.

Just after four p.m., a nurse appeared in the doorway, smiled at Adam and asked Roger to join him in the hall.

"Mr. Durkin, there's a detective here to see you," the nurse said. "I didn't want to upset Adam, so we put him in an office down the hall and told him we'd bring you to the office."

Roger's heart sank, but he did his best not to show it. Turning back to the room, he told Adam and his in-laws he'd be back in a bit. The three looked up at him for a moment, and then went back to their card game.

A minute later, the nurse motioned Roger through a door into a small office. Seated behind the desk, the detective looked to be in his late 30s with sandy brown hair and a slim build. He didn't stand or so much as look up when Roger entered, but instead pointed to the chair on the other side of the desk and said, "Please take a seat, Mr. Durkin."

Roger noticed his mouth going dry but told himself to remain calm and confident as he took a seat in the chair. After a few moments, the detective finally looked up and set down the pen he used.

"Mr. Durkin, I'm Detective Steve McQuillen with the Lands County Sheriff's Office. Thank you for taking the time to meet with me."

Roger wondered if he had any choice in the matter but he simply nodded as he looked across the desk. "Please, call me Roger."

The detective apparently ignored the request as he said, "Mr. Durkin, we have received the results of the DNA sample taken after the assault on your son two days ago."

McQuillen paused, obviously looking for a reaction from Roger, who did his best to appear interested, but not anxious.

"The sample is a match to your brother-in-law, Jack Clement." Again, McQuillen looked for a reaction, and this time Roger did his best to appear surprised. He guessed he was unsuccessful when the detective made some notes on his pad before looking back up at him.

"How well do you know your brother-in-law, Mr. Durkin?"

Roger paused for just a second, during which he decided to be honest about as much as possible. "He's come around a few times this summer, maybe a dozen times or so since my wife passed away a couple years ago." Roger hoped that mentioning Annie's death might draw a measure of sympathy, but that hope passed quickly when the detective skipped right over it and continued.

"Did you have any idea Mr. Clement was capable of violence or had any inclination to hurt and rape your son?"

Roger shook his head. "Jack's got his problems, but no, I had no idea that he would ever hurt Adam, much less rape him."

"What do you mean he has his problems?"

Roger looked down at his hands for a second before replying. "He's had a drinking problem for a long time, and I think he's done some drugs over the years as well."

"How do you know about the drug problem?" McQuillen asked. "Have you ever done drugs with your brother-in-law?"

Roger was still trying to determine where the interview was going, and for the first time, the thought he should have a lawyer crossed his mind. He thought about this momentarily, but then decided to continue, at least for the time being.

"Detective, when my wife Annie died, I was in a pretty dark place. I started drinking, and Jack started coming over occasionally around the same time. A few times he and I shot up some heroin." Roger looked for any kind of judgement or reaction from McQuillen, but he just nodded at him to continue.

"My wife Annie – along with Adam – was everything to me. We didn't have anything to do with Jack while Annie was alive, by her choice, but after she died I guess I just needed someone to lean on. Jack was there for that, even if it was through drugs and alcohol."

McQuillen made notes on his pad as Roger spoke. After a moment, he stopped writing, looked at Roger and then back down at his pad as if searching for his next question.

"Mr. Durkin, are you aware that your brother-in-law is in the burn unit of this hospital as we speak?"

Roger was expecting the question, but he caught himself swallowing hard as the detective voiced the words.

"Yes, I am," Roger said. "My in-laws came down to be with me and Adam after the attack. They told me about Jack's injuries."

"His house practically burned to the ground, with him in it, the same night he raped your son," McQuillen said, pausing again to gauge reaction. "Early indications are Mr. Clement was drinking heavily and under the influence of heroin, fell asleep and somehow knocked a candle over, starting the fire."

Roger thought about saying something, but decided against it.

After a few more notes on the tablet, McQuillen looked back across the desk. "I don't know about you, Mr. Durkin, but I call that karma." Roger saw the faintest hint of a smile cross the detective's face. Again, he appeared to be waiting for Roger to say something, but he remained silent.

"Well, Mr. Durkin, I just wanted to let you know about the DNA sample. Clement's injuries are definitely life-threatening, but if he somehow pulls through, he will be arrested and will face charges that ensure he never sees the light of day. I'll stay in touch and keep you posted."

McQuillen stood and offered his hand. Roger paused for a moment, before shaking the detective's hand and turning toward the door.

"Oh, Mr. Durkin," he heard, just as he passed through the open door. Roger stopped and turned to face the detective.

"If you remember anything else, or if your son does, you'll call me, won't you?" McQuillen took a couple steps to close the distance between them and handed Roger his business card. Roger took it, nodded, and walked down the hallway to Adam's room.

Just as he was about to enter, Tom got up and met him at the doorway.

"What was that about?" Tom asked.

Roger thought for a moment before shaking his head. "Can you and Jan stay with Adam for a couple of hours? There's something I need to take care of before we take him home tomorrow."

"We'll be here," Tom replied. Roger thanked him, walked down the hall and rode the elevator to the ground floor, where he made his way to the hospital's exit.

Chapter Nineteen

Roger jogged through the hospital's public parking lot, jumped in his car and pulled out his cell phone. He searched for the number he hadn't dialed in more than a year, and scrolling through the last names starting with C, found the listing for Dave Carter.

Before he decided to study to be a teacher while at South Carolina, Roger was certain he would be a lawyer. He planned on majoring in Journalism, as the strict writing regimen involved in the discipline would be good preparation for the writing he'd do in his first year of law school. When he realized coaching was his passion, he switched over to the Health & Human Performance college from which he graduated.

During his undergrad years at USC, one of Roger's best friends was Dave Carter. Like Roger, he had every intention of being a lawyer, and unlike Roger, he stuck with the plan. After graduating from law school at the University of Florida, Dave accepted a position with a large criminal defense firm in Atlanta. There he cut his teeth defending DUI, drug and other petit offenses, learning how to argue in front of a judge and jury and becoming quite proficient at it. After a few years in Atlanta, with his star rising, he accepted a position as a junior partner in Indianapolis in the state's most reputable criminal defense firm. He lived in Indianapolis for four years when Roger and Annie moved back to Williams, and the college buddies ended up being within an hour of each other again.

For the first year or so, Roger and Dave got together six or seven times a year, usually with Roger going up to the city to hang out for a night on the weekends. There they hit some of the popular watering holes downtown, and Roger crashed in Dave's guest bedroom for the night. After Adam came along, the visits became much more infrequent, eventually tapering down to a phone call about once or twice a year.

Roger thought for a moment before hitting the send button and, after two rings, he heard his old friend's voice on the line.

"Roger! Man, it's been a while. What's up?" Dave sounded great – upbeat and cheerful as always.

Roger paused for a second, not sure exactly how to begin this conversation.

"Hey Dave," he finally said. "How're things with you?"

The two made small talk for a couple minutes, Dave commenting about how sorry he was about what happened to Annie. Roger assured him that, while he struggled with it for a long time, he finally moved on with his life and things were getting back to normal. Or, at least they were until a couple of days ago.

"That's why I called," Roger said. "I need your help with something."

Dave's reply was instant. "Anything, buddy. You know that."

"Can you meet me in an hour? Somewhere between here and Indy?" Roger noticed beads of sweat formed on his forehead and upper lip. He couldn't remember ever feeling this nervous in his life.

Dave agreed to meet at a coffee shop off the Interstate in 45 minutes. Roger thanked him, told him he'd see him then, and hung up the phone.

Turning on the ignition, Roger looked back up at the hospital. He tried to guess which of the windows was Adam's room and wondered if he or one of his in-laws was looking down at him in the parking lot. The glare of the sun made it impossible to see anything other than a reflection, but Roger sensed being watched. After a moment, telling himself he was just being paranoid, he put the car in gear, headed out of the lot and made his way to the ramp onto I-65 North.

****

Roger pulled his car into the coffee shop's parking lot just before 6:30. He quickly sent a text to Tom letting him know he wouldn't be back to the hospital until after dark and to tell Adam he had to run a few errands and pick up some things before he brought him home the next day. Tom replied quickly he would do so, and just as Roger was putting his phone in his pocket, a silver Mercedes pulled into a spot on the other side of the lot. When Dave got out of the car, Roger stepped out and met his friend near the front door. The two exchanged a quick hug with a couple pats on the back, and Roger said, "Nice car."

Dave looked back at the Mercedes, hit the lock button on the key fob, and smiled when it beeped to confirm it was locked. "Just got it a month ago. Fast as hell." Roger recalled how Dave was always into fast cars, as far back as he knew him. His friend constantly got speeding tickets in college, and Roger imagined that probably hadn't changed much in his adult years.

After placing and receiving their coffee orders, Roger motioned Dave to a table in the back corner of the shop, as far away from any other patron as he could get. They each took a sip from their cups, and Dave stared across the table at his friend.

Roger thought for a moment about where to start, and after one more sip of coffee he decided to jump right in.

"I'm in some pretty big trouble, I think." Dave still didn't say anything, but waited for Roger to continue.

"I guess I should start by saying I'm sorry I haven't called you in a year," Roger said. Dave waved a hand as if dismissing the apology and Roger continued. "I made a mess of my life the past couple years. I started drinking – heavily – and even got into some drug use."

Dave looked a little surprised, but remained silent.

"Anyway, my brother-in-law – Annie's brother – started coming around to our house. He'd bring over some Jim Beam and occasionally a little heroin, and we'd do our best to dull my pain.

"The guy's an asshole – always has been. And when Annie was alive, we didn't have anything to do with him. But after I lost her, I let him into our lives."

Dave had a look on his face like he wanted his friend to get to the point, but to his credit, he allowed Roger to continue at his own pace.

"So, at the end of the summer, I hit my boy. I was drinking all day and I did something stupid. First time I'd ever laid a hand on him, other than an occasional spanking when he was little. After that, I joined AA and haven't touched a drop since. I think that pissed off Jack – my brother-in-law – that he was losing his drinking buddy."

Roger paused for a moment. "For the remainder of this story, I need you to assure me we're under attorney-client privilege."

Dave spoke up for the first time since they sat down. "Are you hiring me?"

"I don't think I have much choice," Roger replied. "I hope you can cut me a break on the fee." Roger tried to smile, but Dave could tell he was forcing it.

"Consider yourself represented," he replied. "You know you can always count on me."

Roger gathered his thoughts again for a moment and then continued. "So, two nights ago, I came home from work and my AA meeting, and Adam wasn't in the house. I searched and searched and found him out in our woods, rolled up in a ball and mumbling to himself. Turns out, he was raped."

Dave lowered his gaze toward the table, "Oh shit, buddy. I'm so sorry."

Roger felt the anger building up inside him, almost as strong as 48 hours earlier when he found out what happened. He took another sip of coffee and allowed the warm liquid to work its way into his body, calming him ever so slightly.

"Adam told me his uncle did it. He was bleeding and in so much pain, but he managed to tell me it was Jack. It was the last thing he said until this morning."

Dave also had to gather himself. He found himself shaking slightly, and it occurred to him Roger's voice escalated to where other people, if listening, might be able to hear what he said. He lowered his own voice in an effort to calm down his friend.

"So, what did you do about it?" Dave asked very quietly.

Roger paused again, lowered his voice and said, almost in a whisper, "I left the hospital and went to Jack's house with every intention of killing him."

Dave looked around again to make sure no one listened. The few other patrons in the shop appeared wrapped up in their own conversations or whatever they were reading, so he looked at Roger to continue.

"When I got to his house, I grabbed a tire iron from my trunk, went inside and beat the crap out of that piece of shit. After my first swing broke his collar bone, just as I was about to swing at his head and end it, I decided instant death was too good for him."

Another pause, as Roger took another sip of coffee and tried to settle the rage inside him once again.

"So instead of killing him, I broke both of his legs and set his house on fire. I tried to make it look like it was an accident, but the injuries will make it obvious that something else happened."

"Is he dead?" Dave asked.

"No, after I torched the place, I called 911 and reported the fire."

Dave rocked back in his chair, nearly tipping over. "You did what?"

"Again," Roger said, "I didn't want him dead. I wanted him to feel the pain Adam's going to feel for the rest of his life. He's in the burn unit. Doctors say it's 50-50 whether he lives or dies."

Roger proceeded to tell him the rest of the story, all the way through the interview with Detective McQuillen just a few hours earlier. When he was finished, he was sweating and could feel his blood pressure escalated significantly. Dave went to the counter and came back with two cups of ice water. After they each took a couple drinks of the water, Dave looked across at his friend.

"So how do you want to play this?" he asked.

Roger thought for a moment. "I guess I need to know my options."

"You know the options," Dave said. "The obvious one is to turn yourself in, throw yourself at the mercy of the court and hope we get a sympathetic prosecutor and judge willing to accept a plea that minimizes or negates completely any jail time. We'd need to work on your story, though, if you know what I mean."

Roger nodded, as Dave continued. "The other is to take our chances. The first chance is whether they connect you to the fire and arrest you. If that happens, the second chance is whether they can prove you did it. If they can, you could be going away for a long time."

Roger looked out the window. The sun was beginning to set and the moon made an early appearance in the eastern sky.

Dave broke the silence. "Don't answer this, but I'm assuming the tire iron has been taken care of." The look that registered on Roger's face told him his friend just realized he had forgotten that important detail.

"What do you think I should do?" Roger asked.

"Let me look into a few things," Dave replied, "and we can talk more about it tomorrow. In the meantime, don't talk to anyone, especially the police. And make sure you tie up any loose ends, if you know what I mean."

Roger knew exactly what he meant, and after thanking his friend he got back on the Interstate and headed south toward Williams. On the way, he took a turn off, parked his car alongside the Driftwood River and, making sure no one was around, tossed the tire iron as far out as he could into the fast-moving river.

Chapter Twenty

Roger arrived back at the hospital just after nine. Tom told him Jan went back to the hotel and after Roger thanked him for hanging around, Tom did the same. As Roger prepared to spend his third and final night in the room's chair, Adam slept peacefully. The doctors scaled back Adam's pain medication considerably that day and the sleep he enjoyed this evening was, for the most part, without the aid of medication. Roger wondered when the nightmares would begin and when Adam would be forced to start reliving what he went through a few nights before.

As he sat there in the dark hospital room, a million thoughts ran through his mind. First was the DNA confirmation that Jack was the rapist, not that there was any doubt in Roger's mind prior to that. He wondered if Tom and Jan knew about Jack yet, but he doubted it since neither of them showed any indication throughout the day. Second, he thought what it would be like to get Adam home the next day. Would the sight of the couch, the living room, or anything else in the cabin bring back the painful memories of what happened? Would his son ever be able to return to any sense of normalcy in that house, or would they have to think about leaving behind all the memories of the good times there to escape the past year's bad memories?

Mostly, though, Roger kept replaying the conversation a few hours earlier with Dave. He knew, even without the tire iron, he would most likely become a suspect in Jack's assault and arson case, and the debate over whether to surrender to the police continued to rage within his mind.

Finally, after more than an hour of tossing and turning in the chair, sleep came reluctantly, at least for a few hours.

When he awoke, the gap between the curtains revealed the slightest bit of early morning light. Roger realized he only slept about four hours, and it was in no way restful. Still, today he was going to take Adam home and start the process of initiating the "new normal."
As he stood quietly by the window looking out over the parking lot that was his view the past three mornings, he wondered what the new day would bring and what advice Dave might have for him. The realization hit him that this morning could be the beginning of his last day of freedom, at least for a while, and the thought was much more sobering than any other that could possibly enter his mind.

Turning back toward the bed, Roger saw Adam lying awake and looking at him.

"Dad, are we going home today?" Adam whispered.

Roger moved away from the window and back toward the bed. "Yeah, buddy. As soon as the doctor comes in a couple hours from now and makes sure you're all set. Are you looking forward to getting home?"

Adam paused for a moment before tentatively nodding his head. Roger felt better as he watched his son get himself out of bed and go to the bathroom on his own. He looked much stronger than he had the day before, and Roger guessed the solid food he ate the previous day gave him back some of his strength. An hour later, Adam ravenously ate everything the nurses brought him for breakfast, and when the doctor visited briefly around 9, he told Roger he would sign the discharge papers, at which time they could head home.

As they drove home and eventually pulled into the long, unpaved driveway, Roger watched for any signs of apprehension from Adam but saw none. For the most part, the boy stared out the window impassively, and neither of them spoke much on the way home. Right before they left the hospital, Adam's doctor pulled Roger aside and told him that at some point he was going to have to ask Adam what he remembered of the attack. And while he didn't advise doing it in the next few days, the doctor recommended, by the following week, Roger should get Adam into therapy and have him start working through the psychological trauma of the event.

Roger stopped the car in front of the house, and Adam quickly got out and headed toward the front door. Inside, he walked through the living room and past the couch without so much of a glance and went straight into his bathroom. Roger waited a moment and then quietly walked down the hallway and stopped to listen near the bathroom door. He heard nothing, and when he asked Adam if he was okay, he said he would be right out.

Tom and Jan came to the house just before noon, each holding two bags of groceries. As Tom and Roger put the groceries in their place in the kitchen, Jan set about the task of making them all turkey sandwiches. Halfway through their lunch, the four of them seated around the small kitchen table, Tom's cell phone rang and he excused himself to take the call. When he came back a few minutes later, his face was pale.

"That was the doctor at the hospital," he said. "Jack went into cardiac arrest about an hour ago. They weren't able to save him."

Jan choked back a sob, and Tom moved over to wrap his arms around her. Roger looked at Adam who either hadn't paid attention to what his grandfather said or had no reaction to the news his uncle died. Roger stood and moved around the table to where his in-laws stood.

"We need to go to the hospital," Tom said, helping Jan up from her seat.

Roger wasn't sure what to say, but offered he was sorry for their loss. He asked Tom if he was okay to drive to the hospital, and when he said he was, Roger led them out to their car. Tom put Jan into the passenger side of the vehicle and moved around to the driver's side where Roger stood.

"I know Jack was the one that attacked – raped – Adam," Tom whispered. "I don't think Jan knows, though. Even if she suspects, he was still our son, and I'm sure she's trying to convince herself he couldn't have done such a thing."

Roger didn't know what to say, so he just waited as Tom continued.

"And I'm not saying you're the one who put Jack in the hospital, but if you were to have done such a thing, I could completely understand." Tom gave Roger two pats on the arm before getting into his car, starting the engine and heading up the driveway.

Back in the house, Adam picked up the plates from the table and put them in the dishwasher. He just finished when Roger entered the kitchen.

"I'm pretty tired," he said. "Is it okay if I go in and lie down for a little while?"

"Sure, buddy," Roger replied. "It's going to take a little while before you get all your strength back, but you'll be outside running around before you know it."

Adam walked over and gave Roger a hug. It was the first physical contact Adam initiated since before the attack, and Roger felt his heart melt as he pulled his son close.

"I love you, buddy," he said. "Get some rest." Adam nodded his head, and walked quickly to his bedroom, closing the door behind him.

Five minutes later, Roger's cell phone buzzed. Looking at the caller ID, he saw it was Dave.

"I was just going to call you," Roger said, without any kind of greeting. "Jack died a little over an hour ago."

There was a pause on the other end before Dave said, "Shit. So, we're looking at murder or manslaughter now."

Roger was conscious enough even on the night he attacked Jack to know what he could be facing, but the words from his friend still sent a shiver down his spine. Murder. Manslaughter. He hadn't opted for the law school route, but he knew enough to understand the penalties for what he did just went up dramatically.

"Roger, listen to me," Dave said. "I did some digging last night and this morning, looking into some similar cases. I don't want to talk over the phone, though. I'll come to your house later this afternoon if that's okay with you."

They agreed Dave would come over around 5, and after he told Roger to "just hang in there" they both hung up the phone.

Chapter Twenty-One

Dave's car pulled up the driveway a few minutes before five. Adam came out of his room a few hours earlier saying he was hungry, and Roger fixed him another sandwich, which he devoured quickly. It was good to see Adam's appetite coming back, Roger thought, and though he continued to look for any kind of adverse signs from him, for the most part Adam appeared to be just working to get his strength back. He was hungry and tired, but that was understandable considering the beating he suffered and the fact he hadn't had nourishment, other than intravenous fluids, during the first 36 hours he recovered in the hospital. After finishing his sandwich, Adam went back to his room to play some video games and watch television.

Tom called a little after four and said, all things considered, he and Jan were doing okay. They were hoping to make arrangements for Jack's body when they arrived at the hospital but were told law enforcement put a hold on releasing him, pending a possible autopsy. When Tom asked why they were considering an autopsy, the doctor referred him to Detective McQuillen who, of course, was not at liberty to answer his question.

Roger probably should have been more upset and concerned about the information Tom passed along, but he knew it was coming. As Dave got out of the car and entered the house, Roger was about 70 percent convinced he would turn himself in to the police. Meeting his friend at the front door, Roger pushed open the screen and allowed Dave to enter the cabin. It occurred to him this was the first time

Dave visited the house. All their other get-togethers were in Indianapolis and Dave mentioned he rarely made it down to Williams.

Dave asked about Adam, and Roger told him he seemed to be doing well so far and that he was in his room playing video games. The two decided to grab a glass of iced tea and to sit on the front deck so they could talk without worrying about Adam hearing them. It was early October and there was still a little more than an hour of daylight remaining, but the warmth of the day already gave way to the cooler Autumn evening.

"I got a call from my father-in-law a little while ago," Roger said. "They're holding the body, at least for now."

Dave nodded. He also suspected this was coming, and considered it along with the other information he gathered.

"I considered some similar 'revenge' cases," Dave began. "I found several cases where children were the victims of assault, and more specifically rape, where the parents decided to take justice into their own hands."

Roger took a sip of his iced tea and nodded his head for his friend to continue.

"None of the cases I found were in Indiana – I only searched the past 10 years – but I found two involving rape. One was in Ohio and the other in Illinois, so we can at least factor in they took place in the Midwest.

"In the Ohio case, a father shot and killed a neighbor after the neighbor molested his seven-year-old daughter. In this case, the father walked in on them during the molestation. The neighbor ran out the back door, the father grabbed his shotgun and pumped several rounds into the neighbor as he was running into the yard next door. The DA, probably sensing there would be a lot of sympathy for this guy's actions, made the decision not to file any charges.

Roger was listening intently.

Dave continued, "The difference between the Ohio case and yours, though, is the father acted immediately without any kind of advanced planning. I'm sure the prosecutors and judge knew that many reasonable people, given the same circumstances, might have done the exact same thing in a rage. It's called a 'depraved heart scenario' and factors in a strong emotional reaction to a traumatic situation.

"In your case, though, I'm afraid they would consider the time that elapsed between the attack and your actions to open up the element of pre-meditation. Throw in the fact you had an opportunity to turn Jack in to the authorities when you were interviewed in the hospital, and failed to do so, and that gives the argument even more strength."

Roger gazed across the front yard as the sun dropped lower toward the horizon. "Tell me about the other case," he said.

Dave shuffled through some papers in the folder he brought with him and found the one he was looking for.

"In the Illinois case, there are a few more similarities to this situation, especially in the timing. Here you had a 20-year-old father of a two-year-old boy, after leaving the child in the care of the father's 16-year-old brother, came to discover his brother had on several occasions molested the toddler while he babysat. When the man confronted his brother about it, apparently the kid smiled, admitted everything, and talked about how much he enjoyed it. The father then proceeded to beat his younger brother with a baseball bat. The kid lived for about a week before they took him off the ventilator and he died from the injuries."

Roger felt like his stomach was in knots, partly from hearing the graphic details Dave just shared with him, but more so from what he thought was coming next.

"Apparently, there were no witnesses to the beating, but the dad knew he was going to be the most likely suspect, so he turned himself in to the cops. The DA considered all the information and ended up filing manslaughter charges against the father. The case dragged on through various delays and continuations, and after about a year the two sides settled on time-served."

Roger pondered the idea of a year in prison and, although it was still a long time away from Adam, it wasn't as bad as he envisioned.

"Listen, Roger. This is your decision to make, and I'm on your side no matter which way you go with this. The way I look at it, the main difference between your situation and the Illinois case is the guy killed a teenager, someone in the eyes of a judge or jury may have been able to be rehabilitated. Your guy was a lifelong drunk and drug user, apparently with a proclivity toward young boys. Our current DA is a pretty reasonable guy, not a grandstander, so I don't see him jumping on a pulpit in this case. But, you never know."

Roger just nodded and then put his head in his hands and started shaking it back and forth. Dave waited a moment to see if his friend said anything, and when he didn't he felt like he should finish his thought.

"You don't have to make a decision right this second, but I think you should do it by this time tomorrow. And, like

I said yesterday, if you choose to surrender we need to get your story together. When you do that, consider the timing of the Illinois case I just told you about and how the father reacted to the admission and demeanor of his younger brother. That is what led him to act in the way that he did."

Dave continued. "And if we go the route of surrender, I would arrange for you to turn yourself into the prosecutor, rather than the police. I can explain why later, but I think we could make some arrangements prior to the surrender that would prove beneficial for you."

When he looked up at Dave, Roger had tears in his eyes. "What's going to happen to Adam?" he said, struggling with each word.

Dave shook his head. "That will be decided by DCS and the court, but I'm guessing they'd give Annie's parents temporary custody, assuming they're willing, while your case is resolved."

Roger considered this, but since they no longer lived in Indiana, he wasn't sure how the process would work. Either way, he knew he needed to have to have a conversation with Tom and now it looked as though the discussion would have to happen that night.

Dave broke Roger's concentration when he said, "Any questions of me? Otherwise, I'd suggest you think things over and have a talk with Annie's dad this evening, if you decide to go the route of surrendering. Call me first thing in the morning and let me know what you decide."

Roger just grabbed Dave's hand and pumped it once, but Dave pulled him into a long hug. "We'll get through this, my friend," he said quietly as he pulled away and headed to his car.

As Dave's car pulled down the driveway the sun was making its final drop below the horizon and, right on cue, the cool air of nightfall surrounded Roger. A chill crept through him but was immediately followed by a sudden burst of warmth, and in that moment his decision was made.

****

Roger wasn't the least bit hungry, but he knew he had to feed Adam. In the groceries Tom and Jan brought over earlier was a family-sized frozen chicken pot pie, which Roger put in the oven. When he went in to check on Adam, the boy was sitting on the floor playing one of his video games, headphones wrapped over both ears. At first, he didn't even notice his dad entered the room, but after a moment he realized someone stood over him. Pausing the game, he looked up at Roger.

In that moment, Roger saw – for the first time since before the attack – the light that burned in his son's eyes. Suddenly, Adam's eyes were once more filled with hope, energy and the love that made the boy so special, and in that one glance all Roger could think of was Annie. It hadn't occurred to him much the past year, mostly because he drowned most of his senses, but Adam was starting to look so much like his mother. Roger was ashamed at himself for not seeing it before, the resemblance so striking.

"Dad, are you okay?" Adam asked.

Roger finally broke out of the trance the second time Adam asked the question. "Yeah, buddy. Just thinking."

Adam smiled back at him and asked about dinner.

"It'll be ready in a bit," Roger said. "Why don't you come out and sit with me?"

Adam turned the game off, and the two walked together out to the living room. The smell of the pot pie was just beginning to escape the oven, and it filled the house with a warm sense of home. Roger did his best to set aside the awful sequence of events that would begin the next day or two. Right now, all he wanted to do was to enjoy some quiet time with his son and do his best to forget everything else.

The baseball playoffs continued that evening and the Cardinals were involved in a Divisional series against the Dodgers. Game one was that night, so Roger and Adam watched the start of the game while they ate the hot, savory chicken pot pie. Adam watched the game intently, and Roger tried to as well, but he found himself staring at his son much more than the television. The memories of the years prior to Annie's death flooded back that night, and he did his best to rein them all in for safe-keeping.

The night was perfect, except the Cardinals lost 3-2, and when Roger tucked Adam in a little after 11, both of them smiled. Adam hugged Roger for what seemed like an eternity, and Roger wondered if Adam had a notion of all the different things running through his father's head that night. When he finally let him go, Roger stood and moved to the door to shut off the light. He felt frozen in place as he stared in at the silhouette of his son, still a little boy in so many ways, but so much more grown up in this past year. Finally, Roger forced himself to pull the door to nearly closed, and he walked down the hall back to the living room.

Sitting on the couch again, Roger stared blankly at his reflection in the dark television screen. He knew what he had to do next, and in his hand rested the cell phone with which he would make the call that could change his – and Adam's – lives forever. Even though it was after 11:30, Roger was certain Tom was still awake, and he knew the conversation had to happen before he went to bed that night. Holding the phone, he stood up and made his way into the kitchen. Subconsciously be began opening cabinets, and didn't realize until he opened the third one that he was looking for a bottle of liquor, even though he was certain he would not find one. Finally, he grabbed a Coke from the fridge and walked out onto the front porch, hitting the dial button on his phone as he sat down in a rocking chair.

****

The following morning came much too quickly and a bright orange sun ascended into a sparkling blue sky to start the day. Roger hadn't slept a wink. After a fifteen-minute conversation with Tom, he walked around the house a few times thinking how he would break the news to Adam. He even had time to consider whether – given the opportunity – he would change anything he did. At least five times he replayed everything that happened the night Jack raped his son, and each time he tried to envision himself doing something different, but the anger that welled up inside of him led him to the same conclusion. In his mind, no other outcome other than Jack's suffering and eventual death was an acceptable punishment for what he did.

At 8 a.m., right on schedule, Tom pulled his car up the driveway. The two exchanged a solemn glance before Tom gave his son-in-law a hug and a pat on the back. Roger

choked back tears as he said, "This is going to be hard."
Tom, also with tears in his eyes, just nodded. Together they
made their way inside the house and went directly to Adam's
room.

After Roger finished talking to Tom the previous
evening, he called Dave and told him his decision. Dave
agreed Roger should talk to Adam in the morning, after
which time Dave would come to the house and escort his
friend to the district attorney's office.

Roger knew he only had a little more than an hour
before Dave would arrive, and he knew he couldn't wait any
longer to talk to his son. Tom waited in the hall as Roger
entered the bedroom, where Adam was just stirring from
sleep.

"Hi dad," Adam said with a smile, as his father closed
the door behind him. "Is that grandpa in the hall?"

Roger stopped just inside the door and again was
taken aback by the resemblance to Annie. "Yeah, buddy. I
need to talk to you about something."

Adam sat up, his relatively short hair matted down
and his eyes still heavy from the night's sleep. Roger moved
over to the bed and sat in the space his son opened for him.

"Adam, what do you remember about the day we had
to take you to the hospital?"

The boy looked down at his hands, which clung
together as if he was trying to crush something between
them. The look on his dad's face when he entered the room
told him something was wrong, but he clearly hadn't
expected the question. He paused for a couple more seconds,
and Roger put a reassuring hand on his son's leg.

"It's okay, buddy. It's just you and me, and you know you can tell me anything."

Another few seconds passed, and Adam finally said, "I remember coming home from school, and Uncle Jack was waiting for me beside his car."

Roger could see the fear building up in his son's eyes, and one part of him hated himself for having to put Adam through this while another part desired another shot at his brother-in-law. His own anger welling up inside of him again, he encouraged Adam to go on.

"I remember him hitting me and dragging me inside the house and putting me on the couch." Tears began to stream down Adam's cheeks, and he wiped his eyes with the right sleeve of his pajamas. "He hit me one more time, and I think I blacked out."

Roger didn't want to ask the question, but knew he had to. "What do you remember next?"

"I remember you finding me in the woods and carrying me back inside the house, and I remember parts of the ambulance ride to the hospital. People were standing over me, and I remember you sitting beside me holding my hand."

Again, Roger paused but then asked, "You don't remember anything between blacking out and me finding you in the woods?"

Adam thought for a minute, then shook his head. Roger couldn't tell if he was being honest with him, or if he just wasn't ready to talk about it. A minute or two of silence passed between them, Roger gathering his thoughts and Adam wiping the tears from his eyes. Surprisingly, it was Adam that broke the silence.

"Dad, why are you asking me this?"

Roger prepared himself for this question, yet he still paused, grasping for the right way to say it.

"Buddy, do you remember when you were growing up and you did something you weren't supposed to do? You didn't do that often – you've been such a good kid your whole life. But do you remember any of those times?"

Adam nodded his head.

"Whenever you did something you weren't supposed to do, your mom and I would sit down with you and make you tell us the truth of what you did, right?" Another nod from the boy.

"We taught you that it was always important to be honest and to own up to your mistakes, to those things that you did that you weren't supposed to. Well, I did something bad, and I need to own up to it."

Adam stiffened as he continued to look at his father. For the briefest moment, Roger thought he saw some hint of recognition in his son's eyes.

"I did something bad to Uncle Jack, Adam. Something I need to tell the police about."

The tears started back down Adam's face, and this time it was Roger who wiped them away for him. Adam started shaking his head back and forth, as if trying to dispel from his mind the thought entering it. Roger let him go for a moment, but then reached up and put a hand on each side of his son's face.

"Adam, look at me," Roger said, but the boy continued to try to shake his head back and forth, the quiet tears now turning into larger sobs. Roger wrapped his arms around his son and pulled him close to him, now whispering in his ear.

"Buddy," he said softly, "your grandpa is outside because I'm going to have to go away for a while, and I might not see you for the next couple of days." Adam was crying softly into his dad's shoulder, now realizing he wasn't going to be able to keep the intruding thought away.

"Your grandparents are going to take care of you until I get this worked out, but there are also going to be some people who are going to have to talk to you. It's going to be really important for you to be brave and strong and tell those people the truth about what you're feeling."

Roger did his best to choke back the sobs wanting to escape, and the trembling little boy in his arms wasn't doing anything to make that easy. Still he was determined to hold it together for his son, at least until he was out of sight.

Roger heard the door open behind them, and Tom put his head through and told him Dave just pulled up and waited in the living room. He nodded to the doorway, gesturing for his father-in-law to enter. Tom did so and stood a few feet from the bed.

Adam pulled his head away from Roger's shoulder, looked at his grandfather and then back at his dad. His swollen red eyes, filled with glimmering tears, sent a stabbing pain through Roger's body, and for a moment he was afraid his heart would shatter.

"I have to go now, buddy, but I'll see you as soon as I can. I promise."

Adam grabbed him and held him tighter than Roger thought possible for a 10-year-old. Both held each other, neither ready to let go when they finally pulled apart. Roger looked into his son's eyes one more time, kissed him on each cheek and the forehead, and stood and walked out of the room. As he closed the door behind him, he heard Adam's pained sobs and the quiet voice of Tom telling him everything would be okay.

Roger dropped to his knees in the hallway and allowed his own pain to escape, although he did everything in his power to make sure his son could not hear him. Dave, seated on the couch in the living room, stood and moved toward his longtime friend. He let him cry for a few moments before putting his hand on his shoulder. After another minute, Dave grabbed Roger's arm and helped him to his feet. Moving to the bathroom, he wet a washcloth and handed it to his college buddy, now also his client.

After he cleaned himself up, the two made their way out to Dave's car and headed down the driveway. Roger turned his head to look back at the cabin, wondering when he would get to see it again. In that glance, the memories of Annie and Adam and all the good times they had together flooded back, and the tears came once more.

Chapter Twenty-Two

Micah rolled over and reluctantly opened one eye to glance at the red glow of the alarm clock next to his side of the bed. It was 7:43, and the soft light emanating through the translucence of the blinds let him know the sun was making its appearance to start the day. Rolling back over quietly, he saw Kayla was still dozing. Her naked back was exposed to him, and his thoughts drifted back to the previous night. They went to dinner at the country club where they enjoyed a cocktail and split a bottle of Cabernet, enjoyed a great dinner and spent the evening dancing until the performing group shut things down for the night.

When they returned home a little after eleven, Micah walked their babysitter back to her house down the block and, when he returned, Kayla greeted him at the door with a bottle of champagne and not a shred of clothing. They only made it through a half a glass of champagne before they were in the bedroom, her beautiful body on top of his.

Staring at her, Micah realized evenings like those had become far too uncommon since Emma came along, and he made a pact with himself to make sure they carved out more time for each other.

As if sensing his eyes upon her, Kayla stirred and rolled over, smiled and kissed him lightly on the lips.

"Now that was fun last night," she whispered. "Especially when we got home."

Micah kissed her again, and nodded his head. "Especially when we got home. We need to do *that* more often."

Kayla rolled out of bed and headed toward the bathroom, not bothering to wrap herself with a robe or anything else. Micah watched as she made her way across the room, and she gave him a look over her shoulder to make sure he was, in fact, watching. She smiled approvingly and, when she reached the bathroom door, stood fronting him for a lasting moment before closing the door behind her. Micah realized again how lucky he was, and he took a moment to thank God for bringing Kayla into his life. When he heard the shower start up, he got up and threw on a pair of shorts and headed down the hallway to check on Emma, still fast asleep in her bed. From there, he went to the kitchen, poured a cup of coffee, and made his way outside to grab the newspaper.

In just his shorts, the October morning was cool with temperatures in the high 50s. He could tell from the glow of the sun it was likely going to warm into the mid-70s and be a beautiful fall day, and he was extremely happy it was Saturday and he would be able to enjoy it with his family. He thought a picnic in the park and a walk through the woods to check out the trees just beginning their change to beautiful autumn colors could be just what they all needed, especially after the magical evening he and Kayla enjoyed the night before.

Walking back through his front door, Micah unrolled the newspaper on the kitchen counter and took another sip of his coffee. As he glanced at the front page, he heard the patter of small footsteps on the wood floor upstairs, followed by the sound of those same little feet making their way down the staircase. A second later, Emma peeked her head through the kitchen doorway. Micah pretended he hadn't seen her, and when he lifted his head slowly to look in her direction,

Emma pulled her head back in their traditional game of peak-a-boo. This went on for about a minute, until Micah snapped his head up unexpectedly and caught Emma in the middle of the doorway.

"Gotcha!" he said. Emma smiled and ran toward him, her blanket in tow. He bent down as she approached and snatched her into his arms.

"Good morning, princess," Micah said, kissing her on the top of her head. "What's for breakfast today?"

She looked up in the air for a moment, then back into her daddy's eyes and yelled, "Pancakes!"

Micah pretended to be surprised, but he knew Emma would eat pancakes every morning if they let her. "You don't like pancakes, do you?" he teased, as he put her back on her feet.

She looked up at him, rolled her eyes and said, "No, I don't like pancakes, daddy. I *love* them!" With that, she giggled and ran into the living room. Micah heard the television come on, and knew his daughter would momentarily be wrapped up in whatever cartoon was on at that time. Going to the pantry, he went about the business of producing the family's traditional Saturday morning pancake breakfast.

Kayla came down a few minutes later, her wet hair cascading around a sheer robe and a smile on her face that made Micah think about taking her right there on the kitchen counter. She saw the look on his face and glanced toward the door to the family room.

"Easy there, cowboy," she said. "You need to get your strength back." She smiled and handed him his cell phone. "This beeped a minute ago. You have a text."

Micah kept his eyes locked on Kayla. When he reached for the cell phone, he grabbed her hand, pulled her close and kissed her one more time, this one lasting quite a bit longer than the two earlier. Kayla finally pulled away and picked up the cup of coffee Micah poured for her.

Reluctantly, he glanced at his phone and looked to see who texted him. When he saw, the name he quickly opened the text.

Let's meet for breakfast Mon morning. I have info re: Henley case you'll find interesting. 7:30 at Haley's. Enjoy your weekend.

Micah looked up at Kayla, who watched him over her steaming cup of coffee. "Good one?" she asked.

"Could be," Micah answered. "It's from Lara Hiller. State Representative Lara Hiller."

"Henley?" Kayla asked.

Micah nodded, looked back at his phone, and typed, *See you then. Thanks.*

****

As Micah predicted, the weather was perfect throughout the weekend, and he, Kayla and Emma spent the majority of the weekend outdoors, soaking in the last days of warmth and sunlight before the gloominess and cold of winter took hold in just a few weeks. Saturday was spent enjoying a picnic lunch and hiking in the park before returning home, where they enjoyed a dinner of BBQ chicken on the deck outside just as twilight was setting in.

Sunday, they did some outside work, raking some of the leaves just beginning to fall. The work took longer than it should have, but that was mostly because Emma insisted on jumping into every pile they assembled, not that Micah and Kayla minded one bit.

On Monday, Micah pulled into the parking lot of Haley's Diner just a few minutes before the meeting time of 7:30, walked in and took a seat in a corner booth. A couple minutes later, Lara Hiller made her entrance. Just a couple inches shy of six feet, Hiller immediately reminded Micah why she was so popular with the voters, especially male ones. Her long legs moved gracefully below a tight skirt that ended a couple inches above the knee, and a tight white blouse stretched perfectly at the breast below her business suit jacket. Her mid-length blonde hair came just past her shoulders and framed a face that was impeccably made-up but obviously required little help from cosmetics. Her confident stride and the way she held herself demanded the attention of every other diner in the restaurant, as it likely did in any other room she entered.

Micah stood up and greeted her, and she moved just close enough as she shook his hand that he smelled just the right amount of her intoxicating perfume, obviously very expensive. Micah had met Lara on many occasions. She was in the midst of her second year in the Statehouse, but prior to that she sat on the City Council in Williams. He always found her to be striking, and extremely intelligent, but something about her that morning, looking the way she did and the way with which she carried herself, made her almost intimidating.

"Micah," she said, "Great to see you, as always." Lara smiled again, as they both sat down opposite each other.

"You too, Lara. How are things?"

The waitress stopped over, handed them menus and told them she'd return with coffee momentarily. When she walked away, Lara looked back at Micah.

"Doing well, thanks," she said. "We're in the middle of the fall session, so unfortunately I need to be up in Indianapolis in a couple of hours. I only have maybe 30 minutes for this."

"Well, then, let's get to it," Micah said. "I appreciate you reaching out to me."

"Listen, Micah." She paused as the waitress brought coffee and took their order – bacon and eggs for Micah and a yogurt fruit parfait for Lara. "You've always been a straight shooter and are extremely fair and unbiased. That's why I called you."

Micah took a sip of coffee and nodded. "I appreciate that. Thanks."

"The news is going to come out on this later this week, but I'm giving you the scoop a few days before anyone else. You've been working on this story, so you deserve it, and this will give you a chance to get background and break the story before anyone else."

Micah worked his hardest to remain stoic, but he was never a good poker player and he was sure Lara could see just how interested he was in whatever she was about to tell him.

"A House sub-committee has been looking into DCS for the past four weeks. I'm chairing the committee and your series is what brought it to light. There are only three of us on the committee, which is probably why we've been able to keep the lid shut on this for as long as we have."

"What have you got?" Micah asked, again trying not to sound too eager.

Lara held up her hand. "Off the record, until the press conference, right?"

Micah nodded.

"We're going to be announcing a hearing for Sandra Bless and Craig Evans," she said. "In addition to the negligence found in the Henley case, there are dozens of others just like it where action should have been taken but wasn't."

Micah leaned back in the booth and rubbed his temple. On one hand, he was glad to hear the committee was looking further into the situation, but on another, he had a nagging question pulling at him and he was not convinced the procedures DCS employed in the Henley case were entirely the fault of the people who worked there. He needed to ask a question, and had to find the best way to ask it, but he knew now was not the right time. So, he waited for Lara to continue.

"You want to ask me something, go ahead," she said.

Micah shook his head as he took another sip of coffee. "I should probably save it for the press conference."

Lara thought about this for a moment. "You're thinking we're deflecting blame here, aren't you?"

Micah stared at her, and thought about the best way to say what he wanted to say. He realized he failed when the words, "Seems like a bit of a witch hunt to me" came out of his mouth.

182

Lara slapped her hand against the table, and the smile that persisted throughout much of the meeting was gone now.

"In no way," she said, "is this a witch hunt. DCS botched this, along with lots of other cases. *People* screwed up, and innocent people died because of it. Your series helped bring it to light."

Now, Micah was growing upset. "Don't use our series to make me the hangman for these DCS employees," he said, his voice growing just loud enough that an elderly couple a few tables over looked his way. Micah noticed them, and toned it down.

When he settled down, he continued. "The Governor, the Senate and the House ignored the problem, too, you know. DCS is an after-thought for you because most of the kids involved are lower income and don't in any way represent your voting constituents."

The face of perfection that Lara Hiller walked in with just 10 minutes earlier was now reddening with a mixture of anger and resentment.

"Go to hell, Micah," she said, standing up and gathering her purse. "This is not what I came here for." With that, she turned on her heel and bolted for the exit. On her way out, every eye in the place – not just the men – followed her until she was out of sight, after which time they all turned to Micah.

He shrugged his shoulders, started to make some notes on the reporter's pad on the table in front of him, and took a bite of the breakfast the startled waitress had just set before him.

****

Micah was at his desk just a little past 8:15, and a wry grin lingered on his face as he considered how much his job had changed in the past few months. What was once a fairly cushy job in a town where not much happened was beginning to resemble his days in Chicago more than he ever imagined. In addition to investigating a riveting case involving murder, DCS and government cover-ups, he was now revving up the politicians just like he had in Chicago and Mobile. Not that he wanted things to be this way all the time, but a little excitement was just what he was looking for.

The creative juices flowing after his brief meeting with Hiller, Micah sat down in front of his computer and began hammering away at a lead to a story he knew he could not run until after the press conference later in the week. Even though Hiller got upset with him and stormed out of the restaurant, he still had every intention of honoring his promise not to run anything until after the news conference, but he wanted his story essentially done at that time so he could be the first one in the state to report the news.

Chapter Twenty-Three

To Roger's surprise, Dave did not take him directly to the District Attorney's office as he expected. Instead, his friend rented a room at a small hotel on the way into downtown, and he pulled the car directly in front of the door to room 107, where he swiped a key and led Roger inside. Before stepping in the door, Roger noticed Dave scan the parking lot and other surrounding areas, but the few people in sight did not appear to be paying them any attention.

Once inside the room, Dave locked the door and motioned for Roger to sit in one of the two chairs flanking a small table. "I want to hear your story before we get over there," Dave told him after both were seated.

Roger sat up a bit straighter in his chair and looked across the table. "Where do you want me to start?"

"At the beginning," Dave replied. "From here on out, I am the prosecutor as far as this exercise is concerned."

Roger nodded, thought for a second, and then began. "On the evening of September 10, I returned home following work and my nightly Alcoholics' Anonymous meeting. It was around 6:30, and when I entered the house it was empty, although my son, Adam, should have been there waiting for me.

"I called his name several times, checked his bedroom and made my way out to the woods behind our cabin, where he sometimes likes to play. I kept calling his name, but got no reply, and when I came to the area of the woods where his fort was, I crawled in and found him sitting in a corner in his underpants with his knees curled up to his chest. He was rocking back and forth and mumbling inaudibly."

Dave nodded, encouraging him to continue. So far, so good, but the most important part of the story was yet to come.

"When I put my arms under him to pick him up and carry him inside, he began swinging at me and saying, 'no Uncle Jack, no!' but I finally managed to get him in my arms and took him inside the house, where I called 911. When they got there, one of the paramedics told me Adam had been raped.

"At the hospital, I waited for the doctors to check on Adam and once he was medicated and asleep for the night, I got in my car and headed over to my brother-in-law, Jack's, house. My intent was to confront him and confirm my suspicions – that he was responsible for the rape. He told me…"

Dave held up a hand. "Before you start into what happens next, give some background on Jack. It's important that the DA knows just what kind of person we're dealing with here."

Roger nodded. "Jack has been a mess his whole life. When my wife, Annie, was alive, she kept him away from us and only spoke to me about him a couple of times. He had always been into drugs and alcohol, had been in and out of jail a couple of times, and Annie and even her parents had little to do with him. After she passed away, for whatever reason, I made the horrible decision to let him into our lives. During that time, I let him get me into heavy drinking, and I even did heroin with him a couple of times."

Dave shook his head. "Leave your drug use out unless the DA asks. Since it's no longer an issue for you, don't even bring it up. It's good you admit to the drinking, though, since we have to discuss the AA meetings."

"Jack would come around every so often, and I did nothing to stop it. I would drink with him on those occasions, and my life started on a bit of a downward spiral. When the new school year started and I saw what my poor decisions were doing to Adam, I made a vow to quit, and thus began the AA meetings."

Dave nodded for Roger to continue.

"So, that night, after I found out what had happened, I went to Jack's cabin and found him inside with the television on. He was barely awake and had a near-empty bottle of whiskey on the table before him, as well as a syringe and a lit candle."

Dave took on the DA persona at this point. "Mr. Durkin, tell me what happened next, but at this point I want to remind you that anything you say is admissible in court."

Roger paused momentarily, but pulled himself back together and continued.

"I stood just inside the doorway and just stared at Jack for a moment. As I was preparing to ask him where he had been earlier in the evening, he looked at me, smiled and said, 'I'm guessing you're here about the boy' or something to that effect. He then said he thought Adam always wanted him to do it, that the way Adam looked at Jack left no doubt he wanted to be touched."

Roger could feel the rage burning inside him again, just as it had that night and when he had told Dave the story in the coffee shop. He tried to gather himself, but Dave reached across the table and put his hand on his arm.

"Don't try to quell the anger," Dave said. "Let the DA see exactly what you were feeling that evening. It's crucial to the depraved heart scenario."

Roger was relieved he wasn't going to have to hold down his anger, since he wasn't sure at all that he could. The night coming back to him clearly, Roger continued.

"After he said that, I was convinced Jack was the reason Adam was in the hospital, and I blamed him for everything bad that had happened in our lives since Annie died. I went out to my trunk, grabbed a tire iron I had in there, and walked back into the house."

Roger knew this was the part where the story diverted from the truth, but knowing this was the only way he was going to be with his son before he was an adult, he had no qualms at all about going in this direction.

"When I got back inside, Jack was still sitting on the couch, apparently unmoved at all about what he had done or the fact I was there. He looked up at me, and when I saw him smile again, probably reliving the rape in his mind, I hit him multiple times with the tire iron."

"Mr. Durkin," Dave said, "where did you hit him?"

Roger thought for a moment and then answered, "The first one caught him on the shoulder, and then I took another swing that hit him on the ribs. I don't know if it was the drugs but neither blow seemed to affect him, and he took a swing at me, so I swung twice more hitting him in both legs."

"What happened next?"

"I think the last swings broke his legs, and he was finally screaming in pain. I backed away, and in doing so my leg hit his coffee table and tipped over the lit candle. A stack of papers caught fire, and the next thing I know the whole table was on fire and the couch had caught as well."

"So, what did you do next?" Dave asked.

"I started to panic," Roger said. "On one hand, I was so angry I couldn't have cared less if Jack burned to death in that house. That thought made me run out of the house and get into my car without any thought of helping him.

"Once in my car, I didn't know what to do, but something told me I should call 911 and report the fire, which I did."

"Mr. Durkin, it's pretty unusual you would be angry enough to beat a man, rendered helpless by drugs and alcohol, start his house on fire, leave him there without any attempt at helping him, and then call 911 so that responders *could* try to help him," Dave said, doing a very good job of rehearsing this for Roger. "As a matter of fact, I don't think I've ever heard of anyone doing any such thing."

Roger thought for a moment. He knew this was just a rehearsal, but he also knew he would be doing this for real in the next couple of hours, and the final part of his story would determine how soon he would be back with his son.

"I don't really know what exactly made me call 911, but I remember the thought hitting me that I'm not a killer. As angry as I was about what Jack had done to my son, and as much as I wanted him to pay for it, I remember thinking about Adam at that point and not wanting him to ever have to find out his father was a killer, regardless of the circumstances."

Dave nodded and smiled. Apparently, Roger passed the test to his satisfaction. The two spent another hour and a half going through the story with Dave making suggestions here and there to get the wording exactly the way he wanted it. Once they were finished, Dave prepared Roger for what was to come next.

"After we leave here, we'll grab an early lunch and then we have a one o' clock appointment with Rick Barnes, the district attorney. When we get there, I'll go in first while you wait outside in the car. I'll tee this whole thing up for him and begin discussions on what kind of deal we can make, and if I'm not comfortable at that point, I'll be back outside and we'll be on our way back to your house to discuss our next move. If I feel good about it, I'll call you and tell you to come in and join us. At that point, Barnes will make you go through your story like we just did."

The thought occurred to Roger this whole thing was playing out in his mind like a work of fiction, and he wondered again how his life had come to this point in time. Dave apparently saw his friend drifting off into his thoughts, and he brought his hand down on the table just hard enough to get Roger's attention.

"Listen, buddy," Dave said. "I know this is really hard, but we're almost there and it *has* to happen. You can't run from this, and if we do it right, I'll get you back to your son as soon as possible under the circumstances."

"That's the part I'm afraid of," Roger said immediately. "the 'under the circumstances' part."

Dave nodded but had nothing to say that would make his friend feel better, so he continued.

"After you finish your story, the DA is probably going to remand you into custody while he determines what charges to file. Those charges will need to be filed within 48 hours, at which time there will be a bail hearing. The bail will be a fairly high amount, which I could definitely help you with, but I'd advise you not to make bail."

"Why not?" Roger asked quickly.

Dave knew this question was coming. "Because, in every eventuality I've gone through in the past couple of days, you will have to agree to serve some time in this case, even with the depraved heart argument. It's possible the DA will choose not to file charges, but I find that highly unlikely. By you staying in rather than posting bail, you'll be credited with the time served, and it will be in a local jail, rather than a state prison. By comparison, that's like spending your time in a Marriott."

Roger wanted to object, but what his attorney said made complete sense. "But if you can keep me out of jail, you will, right?" Roger knew the answer to the question, and the minute it left his mouth he felt stupid and wished he could take it back. To Dave's credit, he had a pretty good idea how his friend was feeling, so he let it go with just a nod.

"What's going to happen to Adam through all of this?" Roger asked after a moment passed.

"I considered that and asked around last night," Dave answered. Roger was impressed as his friend apparently thought of everything. It occurred to him Dave was a better attorney than he would have ever been. "DCS is going to get involved, but I'm going to file a motion to grant temporary custody to your in-laws. I'll talk to them when we're done here about staying local so Adam can visit you and continue his life as normally as possible through this process."

Roger was as content with that as he could be, and the two went over a few final details before finally walking out of the motel room and heading to a quiet restaurant just down the street.

****

A few minutes after one, Dave Carter sat on the visitor's side of the large wooden desk belonging to the top prosecutor for the state of Indiana's 9th District. Rick Barnes was a formidable figure, a little over six-three with dark black hair, strong features and a complexion far darker than that of most Midwesterners used to cold winters and eight months where tanning – at least natural tanning – was not part of the equation.

Dave did some asking around Indianapolis about Barnes and learned from friends who worked with or against him that he was tough, but extremely fair. Since he served as a defense attorney for close to 10 years before switching over to the prosecutor's office, he was considerably more objective than many of his counterparts. Dave was counting on this objectivity as he began the meeting that would determine the next stage of his friend's life.

Moving quickly through the formalities, Dave informed Barnes that he had a client who was considering turning himself in after a "domestic incident that led to the death of his client's brother-in-law." Barnes gave no indication any such case had come across his desk to that point, which led Dave to the conclusion that the local sheriff's office had not yet submitted any paperwork.

Methodically, Dave went through the events of the evening, setting in place details Roger would expand upon when presenting the story to Barnes, while at the same time laying the groundwork for what he hoped would be a sympathetic audience. Knowing prosecutors never took kindly to someone taking the law into his own hands, Dave hoped Barnes would see reason and put himself in Roger's place under the dismal circumstances.

As he spun the story for the D.A., Dave watched for any reaction that might lead him to believe bringing Roger in was not a good idea, but to Barnes' credit, all he did was maintain a stoic look and nod his head. When he finished the story, Barnes looked away and sent his gaze out the large window that looked out over the county courthouse. After he thought for a few more seconds, he looked back across the desk.

"So, if everything you tell me is accurate," Barnes said, "I'm guessing you're angling for a depraved heart scenario. Is that correct?"

"It's a textbook case," Dave replied immediately. "The man's son gets raped and he reacts the way anybody would in the heat of the moment."

"Well, I didn't read that textbook," Barnes said, for a moment making Dave a little uneasy. "But then again, in a case such as this it's tough to find a jury that would blame the man for doing what he did. But again, that's assuming everything you're telling me is true."

Dave held Barnes' gaze as he searched for any sign the defense attorney was lying to him. After a moment, Barnes ended the stare down, stood and walked to the window.

"I suppose you looked into my background and know I was a defense attorney for a long time," Barnes said without looking back at Dave.

Dave replied in the affirmative.

"So, what are you hoping for here?"

Dave didn't like being in the inferior position, so he stood up from his chair. Instinctively, Barnes turned from the window and looked back at him.

"I think you should choose not to file," Dave said after only the briefest moment. "This guy was a loser, addicted to drugs, booze and, apparently, little boys, and because of that this case is a loser for you. You file it and you're essentially telling every child molester out there you have his back."

Barnes let out a sound that was a cross between a snort and a laugh. "And if I don't file it, I'm telling every victim of crime out there it's perfectly fine to take matters into his own hands."

"Tough choice," Dave said. "But, then again, you're probably not getting many votes from those child molesters and drug dealers. The good people who become victims of crime, on the other hand…"

Dave let the sentence dangle out there for a moment. One thing he learned during his years of defense was that every top-level prosecutor, regardless of how righteous he or she was, is still a politician in every sense of the word. After a moment, Barnes smiled at Dave.

"I like you," Barnes said. "Let's sit back down, talk through this for a moment, and then we'll see if we can bring in your client."

Twenty minutes later, Dave summoned Roger up to Barnes' office, and the three sat in a circle around the small meeting table in the corner. To Roger's surprise, an hour later they walked out of the office, got back in the car and headed back to the cabin. Barnes agreed to allow Roger to remain free for the time being while he talked to the police and several others regarding the case. He told them if everything he discovered corroborated Roger's story he would be in touch within the week to share what, if any, charges would be filed.

****

Ten minutes later, Dave pulled his Mercedes back up the cabin's driveway, and before he shifted the car into park, Adam was on the front porch. When he saw Roger open his door and climb out, he flew down the three steps and closed the distance between he and his dad in a second before jumping up into Roger's arms. His eyes, red and blotchy, gave away the fact he was crying most of the morning.

"Hey, buddy," Roger said, choking back tears himself. "Looks like I don't have to go quite yet."

Adam pulled his head off Roger's shoulder and looked him directly in the eyes. "I don't want you to have to go at all. Let's just get out of here."

"We can't do that, Adam," he replied. "We just need to wait this out and see what comes of it."

Adam leaned close to Roger and whispered in his ear, "Grandpa told me Uncle Jack is dead. Is it okay that I'm glad?"

Roger looked at his son and wasn't sure what to say, so he just offered a small nod and made his way toward the front porch. Tom came out of the house and watched the scene unfold in the driveway.

"Good to see you, Roger," Tom said as they made their way into the front door of the cabin.

"Dave, will you stay for dinner?" Roger asked as they moved toward the kitchen.

Dave shook his head. "No, I need to get back to Indianapolis. I still have a few hours of work on a couple other cases to catch up on today. But, thanks."

"No, thank you," Roger said, setting Adam back down on his feet. "You were incredible today."

Roger walked his friend back out to his car, and the two chatted for a couple of minutes before Roger gave his friend a tight hug and watched him pull back down the driveway. Adam was back out on the porch, and Roger motioned for him to sit down in one of the two rocking chairs.

"Buddy, this isn't over yet, so I need you to stay strong," Roger said. "The lawyer we met with and the police still need to look into all of the details, and then they'll decide what is going to happen next."

Adam looked like he was going to cry again, but he willed himself not to.

"Also, some people are going to come over tomorrow," Roger continued. "Their job is to make sure you are safe and taken care of if I have to go away for a little while."

Adam's face showed he didn't like this at all, but still he managed to hold back any tears that wanted to make their way out. "Can't I just stay with grandpa and grandma if that happens?"

"That's our hope, Adam," Roger replied. "But these people have to do their jobs, so I want you to be big and strong and answer their questions when they come tomorrow, okay?"

Adam nodded his head and hugged his dad one more time. "I'm just glad you're home."

****

That night, after Adam finally wound down and fell asleep, Roger and Tom sat out on the front porch. The air was getting much cooler as October progressed, and both needed a jacket as they sat in the rockers and sipped on cups of hot coffee. Roger shared the details of the meeting with Rick Barnes, as well as what Dave told him about the DCS visit the next day.

"Roger," Tom said, "Jan's not doing well at all. Between losing our little girl a couple years ago, and now everything that's happened with Jack, she's in a pretty bad way right now."

Roger felt bad, but he hadn't even thought of the how his in-laws were dealing with all of this. He learned during the conversation Jan hadn't even come to the cabin but instead opted to stay at the hotel. Apparently, the photos and the memories of Annie ever-present in the cabin were just too much for her.

Tom continued, "Everyone's been worried about my heart the past couple of years, but Jan's blood pressure is through the roof right now, and all of this certainly isn't helping her. I really think I need to get her back to Gulf Shores and let her get back into her element. We're going to head out tomorrow."

Roger was taken aback. "But what about Adam? What about DCS?"

Tom looked down at his lap and took another sip of his coffee. "I'll stay for the DCS visit in the morning, but I don't know that I'll be able to get Jan over here. As for Adam, let's cross that bridge when we come to it. If your situation changes, I can be up here within a day, assuming Jan's doing okay."

All along, Roger just assumed Tom and Jan would be there if anything were to happen to him. Hearing that may not be the case did nothing to ease his mind after what was a roller coaster of a day.

Tom stood up a moment later and said he needed to get back to the hotel, but would be back in the morning by eight. Roger thanked him and watched Tom get in his car and pull down the driveway.

Sitting back down in the rocking chair, Roger took another sip of coffee and found himself wishing it was something stronger. He realized then he hadn't been to an AA meeting in over a week, and vowed to try to do so tomorrow if possible.

As he sat on the front porch, the cool October air wrapping around him, the day's events replayed themselves in his mind. The next thing he knew, he was nodding off in his chair, and he forced himself to stand up and head into bed.

****

The sound of thunder rumbling in the distance awoke Roger from a deep sleep. Leaning over, he looked at the red glow of the alarm clock beside his bed and saw it was just past five. A flash of lightning lit up the sky a moment later, and instinctively Roger began counting off the seconds – one, two, three – before the crash of thunder rolled again. Apparently, the storm was nearly on top of them. Roger rolled over to lie on his back and suddenly found himself wide awake.

A moment later, the door to his bedroom creaked open and he saw the silhouette of his son in the doorway.

"Storm wake you up?" he asked Adam, who didn't answer verbally but moved closer to the bed. Roger couldn't remember the last time Adam came into his room in the middle of the night, not even in the days and weeks after Annie passed away.

"Come on buddy, climb in here with me," Roger said, pulling back the covers. "The thunder and lightning woke me up, too."

Adam climbed into the king-sized bed and wiggled his way over next to Roger. He put his arm around his son's shoulders and pulled him close to him, feeling the heat radiating off the boy, and for a moment, Roger thought he felt Adam trembling.

Another flash of lightning lit up the room for several seconds, and Roger took the opportunity to look down at his son, whose eyes were wide open.

"I was having a nightmare," Adam whispered, barely loud enough for Roger to hear. As he said it, Adam moved even closer to Roger.

"Dreams are just that," Roger said. "They're just in your head."

Roger could feel Adam shaking his head, and a warm tear rolled from Adam's face onto his arm.

"No, this one was real," Adam said.

"Do you want to tell me about it?"

Adam began shaking his head, the tears coming a bit harder now. He stayed quiet for a few more seconds and then said, "Uncle Jack was in my room." Adam paused for a couple seconds, apparently trying to hold back the sob that wanted to escape.

"We…we were in my room, and he had my clothes off and was taking his off, too. You weren't home, and he threw me down on my bed, and I could feel him touching me – touching me everywhere. In places he shouldn't have."

Adam was crying more now, but still controlling himself as if he needed to get the rest of the story out.

"He was hitting me, and touching me and doing other things to me, and I was just so scared," Adam continued, some whimpers interjecting themselves between parts of each sentence. "And I was just lying there – I couldn't do anything – and he smelled so bad. Kind of like your mouth feels when you just threw up – that's what he smelled like."

Adam pulled his head off Roger's arm and leaned in a higher position looking directly into his dad's face. Outside the storm seemed to be right on top of the house, the thunder following the recurrent bolts of lightning almost immediately.

Roger thought about saying something as Adam paused, but he held back, knowing his son was somewhere between talking about his nightmare, while at the same time remembering some – or all – of what happened to him.

"Dad?" Adam said after what must have been a couple of minutes.

"Yeah, buddy?"

"I hate Uncle Jack." Adam was crying again, but managed to say. "I'm glad he's dead. Does that make me bad?"

Roger reached up and pulled his son back down to where he was lying next to him again, his head so that it rested on Roger's chest. He was crying hard now, and Roger just held him close to him for a moment before saying, "Adam, your uncle did something really bad to you, and you have every right to be angry, sad, or anything else you need to feel to move past it."

A blast of thunder interrupted the sentence and made the house shake, causing both to jump just a little.

"You've gone through something," Roger continued, "that no one ever – especially not a little boy – should ever have to go through. And your uncle was a bad man, or he had a lot of problems – whatever you want to say about him."

Roger rolled over so he was looking directly into Adam's eyes. "Adam, do you remember that time after your mom left us – after she died – where you asked me 'why' she had to die?"

Adam nodded, but didn't say anything.

"Do you remember I didn't really have a good answer and I told you sometimes bad things just happen to good people?"

Another nod.

"Well, that's definitely true, and there are times in your life where you feel like those bad things happen to those good people all too often." Roger felt himself on the verge of tears now as well, but he willed himself to be strong for Adam.

"As for your Uncle Jack, well, all I can say is sometimes bad things happen to bad people, too, and he got what was coming to him."

Adam's eyes were wide open when the next flash of lightning lit up the room, and this time the thunder took about three seconds to follow. "Dad?" he asked. "Is everything going to be alright, ever again?"

The question caught Roger off guard, and he almost answered too quickly to reassure Adam, but held back the words right before they were ready to come out. He thought for another second or two before he found the right thing to say.

"Honestly, buddy," he started slowly. "I really don't know. Since your mom died, every time I've ever thought things were getting back to normal, and that we were going to be okay, something else has happened that's thrown us off, hasn't it?"

Adam nodded. "Sure seems that way," he said.

"Well, you know," Roger continued. "While I was sitting on the porch last night after you went to bed, it was really getting cooler out there. And as the darkness started to settle in, I just listened to everything going on around me. And you know what I heard?"

Adam thought for a second, but shook his head.

"I heard the sound of some frogs calling out to each other, and in the trees the sounds of the cicadas, and further off in the distance the buzz of cars moving down the highway, and you know what it all made me think?"

Again, Adam shook his head.

"When you and me, or anyone else, has a really bad day and sometimes we're not sure how we're going to go on, these things that exist around us – the animals, the insects, the frogs and everyone and everything else – just keep going on with their lives. And we can sit and wonder all we want why bad things happen to good people, but you know what? Everything is going to be okay if *we* make it okay. It's up to us."

Further off in the distance, the lightning flashed much more dimly and the sound of the thunder took more than ten seconds to follow. In addition, the room was slightly lighter than it wsa earlier as dawn was nearing.

"But what if the bad things just keep happening?" Adam asked.

"Well, buddy, that's when we just have to be our toughest and our strongest, and we have to say we're going to make the best of this, no matter what. No matter how many bad things get thrown our way, we're not going to let them beat us, or define us, or determine how we're going to live our lives."

Roger looked for any sign of recognition from his son, but he could tell he was still processing everything they talked about.

"Do you want to try to go back to sleep?" Roger asked.

"No, I'm pretty awake."

"Me too," Roger said. "How about we get up and get some breakfast going? We have another busy day ahead."

****

A half hour later, just a little before seven, Roger and Adam sat at the kitchen table finishing their bacon, eggs and toast they prepared together. The storm that awakened them was gone, but large gray clouds remained, blocking out any possible appearance of the sun.

When they finished, Roger cleaned up the kitchen and told Adam to go in, take his shower and put on a clean pair of jeans and a shirt with a collar, reminding him of the DCS visit taking place in just a few hours. Adam didn't look happy at first, but Roger watched as his son straightened himself up, visibly willing himself to be strong for whatever would happen that day. It made Roger smile, and for the first time since all of this started, he really believed Adam was going to be okay, no matter how everything turned out.

Roger put the dishes in the dishwasher before going into his bathroom to clean himself up and get ready for the day ahead.

****

Tom pulled into the driveway just after eight, walked past Adam, who came out to meet him, and told Roger he and Jan were going to get on the road earlier than expected. Apparently, Jan had an episode during the night, and Tom worried that if he didn't get her home as soon as possible, she was going to find herself in a hospital. Roger, while concerned what this meant for his case with DCS, told Tom he understood and wished him all the best. He found it a little disconcerting that Tom said nothing about his and Jan's willingness to help with Adam, should that help be needed, but he knew with Jan being first and foremost on Tom's mind, now wasn't the time to bring it up.

About an hour after Tom pulled out of the driveway, another car made its way to the front of the house. Out of the driver side door stepped Craig Evans, senior caseworker for the local office of the Indiana Department of Child Services. Again, Roger experienced the surreal feeling that all of this couldn't be happening with him and his family. He read and heard so many times about situations where intervention by DCS was needed, but never in a million years did he think he would ever be at the center of one of those cases.

Evans walked onto the porch, where Adam and Roger waited for him. He shook Roger's hand, stepped to the side and greeted Adam, and asked Adam to go inside and give him and Roger a few minutes to talk on their own before he would come in and talk with him. Adam looked nervous, but still did his best to be strong.

The two men sat down in the rocking chairs on the front porch after Evans declined Roger's offer for something to drink. Evans reached into the briefcase he carried with him from the car and pulled out a leather portfolio and a pen. Opening it up, he made a note of the date and time and looked up at Roger.

"Mr. Durkin," he began, "the purpose of my visit today, as instructed by the Family Court of Lands County, is to ensure that during the course of your potential criminal case and investigation Adam is living in a suitable environment for a minor. Please understand my involvement is in no way a determination of any guilt or wrongdoing on your part. I am only here to make sure this is a safe situation for Adam, and to acclimate myself to your case in the event any charges are filed."

Roger nodded his head – Dave explained all of this to him the day before, so none of it came as a surprise.

"After you and I talk for a few minutes, I'm going to bring Adam out and ask him a few questions as well," Evans continued. "You are permitted to be present for the entirety of the conversation, but I would ask that you allow Adam to answer the questions on his own. I'm only going to ask a few, and I will not try to trick him in any way."

"I'm fine with that," Roger said. "I've actually been amazed at how well he's handled everything."

Evans jotted a note on his pad and looked back up at Roger.

"So, let's just start from the beginning," Evans said. "Tell me about your home life here, how you and Adam interact, and what a typical day is like for both of you. Is Adam's mother still in the picture? All of those kinds of things…"

At the mention of "Adam's mother," Roger bristled a bit and looked down at his shoes. He assumed Evans would already have details of Annie's passing, but then he realized DCS was just beginning this investigation and would have no information other than what was passed on to them from the court.

"Well, my wife – Adam's mom – passed away a couple years ago from cancer," Roger began. "Before she died, Annie's job brought her here to Williams and the three of us were about as happy as could be."

Roger was amazed again at how fresh the wound of Annie's loss remained for him. Every time he talked about it, the hurt that rested just below the surface came rushing back as if it had just happened.

Evans saw the pain in Roger's eyes, and offered the obligatory condolences.

"It's been a bit of a tough go for us the past couple of years," Roger continued. "I held it together fairly well for the first year or so, but then got into some pretty heavy drinking that made things rough for both Adam and I."

Evans made some more notes in the notebook, and asked, "Are you still drinking?"

"Haven't touched a drop the past two months, and up until the assault on Adam, I was going to meetings every day," Roger said. "They've really helped me get my act back together."

"So, aside from the drinking problems, which you said lasted about a year," Evans said as he looked across at Roger, "describe the balance of your home life."

Roger thought for a moment. "I work as a high school teacher, and up until the time Annie died, I coached baseball as well. Adam is a good kid – makes good grades and rarely gets into any kind of trouble. Since Annie died, he's had to come home to an empty house for an hour or two after school, but he's been good about keeping himself occupied until I get home. He usually just does his homework or plays out in the woods until dinner time."

"How much time is he here by himself on a typical day?"

"About an hour – two at most," Roger replied. More notes in the notebook.

Evans looked up at Roger after a moment passed. "Mr. Durkin, from my understanding of the case, you could be looking at some fairly significant jail time, should the prosecutor choose to move forward with charges. What would be your wishes for Adam's care, should that happen?"

"The only family members still in our lives are Annie's parents," Roger replied. "My hope would be they would care for Adam should I have to go away."

"Are they local and in good health?"

"They live in Alabama, but Annie's dad assured me they would be willing to help if we need it."

Evans made some notes again after Roger gave him Tom and Jan's names and address information. Should the need arise, he would look into both and ensure they could care for Adam.

"Let's go ahead and bring Adam out for a couple of questions," Evans said after he finished writing. Roger opened the door and called to Adam, who was out on the porch in seconds.

Since the adults occupied the two chairs, Adam took a seat on the wooden porch, crossing his legs in front of him.

"Hi, Adam," Evans began, "Do you know why I'm here today?"

Adam nodded.

"Good. I'm just going to ask you a couple questions, and I need for you to tell me the truth, okay?" Another nod.

Evans began by asking Adam about school, his favorite subject, what position he played in baseball and a few other questions obviously aimed at putting Adam at ease and building trust. After he got Adam talking and relaxing just a little bit more, he started into the tougher questions.

"Can you tell me a little bit about how you have felt since your mom died?"

Adam thought for a minute. "Dad and I miss her a lot," he said. "Sometimes I still cry over it, but I'm trying not to do that anymore."

Evans nodded. "It's hard losing your mom. You're a pretty brave guy. Tell me a little bit about your dad and how you guys take care of the house and work through your day."

After a moment, Adam looked up. "My dad works hard – he's a really good teacher. And I know he misses mom a lot, too, but I think he does his best for me making sure I'm okay and taking care of our house."

Evans smiled. "How about your grandparents?"

"They're fine," Adam said. "I don't see them all that much, but they've been here the past week or so."

"Do you feel safe when they're around?"

Adam shrugged. "Like I said, I don't see them too much."

Evans jotted down a couple more notes and then stood up from the chair. "Can you guys show me around the house? And then we'll be finished for today."

Adam handled the tour guide duties, leading Evans into the kitchen, through the living room and into the bedrooms and bathrooms of the small cabin. Evans opened some cabinets and the medicine chest in each bathroom, but for the most part he just observed.

After they finished the brief trip around the inside of the house, Evans shook both of their hands, climbed in his car and drove off. Roger checked his watch and saw the visit only lasted a little more than a half hour. A few minutes later, his cell phone rang and he looked down and saw Dave Carter's name on the caller ID.

"Roger," Dave said, "I just got a call from Rick Barnes. He wants to meet with us tomorrow at 10."

"Any indication on which way he's leaning?" Roger asked.

There was a slight pause on the other end before Dave answered. "I tried to get more information from him, but he just said he'll talk to us tomorrow. I really couldn't tell from his tone of voice."

Roger thanked Dave before disconnecting the call. It looked like it was going to be another day of waiting and wondering.

Chapter Twenty-Four

Roger determined not to let his free day with Adam pass with the two of them sitting around thinking about what might come next. It was a Thursday and he had no idea what Friday would bring, but the plan was for Adam to start back to school the following week. Roger's situation when it came to returning to work was, obviously, much more up in the air. The principal for the school at which he worked offered – actually, insisted – on a leave of absence for Roger while he cared for Adam. Of course, he knew nothing of the attack on Jack, but Roger shared with him a little information about Adam being in the hospital.

After Craig Evans left the house, Roger and Adam jumped in the car and made the 45-minute drive to Indianapolis to go to the Zoo. It was one of their places and, while not the biggest zoo in the country, it is well laid-out and offers most of the major animals people love to see. Their favorite was always the polar bear exhibit, and that afternoon they spent nearly an hour just sitting and watching the giant white bear play in the water, happy as can be. As they drove back into Williams, Roger surprised Adam by stopping the car in front of the famous ice cream parlor downtown that was, without a doubt, Adam's favorite place in their hometown. Together, they sat at the counter and split a huge banana split before returning home for the evening.

When Roger tucked in his son that night, a thought occurred to him that every day since Jack attacked Adam was spent as if he were trying to create just the right memories for Adam in case it turned out to be their last day together – at least for a while. He suspected, after the 10:00 meeting the next morning, he would finally know whether today's memories would be the ones he'd have to hold onto for a while.

Sleep came sparingly that night, and Roger spent most of the time in bed rolling back and forth trying to block out any thought this could be his last night of freedom for some time. He knew, during his meeting the next day, Barnes could very well tell him they were deciding not to pursue charges, but deep down Roger knew that was probably not going to happen. Part of him wished he had a little more time, but the days of wondering what was going to happen had dragged on too long, and he was ready for the next step – unless, of course, the next step involved losing his son.

The last thought he had before he finally fell asleep, at least for a couple hours, was that he had not heard from Tom and Jan upon their return to Alabama. Typically, in past visits, one of them would call to let Roger know they made it home safely. But then again, nothing was typical anymore.

****

The sound of the cell phone vibrating on the nightstand next to his bed woke Roger before the first ring came too loudly at 2:17 a.m. Looking at the screen on his phone, Roger saw it was Tom and knew any call at this time of night would not be good news.

Tom, his voice breaking, told Roger during the drive back to Gulf Shores, Jan had a stroke and Tom had to pull into a hospital in Montgomery, Alabama, just a few hours from home. As Roger was silently saying a quick prayer, Tom said, "Roger, I've lost her."

Roger searched for the words but none came, and a long pause lingered between the two men on the phone. Finally, he said, "Tom, I'm so sorry."

Tom tried to reply, but after a couple unsuccessful attempts, he quietly hung up the phone. On the other end of the line, Roger stared into the darkness of his bedroom and wondered what came next.

He didn't have to wait long. A little after eight his phone rang again. Adam was still in bed, and this time Dave's name and phone numbered appeared on Roger's screen. As soon as Roger picked up the call, before he could even say hello, Dave started talking.

"Roger, I just got a call from a friend of mine in the clerk's office," he said, much too urgently for Roger's liking. "Barnes issued a warrant for your arrest on a charge of second-degree murder. We'll need to surrender this morning, rather than meet with Barnes."

While Roger, deep down, knew this could be coming, the words coming over the line still hit him hard. When he gathered his composure, he told Dave about Jan's death and the uncertainty of what would happen with Adam as the legal case played out.

"I don't know yet," was all Dave could manage. "But I'll bring someone over with me that can take him temporarily while we sort that – and your situation – out."

The call ended with Dave's promise to pick up Roger and Adam just before 10 a.m. As he woke Adam and told him all that transpired in the past six hours, Roger was amazed – and a bit worried – at how maturely and stoically his son took the news. There were no tears and no tantrums as there were through much of the build-up to this moment, and as Adam went into the bathroom, Roger worried he was witnessing the end of his son's childhood.

When Dave arrived at 9:45 in his Mercedes, a red Lexus convertible followed him up the driveway. Both cars stopped, and Roger and Dave stood on the porch as an attractive blonde exited the Lexus and walked side-by-side with Dave toward the front of the house.

"Roger and Adam," Dave said, "I would like you to meet my assistant, Cheryl." On cue, Cheryl smiled, and Roger and Adam, despite the gravity of the situation, couldn't help but smile back. Adam even blushed a bit, thinking deep down how much he liked the way Cheryl looked, and the way she smiled at him.

The smiles on both Durkins faded away quickly, however, when Dave said they needed to get going. Roger bent down to his son's eye level, grabbed him by the shoulders and said, "I'll see you as soon as I can, buddy. I promise."

Adam looked as if he would cry again, but reminded himself of the promise he made to himself and his dad to stay strong. Besides, he didn't want Cheryl to think he was a big crybaby. So instead, he gave his dad a quick hug, looked him in the eye and nodded. Roger, doing his best to hold it together himself, turned and walked quickly toward the passenger side of Dave's car. As they pulled out of the driveway, Roger took one quick glance back, only to see Cheryl and Adam walking into the house.

Chapter Twenty-Five

Lara Hiller, flanked by two other legislators who joined her on the oversight committee, milled about the lectern placed in the state capitol's rotunda as the members of the press settled into their seats for the Friday morning press conference.

At precisely noon, as promised, Hiller stepped to the microphone, looked down at her notes and then up at approximately two dozen reporters and photographers staring back at her. Absent was the white, toothy grin seen so often on the campaign trail and at the various fundraisers she so often frequented. In its place was a fire in her eyes and conviction in her voice as she began to deliver the short prepared statement carefully crafted well in advance of the conference.

"Good afternoon, and thank you for your time today," Hiller began as the television cameras rolled, photos snapped and audio recorders pointed in her direction. It occurred to Micah as he awaited the message to which he was already partly privy, Lara Hiller lived for these moments. There was no doubt in his mind this was when she was at her best, and it shined through in the way she spoke and the way she carried herself. It never failed, every time he watched her address an audience she managed to grab the attention of every person there.

"By now, all of you are aware of the grisly Henley murders in Williams several weeks ago, as well as the circumstances surrounding this terrible tragedy. Since

Williams is my hometown, this crime has affected me deeply, as it does everyone who lives there."

Hiller paused for effect, and Micah shifted in his seat as he wondered how many times she rehearsed every word and gesture of this presentation in the past few days.

"When something like this happens in our hometown – or anywhere in our state for that matter – we go through the stages of grieving, whether we know the victims personally or not. We experience denial, thinking something like this couldn't happen so close to home. When we realize it can, we despair, wondering what our world is coming to. And when all that settles down, we get angry."

Hiller's voice began to rise as she moved through the stages of grief, and the composure that marked her appearance at the beginning of the press conference turned to a subdued rage as she moved to the next section.

"Within the anger, we begin asking questions. Why did this happen? What could have been done to prevent it? Who, if anyone, is responsible? What are we going to do about it?"

She let the last question linger out there, the words practically echoing off the towering dome of the rotunda in which they were seated.

Calming herself, Hiller brought her voice back down to normal levels. "Those four questions have been at the center of an inquiry this committee launched approximately a month ago, and getting answers to those questions has become our mission. The common denominator in this crime and so many just like it is the Department of Child Services."

Scanning the audience, Hiller let her eyes lock in on Micah for the briefest moment and, within that moment, Micah thought he saw the faintest glimpse of amusement.

"DCS does many good things, and the agency helps a lot of children despite some pretty long odds against it, but in this instance and quite a few others like it, DCS failed. *People* at DCS failed. And they failed in a way that cost four children and a mother their lives to a serial abuser, one who could have been stopped with earlier action."

Hiller noticed her voice was rising again, and she tugged with both hands on the suit jacket she was wearing as if to pull herself down a bit.

"The finding of this committee, after reviewing dozens of cases, is that we need to review the processes DCS uses to evaluate cases, the leadership of the organization, the training of the staff and, if necessary, any legal obstacles restricting the organization's ability to effectively serve its purpose."

With the last sentence, Hiller settled her eyes on Micah, letting the stare last just a bit longer. Micah looked away to make some notes in his pad, making note of the words "legal obstacles" and underlining them for emphasis. When he finished jotting, he looked up and saw she was still staring directly at him.

"We'll take questions now."

From around the room, the follow-ups began flying. What was the timeframe? Which members of leadership were at the center of the investigation? Did the committee foresee any criminal charges?

Micah considered these questions and more, but his eyes kept returning to the words legal obstacles written on his pad. When things began to settle down, Micah stood and asked the only question he wanted to ask following his private meeting with Hiller several days earlier.

"Representative Hiller," he began, "you mentioned near the end of your statement a review of 'legal obstacles' preventing DCS from serving its mission. Was this a recurring theme in the cases the committee reviewed and, if so, will you look to introduce legislation to remove these obstacles?"

Hiller smiled at the question. Micah was sure she prepared for it, which was why she brought it up during the statement after getting angry with him during their breakfast meeting.

"Every option is available to us," she said. "Depending on the findings of our investigation."

With that, Hiller and her colleagues left the stage, making their way quickly to the offices adjoining the rotunda. By the time most members of the media were out of their seats in pursuit of another question or photo, the three representatives and their aides were behind closed doors.

As Micah packed up his briefcase and prepared for the drive back to Williams to write and file the story for the next day's paper, he turned his cell phone back on and noticed he had three voicemails. Figuring he could use the commute back to work as an opportunity to return calls, he sat down and jotted notes onto his pad. The first two calls were from reporters with questions on active stories they were pursuing. The third, however, was from his newly appointed supervisor at Lands County CASA, and the message was a relatively short one.

"Micah," the message said, "please give me a call at your earliest convenience. We have a case we'd like you to take."

Even though he knew the call would be coming eventually, Micah was both excited and nervous as he prepared to return the call.

Chapter Twenty-Six

Adam worked the controller of his Playstation 3 as he navigated his race car through the course, semi-focused on the game but bored at the same time. Cheryl talked to him for the first few minutes after his dad and Dave left, but after the brief conversation she moved into the kitchen and started making phone calls. Over the sound of the cars on the television screen, he would occasionally overhear Cheryl from the kitchen, and he knew she was talking to someone about him.

Tired of being sad and especially tired of crying, Adam moved on to being really angry. He was mad at his mom for dying and at his dad for drinking and getting involved with his Uncle Jack, but especially mad at himself for being so weak and letting his uncle get the best of him. Deep down he knew he was the one that caused the situation he was now in – if he was a little stronger, he could have avoided this whole deal. And now, because he failed, his dad was likely going to prison for a long time and he was going to be stuck living with either his grandfather or – more likely – someone he didn't even know.

As the thoughts piled up inside his head, Adam slammed his virtual racecar into the wall, dropped the remote on the coffee table and got up and walked into his bedroom, slamming the door behind him.

A moment later there was a knock at the door. "Is everything okay in there?" Cheryl asked.

Adam ignored the question at first, but when she tried the knob and found the door unlocked, Cheryl entered and saw him sitting on his bed. "You okay?" she asked, still standing in the doorway. Adam nodded but didn't make eye contact.

"I should be hearing from Dave soon about what we're going to do next," she said. "He wants us to just hang out here until we get his call. Are you hungry?"

Adam shook his head, even though he was in fact a little hungry. He felt like his stomach was tied up into knots, and the thought of eating anything made him feel queasy. Cheryl waited for a moment or two longer to see if Adam was going to say anything, and when he didn't she turned and headed back toward the door. Adam was okay with that, but he also liked the way Cheryl looked and didn't want her to leave.

"Cheryl?" She turned back from the door to look at him. "What do you think is going to happen next?"

The pretty blonde sat on the bed next to Adam, and he immediately noticed the soft fragrance of her perfume. She put her hand on his shoulder and turned him so that he faced her. Adam felt a little flutter inside, but forced himself to keep his eyes focused on hers.

"Adam, you've been through a lot and you seem like a pretty tough young man." He liked that she called him a "young man" and not a boy or kid. "Honestly, I don't really know what's next, but I promise you this. Dave and I, along with your dad, are going to do everything in our power to make sure you're taken care of and that you're happy. Hopefully, everything works out and you're with your dad again real soon."

Adam only nodded, but he hoped Cheryl would stay there with him in his bedroom a while longer. To his disappointment, she stood a moment later and told him she needed to make a few more phone calls and he should just "hang tight."

****

When Roger and Dave arrived at the Lands County jail, they were greeted by District Attorney Rick Barnes, who read Roger in on the charge of second degree murder and turned him over to a booking deputy who took Roger's fingerprints, inventoried the few possessions he hadn't given to Dave, took his mug shot and led him to a holding cell. Dave promised he'd see Roger shortly and then pulled Barnes into an office adjacent to the booking area.

"Rick, what's this all about?" Dave said. "I came to you because we were ready to work something out so this didn't have to happen."

Barnes looked away momentarily, then back at Dave. "Well, Mr. Carter, either you didn't tell me everything or your client isn't being completely honest with you."

"What do you have?" Dave asked.

"I'm not going to tell you that just yet," Barnes said, "but in good time. Let's just say after your visit yesterday, I had a couple investigators revisit the crime scene and we found a couple of things that were inconsistent with your client's story. We're still processing the evidence, but we wanted to make sure Mr. Durkin didn't take off."

Dave thought about pressing for more information, but figured it wasn't going to do any good. Instead, he walked out of the office and told the deputy he'd like to meet with Roger. He was led to a visiting room, where five minutes later, Roger sat across from him.

"What changed from yesterday?" Roger asked, before he even settled on the metal bench across the table from his lawyer.

"Barnes wouldn't tell me, but they found something that led to the charge," Dave replied. "He'll have to reveal whatever evidence he has before trial, but the arraignment won't even happen until Monday at the earliest, and more likely Tuesday."

Roger realized at that point he would be spending his first night ever in jail, and it would be at least two or three nights before he'd even have a shot at bail. And, as he and Dave discussed, it was more likely they would pass on bail and allow any time he served in county jail to count against time served when he was sentenced. Even though he steeled himself for this moment multiple times in the past days, the thought he would be stuck in a cell for an extended time hit him hard.

"Roger, do you think there is any chance at getting your father-in-law back up here to take care of Adam?" Dave said. "As you and I discussed, unless I can get a dismissal based on lack of evidence – highly unlikely at this point – you're going to be incarcerated for at least several months. We can try to fast-track this, but there's no way this is over for at least a few months."

Roger looked down at his hands folded on the table in front of him. Without looking up, he shook his head. "Jan just died and Tom's in a bad place right now. I'll call him, but I got the feeling when he left, and when we talked on the phone, that seeing us – mainly Adam – just brings back too much pain for him. I get the feeling like he's checked out on us and just can't handle this anymore."

Dave nodded, stood and walked to the door where he asked a deputy waiting outside to bring a telephone. Once it was on the table in front of Roger, Dave left the room and told Roger he'd give him a few minutes to make the phone call. Through the window, Dave watched as Roger talked to Tom. The look on Roger's face during the phone call, as well as his mannerisms, let Dave know the call was not going well. When he saw his friend and client hang up the phone, he asked the deputy to let him back into the room. As he entered, Roger looked up and just shook his head, a lost look spread across his face.

"Tom said he needs to take care of Jan's arrangements, and he just can't help us right now," Roger said. "He said he'd check in a few days from now, but I get the feeling he's out of the picture for good."

Dave nodded. "Well then, let me see what arrangements I can make over the weekend. DCS won't be ready to act on this until Monday, so that gives me a little time to come up with something. Do you have any other friends or family members close by who might be willing to serve as a temporary guardian?"

Roger shook his head again. "Annie's parents and brother were the only family here, and we tended to keep to ourselves for the most part, so there aren't any friends close enough I could ask to take care of my son. My parents have passed away and I was an only child, so there's no family there either."

"Okay, buddy," Dave said. "Let me see what I can get done over the next day or two, and you just try to hang in there. Do you need anything?"

Roger didn't know what he was allowed to have that his friend could possibly bring him, so he just shook his head, feeling more lost than ever. With no more words to exchange, Dave stood and walked out of the room as the deputy moved around, took Roger by the arm and led him back to the holding cell he'd spent a few minutes in earlier. Apparently, this would be his cell for the time-being.

****

Adam was still sitting in his room flipping through old copies of Sports Illustrated when he heard Cheryl's phone ring. He heard her answer the call in the living room and saw from the clock next to his bed that is was almost 5 p.m. Adam couldn't hear what Cheryl was saying, but she wasn't on the call very long and, a moment later, she knocked on his door. When Adam invited her in, she opened the door and looked down at where he sat on the floor.

"Dave wants us to pack a bag for you and come up to his house near Indianapolis," Cheryl said, obviously trying to sound as calming as possible. "You're going to stay with him and his wife for the weekend. They're really nice – you'll like them."

Adam thought about asking on the status of his father but figured Cheryl probably didn't have any more information than she had earlier, so he decided to hold off. Instead, he resigned himself – as he did quite a few times in the past couple days – to accept whatever his next step would

225

be, grabbed a duffle bag from his closet and began packing a few items of clothes into it.

"How much should I bring with me?" he asked. Cheryl wasn't ready for the question, and she shrugged her shoulders and told him to pack for three nights.

"I can bring you back here once we have a better feel for things on Monday or Tuesday," she said.

Five minutes later Adam folded a third shirt, zipped up the duffle bag and followed Cheryl out the front door, remembering to grab his key and lock the house as he did so. Dave came back from the jail to pick him up, and as Adam climbed into the car, Dave turned and told him his dad said to "hang tough."

Adam nodded, and turned to look out the window as the car turned onto the ramp on I-65 northbound. They rode the rest of the way in silence, and about forty minutes later arrived at Dave's house.

Chapter Twenty-Seven

Back in his office late Friday afternoon, Micah was working on the story for Saturday's paper, detailing Lara Hiller's press conference regarding her team's DCS investigation when his cell phone rang. He returned the call from Chris Rutherford, his CASA case supervisor, on his drive back from Indianapolis to Williams, but the call went straight to voicemail. Looking at the caller ID screen on his phone, he saw this was his return call.

"Hi, Chris," Micah answered.

"Micah, sorry I missed you earlier," Rutherford replied. "And I apologize about this, but the case I was going to assign you was reassigned this afternoon. You're next in line, though, so I'd imagine we'll have something for you next week."

The disappointment on Micah's face was apparent, but there was no one there with him to see it, so he thanked Rutherford and hung up the phone. During the past few hours, any anxiety Micah initially felt vanished, and he looked forward to his first assignment as a CASA. Still, he knew his time would come and that likely by the first part of next week, he'd be starting into his first case.

He turned his attention back to his story, where he was wrapping up the final few paragraphs. The next day's news story was simply going to outline the press conference while an editorial, slated to run Sunday, intended to question the intent of Hiller's investigation and pose the question of whether the investigation was more of a political ploy than an actual attempt to fix a broken system. Micah and his editorial team were leaning toward the former and, in the editorial, contended the DCS investigation was a a knee-jerk reaction intended to shield blame after the Henley murders.

After he finished the final sentence of Saturday's news story, he took one more read-through and filed the story for his news desk. Turning off his computer, he left the building, got into his car and headed home for a weekend with Kayla. It had been quite a week, and after Sunday's editorial ran, he knew the week to come would be even more interesting.

Chapter Twenty-Eight

The weekend passed quickly enough for Adam. He spent most of Saturday with Dave and his wife, who told him to call her Mandy. They were nice enough, but they didn't have kids and Adam could tell they only had him there because there weren't any other options. For the most part, they watched movies Saturday with Dave working through some case files and Mandy coming and going from the room throughout the afternoon. Adam at one point asked Dave if one of the files was his dad's, but Dave only nodded and went right back to work.

Sunday, Adam spent almost the entire day – except coming down for lunch and dinner – in the room the Carters were letting him use. He played a few games on the device Dave borrowed for him, but he spent most of the day drawing pencil sketches in the notebook he brought with him from his house. Lately, Adam found himself drawing more than he ever had before, and he was noticing the more he practiced it, the better he became. When he first started drawing several weeks ago, he thought he wasn't very good at it, but the last couple drawings he finished – he had to admit – were good. He noticed his detailing was getting much better, his pictures had more depth, and he was getting to where he could look at something and immediately translate it to the page.

He liked the way he felt when he was drawing and he loved the sound the pencil made as it glided along the page. When he was drawing, especially as he improved, he felt completely pulled into the scene before him. It was as if he were floating outside his own body and existing on the page on which he worked.

Adam didn't even notice Dave's presence in the room until he felt the hand on his shoulder. Seated on the floor next to the bed, he looked over his shoulder and saw Dave seated on the bed behind him.

"I didn't even hear you come in," Adam said.

"You're pretty wrapped up in that drawing," Dave said, looking at the page Adam was working on. "It's really good."

Adam appreciated the compliment, but felt a little invaded as he wasn't sure he wanted anyone to see his work yet.

"Can you take a break for a few minutes?" Dave asked.

Adam nodded.

"I need to talk to you about what the next few days are going to bring," he said. "Are you up for that?"

Adam figured he was as prepared for this conversation as he could be, so he nodded again at Dave. Subconsciously, he stood so as to be eye to eye with the lawyer.

Dave spent the next few minutes talking about Adam's dad, telling him Roger would be arraigned on Tuesday morning. He explained to Adam that an arraignment was where a judge looked at the evidence and the charge against a defendant and decided whether there was enough evidence to hold a trial. He also explained this was where the judge would typically set a bail amount, if he chose to allow bail at all. When Adam heard that regardless of the bail amount his dad likely was going to stay in jail for the time-being, he knew things weren't going back to normal anytime soon, if at all.

"Adam, I'll be able to explain more of this later this week, and after I see what evidence the DA has tomorrow, I'll have a better idea of what our next steps will be."

Adam processed everything Dave said, and he was still willing himself to be strong. He was sick of people seeing him cry and was determined to not let that happen unless he was alone. "So, will I stay here?"

Dave looked down at the drawing again, and Adam instinctively turned over the notebook so he couldn't see it any longer. Dave seemed to understand the way Adam felt, and he didn't say anything about it.

"At some point tomorrow," Dave finally said, "either me or Cheryl will take you to meet with someone at DCS. It could be Craig Evans, the man who met with you at your house last week, or it could be someone else there. They are going to help us determine the best place for you while your dad's case is resolved."

"Can't I just stay here?" Adam asked, not because he necessarily liked living with the Carters, but because he figured it was likely better than having to start over again with someone he didn't know. At least Dave was his dad's friend.

"Mandy and I were just talking about that downstairs," Dave said, obviously ready for the question. "We don't think you staying here is in your best interest. You need to be able to go to school, and I'd imagine that you want to be able to stay in *your* school and not have to switch to one up here."

Adam hadn't thought about school, but he had been out for a couple weeks now and knew he had to go back eventually. Honestly, he didn't really care whether he went back to his old school or not, but the thought of being a new kid in a school where no one knew him didn't sound too appealing either.

After a moment, Adam looked back over at Dave and asked where he thought he would end up.

"DCS will likely make a recommendation for a temporary foster home," Dave said. "Before that happens, we'll go in front of a judge that handles these kinds of things, talk about this case and all the factors involved, and then get things worked out from there."

"What's a foster home?" Adam asked. He didn't like the sound of that at all.

Dave explained a foster home was a place where kids with uncertain family situations were placed while their cases were resolved. In some cases, a foster family might have one or two kids, and in other cases there were more.

"So, I might have some other kids there in the house with me?" Adam asked. He didn't know if he liked that idea or not.

"Yes, you probably would," Dave said. "At least one other, and probably two or three others."

Adam turned his page back over and started sketching again, not really caring at this point whether Dave looked at his drawing. A moment later, Dave patted him on the shoulder and told him he'd come back in a bit when it was time for bed. Adam didn't acknowledge him, and focused instead on the pencil as it worked across the page.

Chapter Twenty-Nine

The near-deafening roar of thunder shook the house, waking Adam in a sweat from a fitful sleep that lasted through much of the night. Rolling over, he looked at the glowing red numbers on the clock next to his bed and saw it was 5:41 and, other than the lightning sporadically lighting the sky, was still dark outside. All night his sleep was disturbed by various dreams, none of them good, and all of them having to do with him feeling lost and alone. The roar of a morning thunderstorm seemed an appropriate way for the uncertain day ahead to begin.

As he lay in bed, Adam quivered as he thought of the dream he had right before the thunder woke him. In it, he was sitting in the sand at a beach. He didn't recognize the beach as one he'd been to before, but the waves were large like he saw in California, much bigger than any he witnessed on the east coast trips he took with his parents. Plus, it wasn't a long, sandy beach like those in Myrtle Beach or Miami. This one was maybe a hundred yards long and bordered at each end by large boulders protruding out into the water, allowing the breaking waves to crash and send huge spouts of water up into the air.

Adam loved watching the water crash into the huge rocks, and as the spray fell back into the ocean it created a curtain-like shroud, almost like sheer drapes. He could see through it, but not clearly, and anything on the other side of the curtain was distorted. In the dream, though, there was an image to see each time a new shroud formed. In the first one, it was his mom behind it, and she was waving to him beaming with the incredible smile that formed an indelible image in his memory. The image made him feel warm, although in the dream he wore a heavy coat, but when the mist fell away the vision of his mom was gone.

A moment later the next wave met the rocks and a new curtain formed. Behind it this time was his dad, although it wasn't the strong, handsome man he knew while his mom was alive. Through the mist, Adam could see this version of his dad was in one of his drunken states, complete with the glossy eyes and uneven stupor as clear in the dream as they were in real life. Through the spray of water, Adam saw his dad was stumbling, fighting as hard as he could to keep his balance and, as the last of the mist faded, so did his father, seemingly disappearing into the ocean for good.

The third wave in the dream was the biggest of all, starting far out in the water and building as it approached land before finally cresting down over the rocks. It hit so hard Adam could feel the resulting splash all the way up the beach. Looking through the misty curtain, this time Adam saw his Uncle Jack, as clear as real life and standing much larger than the vision of his parents had been. Because of the way the wave hit, the mist moved towards him on the beach, bringing Uncle Jack closer with each passing second. Jack was naked, wearing nothing but that horrible smile that haunted Adam's dreams for the past few weeks.

The yellow, gapped teeth in the mouth that emitted the horrible smell of stale cigarettes and old booze moved closer and closer to Adam as he sat in the sand, unable to move and mute as he attempted to scream. And just before Jack's grotesque, sagging body fell upon his helpless nephew the thunder brought a welcomed end to the ghastly nightmare.

Another flash of lightning lit the room, making Adam feel better as he realized he was alone.

Chapter Thirty

Roger's second morning in county jail started just like the first one, but with just a little less trepidation as he had a better idea what to expect. Movies and television shows paint a certain picture of incarceration that makes it scarier than actuality, as Roger found out during his first day in jail. The guys with whom he shared a cell block weren't particularly scary in any way – most of them were guys with drug problems who were arrested for theft or other comparatively minor infraction. While he knew state prison would be a much different situation should it come to that, the county jail was a walk in the park by comparison.

Wake-up came at six and a half-hour later Roger was dressed and headed with the rest of his pod-mates into breakfast, which consisted of some of the worst eggs he'd ever eaten, something resembling ham, as well as toast and strong, bitter coffee. He learned during his first day it was good to drag out meals as long as possible, because other than eating, there's not much else to do during the day. A guard controls the one television in the pod, and he tends to keep the content extremely safe, balancing between local news in the morning, ESPN Sportscenter through the day, and more local news at night until lights out.

One hour a day is spent in the rec area, with some guys shooting a basketball at a hoop with no net but most of them just sitting around talking. That was how Sunday went, and Roger knew Monday would be more of the same if it weren't for his upcoming arraignment and the meetings with Dave in preparation for the hearing.

As he awoke Monday morning, dressed and ate his breakfast, Roger stared blankly across the table until a large, hulking man stood across from him. Another inmate, the guy had to be six-six or six-seven and well over three hundred pounds. As Roger's eyes moved up to the man's face, he saw he was black and beaming with a cheery smile that surprised Roger in this mundane setting.

"What you doing here?" the deep, bellowing voice asked. It was not an intimidating sound, as Roger thought it should be coming from such a prolific figure. Instead, the voice – albeit strong and forceful – sounded happy and upbeat. Still, the question caught Roger a little off-guard, as he wasn't sure if the man inquired about his location at this particular table, his presence in the jail or his reason for being on earth.

Roger stumbled at first as he tried to answer, but finally managed, "A little misunderstanding with my brother-in-law."

The man just stared at him for a moment, but then his smile turned to a toothful grin as he emitted the loudest, most booming laugh Roger ever heard. Doubling over his substantial midsection as he laughed, the man sat down across from Roger. "That's a good one," he said. "A little misunderstanding. Nice."

"How long have you been here?" Roger asked, as they each took a bite of lumpy oatmeal on the plate in front of them. Roger grimaced at the taste and texture, but knew he needed to eat whatever they gave him each day. It would be the only way to stay strong and keep any kind of mental edge for whatever hardships stood before him.

The large man took another bite from his plate before looking back across at Roger. "Name's Sandy, and I've been here about a month. You're new." It occurred to Roger the name Sandy didn't fit the hulking man seated across from him, but he kept that to himself.

"I'm Roger. Just got here yesterday. Not much to do in here, is there?"

"Aw, it's not that bad," Sandy replied. "This is my first stint, but I've heard from some of the other guys this place is a lot better than other jails, and definitely a lot better than prison."

"Well, if every day takes as long as the first 24 hours yesterday, I'm going to lose my mind or die of boredom," Roger said.

Sandy laughed again, although not nearly as deeply as earlier. "You'll learn how to make the days go by. Make friends with the guards and work your way into the library. I do a lot of reading, and even a little drawing. How long are you going to be here?"

That question occurred to Roger in the past day, but hearing the question verbalized caught him off-guard just a bit. "I really don't know. Arraignment is tomorrow."

"What's the charge?" Sandy asked again.

Roger wondered for a minute if he should answer, but figured if Sandy was in good with the guards he could probably find out from them. It also occurred to Roger that having this big guy on his side would not be a bad thing as long as he was stuck in the jail.

"Second degree murder," he said, just barely above a whisper.

The smile that seemed to permanently reside on Sandy's face faded for the first time since he introduced himself to Roger. "No shit," he said. "I certainly didn't expect that answer coming from you."

"Tell me about it," Roger said. "Never thought I'd be here."

Roger could tell Sandy was resisting the urge to ask for more details, but having spent a month in the jail he knew one thing you never do is have conversations about your case with another inmate unless you've already been convicted.

"Well, a couple things to know here," Sandy finally said. "Keep to yourself as much as possible, use your time here to better yourself, and eat as little of this fucking oatmeal as you can."

Roger almost choked on the spoonful he just put in his mouth, and once he managed to swallow it, he started laughing almost uncontrollably. He realized how good it felt to laugh, and as the guard in the dining hall announced it was time to return to the pods, he stood and thanked Sandy for the advice.

"I'll see if I can get them to bring you a book," Sandy said as they headed off to their separate pods.

****

A little over an hour later as Roger lay on his bed, he thought about the second piece of advice Sandy gave him. Realizing he hadn't had any kind of physical activity in well over a week, he got down off his bed onto the solid concrete floor. Spreading his hands out to shoulder width straight down from his chest, and working his feet up onto his toes, he began doing push-ups and continued until he couldn't hold himself up any longer. He didn't even count – just kept going until his arms could no longer support his weight. When that happened, he immediately rolled over onto his back and began doing crunches until his abs were throbbing.

After a one-minute rest, he repeated the protocol and then did so a third time. As he was finishing his third set of sit-ups and working up a little bit of a sweat, a guard appeared at his door.

"Durkin, your lawyer is here."

Roger popped up off the floor and realized he felt exhausted, but also really good from the physical exertion.

The guard led Roger down the hallway of his pod to the meeting room he used the previous day to meet with Dave. As he entered, his lawyer stood across the table from him and noticed the beads of sweat on his client's forehead.

"You okay?" Dave asked.

"Yeah," Roger said, "I feel pretty good, all things considered."

"Well, good," Dave said. "This is going to be a big week for us."

Dave began by discussing the arraignment coming up the next day, telling Roger it was going to be very brief and the judge was simply going to ask Roger if he understood the charges before him. This would be the only thing Roger would be expected to say during the hearing. The balance of the arraignment would involve the prosecution presenting the evidence and outlining the case it would make against Roger. After that, Dave would issue a motion to dismiss based on lack of evidence, but he reiterated to Roger the motion would likely be rejected.

"Do we know what evidence they have yet?" Roger asked.

"No, but I'll probably find out at least some of it today," Dave said. "They don't have to offer full discovery prior to the arraignment, but they have to lay out everything they have at this point during the hearing."

Dave then explained that, assuming the judge deemed sufficient evidence to hold over for trial, a bail amount would be set.

"Are you sure I can't just pay the bail so at least I can be out to spend time with Adam until the trial?" Roger asked. "I don't want to spend any more time in this place than I have to."

Dave shuffled some of the paperwork in front of him, obviously trying to find the best way to phrase his response. After a moment, he looked across at Roger.

"Let's cross that bridge when we come to it," he said. "We'll see what kind of evidence Barnes has and the amount at which the judge sets bail. If we're looking at trial or the likelihood of any kind of prison sentence, trust me when I say this, you would much rather serve that time here than upstate."

Roger nodded. They already went over this and, as boring as county jail was, he knew it was a day at the beach compared to what state prison would be like.

"Roger, there's one other important item we need to discuss today," Dave said. "And that's what to do with Adam if you're going to be locked up for a while."

Roger kept his gaze on Dave, but didn't say anything.

"Mandy and I would be happy to keep him for a little while, but he needs to get back to school soon and it's going to be best for him if he's not starting over at a new school. He doesn't have much stability in his life right now, so his friends at school could be the best thing for him."

"But where's he going to live?" Roger asked.

"I have a two o'clock meeting this afternoon with a caseworker at DCS," Dave said. "I'm going to lay out the preliminary case for her and ask her to begin considering temporary foster care opportunities in the Williams area, should we need to go that route for Adam. She's going to want to talk to Adam, but I'll be right there with him."

"Why do they need to talk to Adam?" Roger asked.

"They're going to want to make sure immediate action isn't warranted. With the charge you're facing, DCS will be concerned for Adam's safety should he be left alone in your care if you were to make bail. Once Adam tells them what a good dad you've been, the way you've kicked your drinking problems and how well you treat him, it should eliminate that concern. At that point, they'll start looking into temporary care options should they be needed."

Dave could tell Roger was concerned about the DCS meeting. "Look buddy," Dave said. "You don't need to worry about this right now. Let's just focus on the arraignment and getting our case together. I will make sure Adam is well cared for until you're together again, and I promise your case will be my top priority until it's resolved."

This seemed to offer some relief for Roger, who offered a forced smile as he looked at Dave.

"Do you want me to bring Adam by here this afternoon?" Dave asked.

Roger thought about this for a second, but he really didn't want his son to see him in the orange jumpsuit if it could be avoided, so he shook his head. "Let's wait one more day and see how the arraignment goes. Maybe I can see him after that, one way or another."

"Whatever you like," Dave said as he stood up from his chair. The two shook hands, and as Dave exited through the visitor door, Roger was led back into the jail by the same guard who brought him in an hour ago.

The guard was carrying a book in his left hand, and as he locked Roger back into his cell, he handed it to him. "Sandy said you'd like this one," the guard said.

Roger sat down on his bed and looked at the cover.

A Time to Kill by John Grisham. He'd already read it, but Roger smiled. Apparently, Sandy was well-connected in the jail.

Chapter Thirty-One

Tuesday morning's routine was much the same for Roger as was Sunday & Monday, but with one big difference. Immediately after breakfast, Roger was led back to his cell, given the suit Dave left for him yesterday, and told to change clothes and be ready to meet his lawyer in 15 minutes. As soon as he was changed, a guard led Roger back into the meeting room in which he met Dave the previous day.

Dave, seated in his customary position, was also in his courtroom finest. After an exchange of "good morning" and a handshake, Dave jumped right into the business of the day.

"Before we get into the arraignment, I want to bring you up to speed on my meeting with DCS yesterday," Dave said. "I met with a young lady who is relatively new to the agency, but we also brought Craig Evans into the room. I let them know I was only speaking with them on a preliminary basis, but the hope was they could begin to lay the groundwork for a quick placement in the event it is needed."

Roger was following along so far.

"Evans allowed the young caseworker to lead most of the meeting, but my request was a little different in that DCS doesn't handle many cases on a preemptive basis, so I guess he felt he had to offer a little guidance at the end," Dave continued. "Since I have worked with them in the past and offered them some pro-bono assistance, I think he is making a few concessions for me that he might not otherwise."

"Dave," Roger interrupted, "I don't know if I've said it yet or not, but I want you to know how much I appreciate everything you're doing for me. Regardless of how this turns out, I know there is no way that I can ever repay you for this."

Dave waved a hand dismissively. "You would do the same for me if the situations were reversed."

"Yeah," Roger said, "but I feel bad I haven't made more of an effort to keep in touch these past few years. You really are a great friend."

Dave could see his college buddy was choking up a little bit. "Roger, some friendships have bonds that don't need constant contact to stay strong. Let's just stay focused and try to get the best outcome today."

"Sounds good," Roger said, glad his friend was keeping him on task.

"As for the arraignment today, in all likelihood, Barnes has enough to hold this thing over for trial or we'd already be working on a deal of some kind," Dave continued. "He knows we're going to use a depraved heart defense – and we have a pretty good case for that – but he also wants the public – his voters – to know he will not tolerate anything that can be perceived as vigilanteism."

Roger nodded.

"Once the judge determines there is sufficient evidence to go to trial, he is going to set a court date and will determine whether to issue bail. I'm still up in the air as to whether you should pay the bond, but let's have that discussion after we hear the amount. At that point, we would likely start talking about making a deal with the goal of the least possible jail time."

"Do you think Barnes will be willing to deal?" Roger interjected.

Dave nodded his head. "I'm sure of it. He wants to go on record as being tough on all kinds of crime, even those of retribution by someone who has suffered a horrible tragedy. But he doesn't want to be the prosecutor against an otherwise good citizen who looked for some personal justice on a guy who raped and beat his son. Trust me. He doesn't want this to end up in a courtroom."

"What happens to Adam through all of this?" Roger asked.

"Once the judge holds this over for trial," Dave said, "DCS and the juvenile court will move forward with what's called a CHINS hearing. It stands for Child in Need of Services. In that hearing, it will be determined that Adam is in a situation where he needs someone to impartially evaluate his situation and make a recommendation for his best interests. He'll be assigned a Court Appointed Special Advocate who will spend a lot of time with Adam, meet with you and act as an intermediary between you – the family – and DCS. Once he or she has done this, there will be a recommendation made to the court. In this case, unless your father-in-law comes back into the picture, it is likely Adam would be placed into a foster home."

Roger knew most of this already, but he appreciated the refresher anyway. "And once my jail time – however long that is – is over, Adam will be returned to me, right?"

"Most likely," Dave said. "Unless the CASA, DCS or the judge overseeing your case determines you are unfit for whatever reason."

"Unfit? Why would they think that?"

Dave paused, obviously searching for the best way to answer. "Well, the findings of your criminal case will play a large role in Adam's outcome. Plus, they'll also consider your drug and alcohol use and will want to ensure all of that is truly behind you. For all three of those parties, Adam's safety is their primary concern – not whether you are reunited with him when all of this is over."

Roger hadn't been prepared for this answer. He assumed once his case and any subsequent jail time were concluded, he would once again have the opportunity to be with his son. Hearing that may not be the case, depending on the conclusions of a bunch of strangers, made him even more uneasy than he was already.

Dave could see his friend rolling everything over in his mind. "Roger, remember," he said. "One step at a time, and for today, that step is our time in the courtroom, which we need to get to."

Roger glanced at the clock on the wall over Dave's right shoulder and saw it was just before ten. The arraignment was to begin at 10:30. "I'll see you over there," Dave said as he collected his briefcase and left through the visitors' door.

The guard took Roger by the arm, led him through the inmates' door and down a hall to a van waiting to take him on the half-mile ride to the county courthouse. As the van door slammed shut beside him, Roger closed his eyes for a moment in hopes the dozens of thoughts running through his mind would calm down in time for his appearance in court.

****

"All rise, this court is in session," the bailiff called. "The Honorable Catherine Dern presiding."

The judge entered from her chambers and made her way up to the large wooden bench perched about five feet off the floor and housed in dark, rich mahogany. Roger had time to reflect this was his first time inside a courtroom, and he was somewhat surprised to see the appearance was very close to what he'd seen on television and in the movies.

"Please be seated," Judge Dern said, as she took her seat on the bench. "This is the case of the State of Indiana versus Roger Durkin. Who is representing the State?"

"District Attorney Rick Barnes, your honor," Barnes said as he stood and instinctively buttoned his suit coat. As quickly as the coat was buttoned, Barnes unhooked it and returned to his seat.

Dern looked toward Roger's table. "And the defense?"

It was Dave's turn to stand. Roger noticed he left his jacket unbuttoned. "David Carter, your honor."

The judge nodded as Dave returned to his seat. She turned her gaze toward Roger, then looked down at the papers on the desk before her. "Roger Durkin, the state has entered charges of second degree murder in the death of Jack Clement. Do you understand the charges before you?"

Dave rehearsed this with Roger, but as he stood at the judge's request, Roger noticed his legs were wobbly and had to steady himself just slightly by touching the table in front of him. "Yes, your honor," he managed, although more shakily than he intended.

Dern made a notation quickly and then looked back up at Roger. "And are you prepared to enter a plea at this time?"

"Yes, your honor," Roger said, steadying his voice now. "Not guilty."

Dern nodded, made another note and said, "Thank you, Mr. Durkin. You may take your seat. A not guilty plea has been entered into the record. Let's move into the evidentiary hearing. Mr. Barnes?"

Barnes stood, buttoned his jacket once again, and shuffled a couple of papers on the table in front of him. He cleared his throat and began.

"Your honor, on the evening of Monday, September 10, the defendant, Roger Durkin viciously beat and injured the victim – his brother-in-law – before setting fire to Mr. Clement's cabin, leading to third-degree burns that resulted in the death of Mr. Clement days later."

Roger did his best – as instructed by his attorney – to keep quiet as the charges and initial evidence were laid out, but it was taking all his will power to sit still as Jack was referred to as a victim. Dave could tell he was struggling to listen to Barnes presentation, so he patted Roger's arm as a non-verbal way to ask him to just calm down.

Barnes, as if sensing the internal struggle taking place within Roger, looked right at him as he continued. "To Mr. Durkin's credit, he came forward with his attorney several days after Mr. Clement's passing and confessed to the attack on his brother-in-law. Mr. Durkin said the attack was not premeditated, and he had only gone to Mr. Clement's house with the intention of confronting him on the charge that Mr. Clement had attacked and raped Mr. Durkin's son, Adam.

Once Mr. Clement admitted the rape, per Mr. Durkin, the defendant went back out to his car, grabbed a tire iron from his trunk and returned to the house where he struck the victim multiple times in the shoulders and legs, basically rendering Mr. Clement immobile."

Roger was a little surprised that, to this point, all Barnes did was repeat the story Roger confessed to in Barnes' office days earlier. He could tell by the look on Dave's face he was also waiting for whatever Barnes had coming next.

"After beating the victim, Mr. Durkin claims he accidentally knocked over a lit candle that ignited some papers on the table before engulfing the entire room in flames," Barnes continued. Roger noticed how polished the district attorney was and how flawlessly every word was enunciated, with just the right amount of emphasis on the most important elements of the story.

"Since Mr. Clement was unable to move at that point, he was obviously not able to help himself as his house went up in flames, and Mr. Durkin – admittedly – did nothing to help him exit the building. Per his confession, as he was leaving the house and preparing to drive off, Mr. Durkin felt some apprehension about letting his brother-in-law die in the house, and he decided to call 911. What's interesting, though, is that he made the 911 call anonymously and then apparently threw the cell phone into a creek bordering Mr. Clement's property. Officers recovered the cell phone during our investigation last week."

Barnes paused briefly and took a drink of water from the glass on the table before him. He shuffled some papers again, before looking at the defense table and continuing.

"Your honor, it is the determination of my office that Mr. Durkin is not being truthful in his statement that his only intention that night was to confront Mr. Clement, and we also believe he willfully started the fire that led to the injuries and death of the victim."

As the district attorney took his seat, Judge Dern had an unsettled look on her face as she looked toward the defendant's table. "Mr. Carter?"

Dave paused briefly before standing. As he told Roger during the lead-up to the hearing, he didn't plan to play many cards during this portion of the case. He knew deep down this was not the kind of case a judge – also an elected official – wanted any part of, but he also knew there was very little chance of having the case dismissed at this point.

"Your honor, as Mr. Barnes stated, my client confessed to actions that inadvertently led to the death of Mr. Clement," Dave stated. "These actions came about as a highly emotional reaction to my client learning that Mr. Clement – in no way a victim, as the State would have you believe – brutally beat and raped Roger's 10-year-old son."

Dave looked at Roger and offered a look of compassion, ensuring the judge could see it.

"It is our contention," Dave continued, "that the State has escalated the charges well above the appropriate level and has done so without any evidence of intent or motivation."

Dave took his seat, and Roger knew exactly what his attorney just did. Even if the judge was going to hold the case over, which was likely, he planted the seed from which would spring the defense and establish the basis for any possible plea deal.

The courtroom stood quiet for a few moments as the judge read through some papers and made some notes on the bench. Finally, she adjusted her reading glasses and looked out upon the court.

"It is my finding there is sufficient cause and evidence to hold this case over for trial," Dern said. "Let's discuss trial date and bail."

After brief discussion between the attorneys, with each of them reviewing their calendars, they agreed upon a trial date just less than three months away – January 8.

"As for the issue of bail," Barnes said. "The State agrees to bail, but in the amount of $500,000. Based upon the charges, and with Mr. Durkin's few remaining ties in the area, we are concerned with the possibility of flight."

The judge appeared as if she felt the DA was going a bit overboard, but she looked down at the defense table.

"Your honor, that amount is absurd," Dave said. "Mr. Durkin has never been charged with a crime before, is an upstanding citizen, and has his son to think about. There is zero flight risk in this case."

The judge had apparently already made up her mind. "Bail is set at $100,000." With that, she tapped her gavel and was off to her chambers. Dave spoke briefly to Roger before he was led back to the same van that brought him to the courthouse just an hour earlier.

****

Roger was sitting on the cot in his cell, his back against the cold cinder block that lined three walls of his cell, and reading the Grisham novel Sandy sent his way when a guard approached and let him know that Dave was waiting for him in the meeting room. The guard led Roger down the hallway in what was becoming a routine route for him. When he entered the room, he noticed Dave traded the suit he wore for that morning's arraignment for a pair of jeans and a button-down shirt. Roger hadn't really expected to see his attorney until the morning, so as he sat down across from Dave, his eyes implored him to skip any small talk and get right to the point.

"DCS followed the outcome of the arraignment this morning," Dave began before Roger had even settled into the hard metal chair. "Evans called me while I was having lunch and wanted to know what we were going to do about bail. Either way, he wants to move forward with a CHINS hearing tomorrow."

"What's a CHINS hearing, again?" Roger asked. It sounded familiar, so he thought Dave already explained it to him, but with everything going on right now, he couldn't remember what it meant.

"It stands for Child in Need of Services," Dave answered. "It's basically a hearing where the court determines Adam needs state-supported services, assigns him a case worker and a CASA and starts the process of deciding upon placement."

Roger nodded. He knew this was coming, of course, but it didn't make it any easier. "I'm going to ask one more time, and I know what your answer is going to be, but what do you think about me just making bail and taking my chances with the outcome? As far as I'm concerned, time away from Adam is the same whether I'm spending it here or up in Fort Wayne. I don't want him to see me like this – in here – and I can't imagine what's running through his head right now."

Dave leaned forward. "We've been over this," he said. "The time away from Adam is not the same. Here it is relatively quiet, secure, and you get out of your cell a few times a day. Depending on how this all goes down, if you get sent to maximum security you're looking at 23 hours a day in a cell and a lot of much tougher dudes sharing your space with you. It's not the same."

Roger hated his continued need these reality checks, but he knew Dave was only doing it for his own good.

"Look, Roger," Dave continued. "I work for you. You call the shots here. If you want to make bail and take your chances, we'll make that happen. It's not what I recommend, but it is your call. But I would request one thing before you make your final decision. Stay in here two more days and think it through. After that, what you tell me to do, I'll do."

Roger thought Dave's request was a fair one, so he nodded his head and asked what he thought would happen during the CHINS hearing. Dave explained that since Adam had no family options in the area, the court would move for immediate placement in a temporary foster care situation. Based on the legwork Dave already did with DCS and Craig Evans, they located a local foster family that would take care of Adam until Roger's case was resolved. Once Roger was free, or if he was going to have to spend an extended time incarcerated, the court would determine a long-term solution.

As Dave was finishing up the summary of what would happen during the hearing the next morning, Roger looked across the table as tears welled up in his eyes. "Dave," he said. "Adam is all I have left. He's it. I've lost my parents, my wife, my job and pretty much my whole life, regardless of how this all turns out. But I have Adam, and if I lose him, I might as well be dead."

"You're not going to lose him," Dave said. "I promise you that."

Roger thought the promise sounded a bit hollow, but he appreciated the words nonetheless. Dave told him he would be back tomorrow afternoon once the CHINs hearing concluded and he had an outcome to report.

Chapter Thirty-Two

Adam passed the first few days of the week in much the same way did the first weekend with Mandy and Dave. The weather improved on Monday, and he spent a little time both Monday and Tuesday outside with his plastic army figurines, but he mostly liked the video games Dave and Mandy allowed him to play as much as he wanted. He liked the couple – they were nice to him, didn't tell him what to do, and let Adam make most of the choices for meals, allowing him to choose his favorites pretty much every night.

Dave kept Adam up to speed on the progress of dad's trial, and he also told him what was coming up the next morning with the DCS hearing. Adam resigned himself to the fact he would likely be spending his last night with Dave and Mandy, and while he was a little bit afraid of what was to come next, he found he could be a lot braver in just about any situation lately. He wasn't crying about his dad, his mom or pretty much anything else the last couple of nights. In fact, he noticed that nothing made him really happy or sad anymore. In a way, everything just *was.* It wasn't necessarily, good, bad, happy or sad. It just *was*.

As they sat down to dinner Tuesday evening – Mandy prepared spaghetti and meatballs with garlic bread, Adam's *absolute* favorite -- he tried his best to enjoy the pasta noodles and homemade sauce. It looked good and smelled incredible, but as he ate more slowly than normal, he realized things didn't even taste as good right now as they usually did.

Adam didn't even notice Dave kept looking at him between bites of the pasta, and after a minute Dave broke the silence that persisted through the first few minutes of the meal.

"I'm going to take you to see your dad tomorrow," Dave said, and Adam's attention immediately went to the lawyer. It almost brought a smile to his face.

"Really?" Adam asked, setting down his fork. "I can see him face-to-face?" Adam talked to Roger once over the phone during the weekend, but he hadn't seen his dad since he turned himself in the previous week.

"Yes, for a little while," Dave said. "I think it's important you guys talk and spend a little time together."

Adam didn't say anything, but he dug into the plate of spaghetti with a little more fervor than he had previously. Mandy hadn't said anything the entire meal, and Adam didn't see it, but a tear leaked from her eye as she looked across at Dave and down at the boy at her table.

****

Dave told him he would bring Adam with him to visit, but Roger was surprised at how nervous he felt Wednesday morning as he finished his breakfast and thought about seeing his son in the next couple hours. Sandy sat across from him for the third straight morning, and they talked briefly about Roger's arraignment the previous day. Sandy asked Roger if he planned to make a deal, but Roger just told him he and his attorney hadn't gotten that far yet. Even as they chatted, Roger's mind just kept going back to Adam and what he would say to him in just a little while.

With the CHINs case coming up later in the day, Roger also knew today's visit with Adam could be the last for a while. Dave warned him after the CHINs hearing, Adam would likely be transferred to a temporary foster home, where he would begin the process of settling in for as long as he'd be there. The foster parents were a couple in their mid-50s who lost two sons in a car accident years earlier, and they decided five years ago to open their home to children in need. Currently there were three other children in the house including two sisters that were 11 and 9, and another boy who was 13. Roger was glad Adam would have other kids in the house around his age, but he hoped and worried Adam would fit into the mix. More than that, he hoped Adam would only have to be there for a short time and he'd be able to work out his situation as quickly as possible.

"Hey man, you still here with me?" Sandy said, breaking Roger from his daydream.

"Yeah, sorry," Roger answered. "Just thinking about seeing my son in a little while, and everything that happens after that." Roger hadn't filled Sandy in on everything yet – after all, they only met a couple days earlier and couldn't be classified as friends so soon.

"I got you," Sandy said. "I can't imagine what it would be like to have kids on the outside while you're stuck up in here."

"You don't have any children?" Roger asked.

"None that I know about," Sandy said, breaking into a loud belly laugh.

Roger chuckled politely, but didn't find the joke nearly as funny as Sandy apparently did. "They're going to put my boy in foster care until I get my situation resolved."

Sandy stopped laughing. "Man, that's rough. I'm sorry."

They went back to picking through what passed as eggs in this place, but Roger really wasn't hungry and hadn't been all morning.

As the guards announced the end of breakfast and herded the inmates back to their pods, Sandy patted Roger on the back and told him he hoped all went well with his son. Roger thanked him and headed off, knowing within the next hour he would be sitting across from Adam and trying to figure out the right thing to say. As hard as he tried since the previous evening, he still had no idea what that would be.

****

Visitation was handled differently with Adam than it was any time Dave came to see him. Dave stayed out of the room, but he arranged something with the guards because the table that normally stood between the two chairs was moved to one side of the room and the two chairs sat close together facing each other. When Adam came through the door and saw Roger, he immediately ran and jumped up into his father's arms. The guards looked for a moment as if they were going to pull him off Roger, but decided to let it go. Still they watched the exchange closely, obviously making sure Adam wasn't passing anything over to his father other than a hug.

After what seemed like three minutes of Adam squeezing Roger as hard as he could with his face buried on his dad's shoulder, Adam relaxed his arms and moved his face in front of his dad's. Tears streaked down his face, as they did Roger's, but it was a soft, subdued cry very unlike the outbursts Roger witnessed before from his son.

"How are we doing, buddy?" Roger finally asked, doing his best not to choke on the words.

"Doing okay, I guess," Adam answered after a minute. Roger's arms quickly grew tired from holding his boy who, while skinny, was probably closing in on 100 pounds. As Roger lowered Adam back to his feet, he motioned for the two of them to take a seat. The guard who stayed through the initial part of the visit left the room and closed the door behind him.

"How are you doing, dad?" Adam asked.

"I'm adjusting," Roger said. "It's pretty boring in here, and I miss you like crazy, but I'm doing some reading and trying to work out – doing a lot of push-ups, sit-ups and things like that. I sure miss our pizza nights, though."

"Me too," Adam said, looking right into Roger's eyes. The two sat in the metal chairs, both leaning in with their elbows on their thighs, and their faces were only a foot or so apart. "Do you think we'll ever get to do that again?"

Roger was taken aback by the question. In the past week, the thought occurred to him – plenty of times – that he might be going to prison for a long time, but it broke his heart to think Adam was afraid of the very same thing. Roger broke eye contact with Adam as he did his best to fight back more tears. Finally, he composed himself and looked back at his son. "Adam, we're going to find a way through this and we'll be back together soon. I can't promise you when, but we'll find a way to make sure it doesn't take too long."

"I just don't understand," Adam said. "Why are you being punished because you made Uncle Jack pay for what he did to me? Isn't that just self-defense?"

At that moment, it seemed to Roger as if his son had matured by years over the past week since he saw him last. As he looked into Adam's eyes, they looked older than he had ever seen them, and the thought made Roger more than a little depressed. Still, he wasn't sure whether he should ask Adam if he remembered everything that happened, but he was positive he shouldn't be talking about his case in this room with his son.

Adam broke the silence as if he could see Roger was struggling to figure out what to say next. "Dad, I remember everything he did to me," Adam said. "It's all come back in the past few days, usually when I've been lying in bed and missing you."

Roger could no longer hold back the tears, and as he began to cry, so did Adam. "Buddy, I'm so sorry. I'm just so sorry." Roger let his face fall to his hands and although he could choke back any sobbing, the tears now flowed freely. "I should have been able to protect you. It's all my fault."

Adam was now crying freely as well, but he reached his hand down and put it on top of Roger's head, causing his dad to look back up at him. "Dad, I'm okay," he said. "The memories of that day, all that happened, have come back to me but not in nightmares or anything like that."

Adam paused as if searching for the best way to say what he wanted to get out. "Uncle Jack was sick, but not the kind of sick that gets better. Not like when I have a cold or the flu or anything like that. There was something wrong with him – something evil. And when I wake up in a dream and see his eyes – those black, evil eyes – well, at first it scared me. But now I just see them for what they were – cold eyes that belonged to a sick man who was never going to get better. You just made sure he was never going to hurt me or anyone else again."

Roger reached over and pulled his son close to him. "If only I'd have seen it sooner," he whispered. "If only I had seen it sooner."

They hugged for a moment longer, and there was a knock on the door. "Five minutes," warned the guard as he looked through the window.

Roger pulled himself together, as he wanted to end the visit on a better note and didn't know when he'd get to see Adam again.

"Listen, buddy," he began. Both dried the tears on their cheeks with their hands. "Dave has told you about the foster home, right?"

Adam nodded.

"At first, I was worried about you going there," Roger continued, "but you've shown me during these past few weeks what a tough guy you are. I know you're going to be okay until we are together again."

"I'll be fine," Adam said. "But how long do you think I'm going to have to stay there?"

"I don't know," Roger answered, "but like I said, Dave and I are going to do everything we can to get this all worked out just as soon as we can."

"We need each other," Adam said, and Roger just about lost it again.

"I know we do, buddy. I know we do."

The guard entered, followed closely by Dave, who put his hand on Adam's shoulder. Roger and Adam both stood, hugged each other much more briefly than before, but didn't say another word before Adam turned and walked out the door.

Deep down, Roger felt like he was watching his little boy walk away for the last time and that, the next time he saw Adam, he'd be looking at a man. Roger cursed Jack for taking away Adam's innocence, but more than that he was angry at himself for letting it happen.

Chapter Thirty-Three

Micah was pissed. He and his team just finished the weekly editorial planning meeting, and all around the table were reports of getting stonewalled by every potential source for the ongoing DCS story. Lara Hiller had mostly shut down communication with the media – highly unusual for her – but she had completely shut out Micah since the day at the Statehouse. In addition, everyone at DCS was in self-preservation mode, understandably so, and were ignoring repeated requests for interviews. This left Micah and his team with very little to report other than speculation, and you could only use the phrases "could not be reached for comment" or "didn't return repeated calls" so many times before readers grew tired of them.

In addition to the story for which he had such high hopes now going off the rails, Micah's company, like many others involved in printing newspapers in 2014, was falling on extremely hard times. Circulation over the past five years fell more than 30 percent and, while it seemed to be leveling out, online and digital readership was not delivering the same kind of returns the print product did. In addition, advertising was down significantly for the year, meaning upper management was looking for any way possible to cut expenses wherever it could. For a while they resisted cutting into personnel, but late that year it had become obvious they could not responsibly continue carrying the number of staff they had in the past.

For Micah's team, this meant changes to the newsroom. First came consolidation, with responsibilities for the company's other newspapers falling onto the desks of some of the reporters and editors at Micah's papers. After that was attrition, where the company opted not to replace employees that left the company. After six months of this type of cost cutting, Micah and each of his current team members were being asked to do a lot more than they did formerly. Micah knew this was seriously impacting the quality of work his employees were turning out, but he also knew each of them was doing the best he or she could.

So, when the phone rang just before lunch on that Thursday morning, Micah wasn't in the best mood as he picked it up. "Micah Sanders," he said, much more gruffly than normal.

"Micah, this is Chris Rutherford," the voice on the other end of the line said. "Is now a good time?"

"Yeah, Chris. Sorry," Micah replied. "Now is as good a time as any."

"We've got a case that we'd like you to take," Rutherford said. Micah had expected this call, but he wasn't very happy to be having it with the way things were going today. "This should be a really good first case for you, as it shouldn't be terribly time-consuming and looks to be fairly straight-forward. Can you come down to the office later today so we can review the file and set up the meet?"

Micah pulled up his daily calendar on his laptop, and despite all the challenges he was facing at work, he saw his afternoon was open. "Sure, how about 3 this afternoon or so?"

"Sounds great," Rutherford said. "I'll see you then."

Micah hung up the phone and looked at his watch. It was almost noon and the rumbling in his stomach told him he needed to think about getting some lunch. Knowing he needed a diversion from the frustrations at work, he picked up the phone, called Kayla and said he was bringing home some lunch for she and Emma. Micah heard Kayla pause on the other end of the line and knew she was surprised, since Micah almost never came home for lunch on a work day.

"Everything okay?" she asked.

"Yes," Micah said. "It's just turning into one of those days, and I would really love to see my two favorite girls."

"Well, I know two girls who will be very happy to see their favorite guy," Kayla replied. Micah hung up the phone, promising to be there within a half hour with some burgers, fries and milkshakes.

****

When Micah walked through the front door holding a large sack and a drink carrier, Emma hit him full stride with a big hug, almost knocking the milkshakes out of his hand. He recovered as he bent down to kiss the top of her head, and she clung to his left leg as he walked – with some difficulty – toward the kitchen. Kayla wore a tight pair of jeans and a sheer white blouse, and she leaned against the counter as Micah walked in. "Well, isn't it a nice surprise to see you this afternoon?" she said.

In addition to Kayla's sexy attire on a day where Micah knew she had nowhere to go, she wore make-up, something she never did when home alone with Emma. "You look incredible," Micah said, setting their lunch down on the counter and wrapping Kayla up into his arms. They kissed, longer than they usually would in front of Emma, and she responded by rolling her eyes and saying, "Yuck, you guys are gross."

They both laughed, but the look Kayla gave Micah told him he better make sure to save some time for some extracurricular activity before heading back to work. As they all sat down to the table and divided up the food, Micah told Kayla he was receiving his first CASA case that afternoon. He purposely avoided conversation about work, as he didn't want to let anything ruin the nice mood they all felt.

Emma rambled on about something she watched on television that morning and about a toy she saw. Micah loved the way her little face lit up when she talked, and he noticed how much her character was developing over the past few months. He could tell she was picking up a lot of things from her classmates in day care, but she was also developing her own personality, and Micah realized again right then how lucky he was to have his little family. His mind drifted to his meeting later that afternoon where he would learn about a child – or children – that were not nearly as lucky.

Forcing his attention back to his daughter, he finished listening to the story Emma was telling, smiled and took a big bite of his burger.

After they finished lunch, Emma went back to the movie she had paused on the DVR, and as Micah was rinsing out the plastic cups before throwing them in the trash, he felt Kayla move close behind him and slide her hand down the front of his pants. "Got time for a quicky?" she whispered in his ear.

They were in their bedroom in a second, and both of them had their clothes off a few seconds later. Fifteen minutes later they were cleaning up in the bathroom, and

Micah peaked out the bedroom door to see Emma hadn't moved a muscle.

Micah pulled Kayla close to him in the bathroom, and he gave her another long kiss. "Man, I needed this today," he said.

"I got that feeling when you said you were coming home for lunch," she said. "Everything okay?"

"I think it will be," he said. "Things are just a little rough at work right now, but we'll get through it."

"Well, you better get dressed and get back there," Kayla said. Looking at his watch, Micah saw it was just shy of 1:30 and, knowing he had the three o'clock meeting at the CASA offices, he had a better idea. Rather than put his work clothes on, they both put on sweat pants and tee shirts, went out into the living room where they sat on the floor right beside Emma and started watching her movie with her. She looked at them as if a little surprised, but didn't say a word and, a moment later, she laid down so her head rested on Micah's lap. A feeling of total contentment spread through Micah, and he realized what a great decision he made in coming home for lunch. Talk about an hour turning around an entire day.

****

Micah's car rolled into the parking lot at the offices for Lands County CASA just before three, and a moment later he jogged up two flights of stairs, entered the office and greeted the assistant at the front desk. As he walked down the hallway toward Chris Rutherford's office, he looked through the doorway to see Marianne Cawley on the phone. She smiled and gave him a thumb's up, and a moment later, Rutherford greeted him and told him to take a seat.

Laying open a folder in front of him, Rutherford wasted no time in starting right in. "Your case involves an 11-year-old boy named Adam Durkin."

Micah listened as Rutherford laid out the details of the case, including the sexual abuse by Adam's uncle, the retaliatory measures taken by his father, the details surrounding the death of Adam's mother and the way in which Adam's grandfather had essentially run away from any responsibility. In about ten minutes, the CASA supervisor painted the picture of a little boy that had everything going for him up until a few years earlier and now found himself with no one in his life if his father received a long jail sentence.

The training Micah went through to earn his CASA certification had presented numerous case studies, and all of them had been real-life cases, but in that moment, he realized that none of them had been real to him. Knowing now he would soon be meeting a little boy that was so alone really drove home for him the importance of the role he had undertaken, but also made him a little ashamed of himself for getting so worked up about the trivial issues he was facing at work.

Rutherford finished up the debriefing, and Micah looked across the desk at him. "So, when do I get to meet Adam?" Micah asked.

"We'll set it up for tomorrow," Rutherford answered. "He has been staying with his dad's attorney and his wife all week. Apparently, they are friends of Mr. Durkin's, but he is scheduled to be moved to a temporary foster home tomorrow so he can start back to school next week. The meeting will likely be in the afternoon after they transition Adam. Will that work for you?"

Micah nodded without checking his calendar. "I'll make it work no matter what."

Chapter Thirty-Four

Friday morning arrived, and Roger couldn't believe he had been incarcerated an entire week. In some respects, it hadn't felt like a week, but in others it seemed as if he hadn't seen the outside the jail's walls in months. Like most that spend any time in jail, he was becoming accustomed to the slower pace and the drudgery of the daily routine and, as he told Adam, the workouts he did each day were keeping his spirits up and making him feel a lot better than he would have otherwise. He realized as he climbed off his bunk that morning that he felt stronger than he had in years.

Dave was scheduled to come by that morning, and he told Roger he wanted to start talking about approaching Barnes with an offer to make a deal. Dave said it was important to start the negotiation before Barnes did so they could set the terms of what they felt was acceptable. If they waited for Barnes to make the first offer, and Dave seemed fairly certain Barnes wanted to make a deal, Roger would be forced to go on the defensive in the negotiations, rather than take the offensive.

The guards seemed to ease the restrictions during the week. Roger ate breakfast with Sandy every morning, and he felt as if a friendship was beginning. After breakfast, contrary to how it was when Roger first entered the jail, the guards allowed Roger, Sandy and a few others to sit around the table and play cards for an hour or so. Sandy had told Roger word had spread around the jail as to what Roger did to Jack, and that garnered him instant credibility, not just amongst the other inmates, but the guards as well.

Roger learned that in jail, and in prison per Sandy, the lowest form of vermin on earth was someone that preyed upon children sexually. Therefore, what Roger did to protect his son earned him significant respect and placed him high atop the jail hierarchy.

After a half hour or so, Roger and Sandy were the only two left at the table, and in the middle of a game of gin rummy, Roger looked across the table and said, "My lawyer's coming today and wants to talk deal."

Sandy nodded. "You should. The prosecutor wants no part of this case, I'll tell you that much."

It occurred again to Roger how smart Sandy was, and again he wondered why the guy had spent so much time inside the walls. "How'd you find out about my case?" Roger asked.

Sandy kept his eyes down on his cards. "Guards talk. I listen."

Roger waited to see if he'd say anything more, but when he didn't Roger spoke up next. "Sandy, you haven't told me yet why you're in here." Again, Sandy remained silent, which told Roger that, while they were becoming friends, they weren't yet that good of friends.

"If you were me, what's a good deal?" Roger asked, changing the subject.

Finally, Sandy looked up from his cards. "I'm no lawyer," Sandy said, "but I read a lot and I've listened to a lot of other inmates talk about deals they make. If you can get a sentence of less than three years and avoid maximum security, you should consider taking it."

Roger looked like he'd been hit in the face with a two-by-four. "Three years?"

Sandy nodded. "Dude, you're up for second degree murder. If the state wants to push this, you could be looking at 25 years or more."

Roger already had this discussion to some extent with Dave, but he also partially dismissed what his attorney said as he figured he was only looking at things through the eyes of a lawyer. Hearing this coming from someone that had done time – significant time, apparently – made it hit home a little more, and he knew he could be looking at a long stretch in jail.

Finally, the guards rounded up Roger and Sandy and led them back to their separate pods. Back in his cell, Roger laid on his bunk and started into his second book of the week. He hadn't been much of a reader since college, but since he had nothing better to do, he figured it was as good a way as any to pass the time.

An hour later, a guard showed up in front of Roger's cell and told him Dave was waiting for him in the visitor's room. When he walked into the room, Dave was seated and looking down at some papers, but smiled as he looked up at his client. "You look good," he said, obviously trying to lighten the mood. "Jail seems to agree with you."

Roger wasn't amused. "Screw you," he said, but he only partially meant it. "Thanks for coming in today."

Dave started right in as Roger took his seat. "I want to send an offer to Barnes today. I get the feeling that if we don't do it today, he'll start the process on Monday."

Roger nodded and Dave kept going. "So, the way I look at it, Barnes wants to prove a point, and that is no matter what happens to you, it is never permissible to take the law into your own hands. Laws are there for a reason, as are police departments and courts, and people who try to deal with crime by committing more crime are going to pay for it – in his eyes."

"I get that," Roger said, "but based on my short time in jail, I still believe jail would have been too good for Jack."

"Be that as it may," Dave said, "that's not how Barnes is looking at it, and it's likely not how the court would look at it, although I don't think it would be difficult to find a sympathetic jury. At this point, that is our biggest – and probably only – advantage."

Dave laid out for Roger again all the evidence Barnes would use against him. Basically, he had a confession, a motive and, through Roger's decision to call 911 after he attacked Jack, a pretty strong case that Roger knew what he was doing and was not out of his mind when he committed the offense. That placed any kind of depraved heart scenario in limbo as, if the case went to a jury, they would have to determine if Roger went to the scene with intent to kill, or if that didn't matter under the depraved heart clause.

"So, let's look at this from a worst-case scenario," Dave said. "If somehow Barnes could get this through a jury trial without the jury being sympathetic to the position you were in, and if he could get a guilty verdict on a second-degree murder charge, in Indiana you would be looking at likely a minimum of 10 years, maybe even 15. The judge would have wide latitude on the sentencing, based on the mitigating factors, but that is probably a fair estimate."

Roger stayed silent as Dave continued. "So, the next scenario is Barnes decides he wants to make an example out of you but is worried he won't be able to get a murder conviction. In that instance, he may lessen the charge to first-degree manslaughter. In this case, you'd likely be looking at five years or more."

Dave continued by explaining that in both cases, his strategy would be to get the jury to sympathize with Roger and to put themselves in his shoes on that fateful evening. To do this, he would have to introduce Roger's alcoholism and bring to light how he came to invite Jack into his home, to trust him and to allow him to be around his then 10-year-old son. What was worse for Roger, though, is that Dave would have to call Adam as a witness and have him tell the jury what he remembered about Jack – how he touched him, looked at him in the shower, and eventually raped him. For Roger, that was more than he could bear.

"Let's find a way to get a deal done," Roger said. "No matter what happens to me, there's no way I'm putting my son up there and making him rehash that terrible night. It's time he's able to move on from this."

Dave nodded. "I thought you'd say that."

At that point, the two men continued talking, Roger making his case for the shortest sentence possible and Dave playing Devil's advocate and presenting everything Barnes would likely throw at them during negotiations. After about twenty minutes, Dave looked across the table and told Roger he had an idea for their initial offer.

"We'll start the bidding low," Dave said. "We'll offer three months in county jail, including time served and two years' probation. Barnes won't accept that, but it will at least start the discussion. We'll then see what he comes back with, and we'll know just how reluctant he is to take this thing to trial."

Roger thought about it for only a moment, but knew if he had to he could deal with three months in his current location. He told Dave to go ahead and make the offer.

Before leaving, Dave told Roger that Adam was going to be moved to the foster home early that afternoon and that he would be meeting his CASA by late afternoon.

"Tell me again what's the point of the CASA," Roger said.

Dave explained the advocate would meet with Adam and work to determine his frame of mind including his relationship with Roger. Since Adam had already been ordered into temporary foster care, they wouldn't have to deal with that aspect of the case, but the CASA would help the judge determine if a long-term placement is necessary.

"You mean if I'm sentenced to more than just a few months in jail?" Roger asked.

Dave paused for a moment, looking for the right words. "Yes, definitely in that instance. But the CASA and the court will also consider your ability to take care of Adam, even after you are released. Their number one concern is the safety of the child, not the happiness of the parent."

"Will they want to talk to me?" Roger asked.

"Probably not right away," Dave answered. "Of course, they'll monitor your case and if you're going to be released in short order, they'll want to make sure it's safe for Adam to be returned to your custody when that happens."

Roger wasn't sure what to ask next, but he knew there was nothing he could do at this point to alter the course of his or Adam's life. In a few short hours, his son would be in a new home with people neither of them knew and would meet with adults that had a major influence on the rest of their lives. Again, Roger hated the position in which he found himself, but as he started to do more and more often in the past week, he resigned himself to accept that which he could no longer change.

Dave told him he would be in touch late that afternoon if Barnes countered their offer, but he told Roger that Barnes would likely want to make him sit through another weekend in jail before offering any kind of reply. Roger wasn't surprised by this, and he asked Dave if he could write Adam a note to take to his son before he went into foster care. Dave liked the idea, and passed a pencil and paper over to his client. When Roger finished a few minutes later, he folded the note and handed it back to Dave, who got up, shook his friend's hand and once again left the jail.

Chapter Thirty-Five

Adam was more nervous than he thought he'd be as he walked into the relatively small white house on Franklin Street in downtown Williams. He was familiar with the area, as the park he played in not far from his elementary school was just down the road, easily within walking distance. Craig Evans from DCS walked ahead of him, and Mandy came along to make sure he was okay. She offered to hold his hand, but Adam declined as he didn't want to look like a wimp.

Evans knocked on the door and a moment later it a skinny lady with dark hair and just a little gray starting to creep in on the sides answered. When Adam was introduced to her, he was told to call her Mrs. Dayne. Behind her was Mr. Dayne and, as far as Adam could tell, they seemed happy to see him. Seated on the couch were Adam's three new foster siblings, all of who were apparently told to wear some decent clothes, sit on the couch and look presentable.

Adam met each of them – Billy was the other boy and was 13, Sara was 11 and Joanie was 9. Billy and Sara barely made eye contact with Adam, but Joanie ran up and gave him a big hug. At first, he thought he found the hug a little strange, but it made him smile. Adam kept his place next to Mandy while she and Evans had a brief conversation with the Daynes. A moment later, Mandy leaned over, gave Adam a hug and told him she'd see him soon. Two minutes later, she and Evans left in their separate cars and Adam was left alone with his new "family."

Mr. Dayne led Adam down the hall to one of the bedrooms, followed closely by Billy. In the room were two twin beds, and it was obvious from the clutter on the bed closest to the window which one was Billy's. As if to confirm it, Billy moved ahead of Adam and sat down on his bed.

"This will be your room," Mr. Dayne said to Adam, as he lifted onto the bed one of the two small suitcases Adam had brought with him. "You can unpack your stuff, and you'll have half of the dresser over there and half of the closet. We moved Billy's stuff around yesterday to make room for everything."

Adam glanced over at Billy, who still had not said anything other than hello. He was just staring at Adam and Mr. Dayne and seemed to be protecting his turf.

"Billy will show you the rest of the house after you unpack," Mr. Dayne said, and left the room.

Adam began unpacking, and had just about finished the first suitcase when Billy said, "Make sure you keep yourself on your side of the room. I had the room to myself until you showed up."

Adam thought of a few snide replies before deciding to take the higher road and said, "No problem."

When the unpacking was done, Billy led Adam quickly around the house, showing him the small living room, kitchen, the girls' bedroom, the master and, finally, the basement. The basement was carpeted with wood paneling on the walls. In the center sat two couches, a recliner, a coffee table and a big screen television.

"This is where we sit around and watch TV and play XBox," Billy said. "Do you play?"

Adam hadn't spent a lot of time with video games until his past week with the Carters, but he nodded his head as if he'd been playing for years. Billy seemed satisfied to have another boy in the house to play games, and he led him from the walkout basement into the backyard. It was small, but had a swing set with a slide, as well as basketball hoop that stood on a small patch of pavement. Adam immediately missed his woods and the huge area he played in throughout his childhood, but as he did with most situations the past week, he resigned himself to his new reality.

Billy led Adam back around to the front of the house and through the garage, where Joanie waited at the door.

"Hi, Adam," she said smiling. "Do you want to play with me?"

Mr. Dayne looked her way and told her to give Adam a break and allow him a chance to settle in.

"It's okay, Mr. Dayne," Adam said. "We'll play later, Joanie."

"Adam, your CASA will be by soon to meet you," Mr. Dayne said. "When he gets here, we'll send the other kids down to the basement so you can have some privacy."

Mandy prepared Adam on what the CASA visit would entail, and she told him it was important Adam answer all the questions and be completely honest with his CASA.

"We love our CASA, don't we, Sara?" Joanie asked. "Her name's Kim, and she's really nice."

Sara nodded, but still hadn't said anything since Adam's arrival. Adam hadn't yet hit the age where he noticed girls much, but he thought Sara was cute and wondered why she hadn't said anything to him. He figured maybe she was just a little shy, but hoped she'd open up more as she got to know him.

As if she could read Adam's mind, Joanie leaned over and whispered to Adam, "Sara thinks you're cute, and so do I." Giggling, Joanie slapped Adam on the back and ran out of the room.

****

Micah pulled his car into the driveway of the small house precisely at 4:30. Taking a deep breath as he turned off the car's engine, he picked up the notepad from the passenger seat and then remembered what he learned in his training. No notes or written observation during the first meeting, the trainer told the class. Just talk, listen and work to build rapport were the goals of the initial visit.

Mrs. Dayne met Micah on the front porch before he could ring the doorbell and, after a brief introduction, she led him into the living room. Mr. Dayne had already herded the other kids to the basement, so Adam was alone on the couch. When Micah entered, Adam stood as Mrs. Dayne introduced them.

"Nice to meet you, Mr. Sanders," Adam said.

"Call me Micah." Mrs. Dayne, seeing they were fine on their own, left the room and went to the basement to be with the rest of the family.

Adam sat down on one end of the couch, and Micah took a seat on the recliner to Adam's right. During training, Micah learned it was important at first to give the child some space, but not to provide too much distance. As it was, he sat just about four feet from Adam.

"So, you just got here today?" Micah asked. "What do you think so far?"

Adam shrugged his shoulders as if to say it was too soon to tell, but he offered, "The Daynes seem nice."

Micah nodded his head. "How about the other kids?"

"I really haven't spent any time with them," Adam said. "Billy showed me around, but he hasn't really said much, other than he likes to play video games."

"What do you like to do?" Micah said.

"My favorite thing has always been hanging out in the woods behind my cabin," Adam replied. "I have a fort back there and it's a really cool place. I haven't been back there in more than a week, though. I'm going to miss it."

"You're not a big fan of video games?" Micah asked.

"They're okay, but I like being outside a lot more."

It occurred to Micah that Adam seemed to be really mature, and he liked that Adam's interests were geared more toward outside activities than sitting in front of a television. Micah and Kayla had worked hard during Emma's first few years to make sure that they did a lot of outdoor activities, and they allowed very little screen time for their daughter. Micah imagined Adam's parents must have taken the same tact with him.

"So, growing up, I guess you spent a lot more time outside than in," Micah asked.

Adam nodded. "Before my mom died a few years ago, she and my dad used to take me on all kind of outdoor adventures. We'd go hiking, canoeing, white water rafting, runs in the park – those kinds of things. My mom always seemed happiest when she was outdoors and we were all together, and my dad was happiest when my mom was happy."

Micah was impressed with the maturity Adam showed and with the ease he could talk about his mom.

"I'll bet you miss your mom a lot, huh?" Micah said. "I lost my mom when I was pretty young, too. I was just a little older than you were, in fact."

Adam looked sad, but he held Micah's gaze. "Really?" He asked the question as if he could not believe anyone else had gone through the same tragedy he had.

"Yeah, I was 13 when she died," Micah said. "It was a car accident. One day she was there with me, and then she went to the grocery store and I never saw her again."

A single tear escaped Adam's eye, but he wiped it away and willed himself to be strong. "My mom died of cancer. It was really hard on my dad and me."

"Tell me about your dad," Micah said.

"He hung in there for me for a while after mom died," Adam said. "He's always been a great dad, but he started to drink a little bit, and then a lot. Still, he never wanted to hurt me and always tried to protect me. I think he just missed mom real bad."

Micah nodded. "I can imagine."

"Micah, can I ask you a question?" Adam asked.

"You can ask me anything," Micah replied.

"Are you married, and do you have kids?"

"I am married, and I have a daughter," Micah replied. "She's four."

Micah could tell Adam was feeling him out and trying to determine just how much he could trust him. So far, he had established a strong initial bond by sharing the information about his mother and talking openly about his own family.

Adam looked as if he was trying to decide how or if he should ask the next question. After a moment, he said, "Would you do anything to protect them? I mean anything?"

Micah didn't have all the details of Roger Durkin's case, but he knew Adam's father was in jail awaiting trial on a second-degree murder charge. He figured Adam's question had to have something to do with his dad's case.

"Yes, I think I would do just about anything to protect them," Micah replied.

"My dad protected me from something else bad happening, and he's in jail," Adam said. "I don't think that's fair."

Micah could hear anger stirring in Adam's voice. He was glad he could get Adam to open up so quickly, but at the same time, it was important in this initial meeting that he got some information to help him with recommendations going forward. The conversation was heading in a direction Micah felt endangered what he needed to accomplish today, so he wanted to change the subject without making Adam feel as if he wasn't willing to listen.

"You and I will have a chance to discuss your dad's case soon," Micah said. "Can you tell me a little bit about the time after your mom passed away?"

Adam paused for a second but then told Micah as much as he could remember of the past two years, including the fun he and his dad occasionally had going to the state park, eating pizza and watching baseball games. He also told Micah about the times his dad would drink so much that he couldn't get him to eat any dinner. On those days, Adam would just stay outside and hole up in his fort as much as he could. Adam purposely left out any mention of the time his dad hit him, as well as everything about Uncle Jack. He liked Micah well enough, but he wasn't even close to feeling comfortable talking to him about any of that yet.

Almost an hour had passed as Adam finished telling Micah about his relationship with his dad – most of it, anyway. As he finished, Micah stood up and handed Adam a business card with a phone number written on the back.

"Adam, we'll be spending more time together, but I really enjoyed meeting you," Micah said. "That's my cell number, and you can call it any hour of the day if you need anything."

Adam recognized the logo on the business card. "You work for the newspaper?" he asked.

"I do," Micah replied. "I'm the editor there, meaning I'm in charge of the news we put in the paper every day."

"Cool," Adam said. "I got to take a tour with my class a couple of years ago, and we saw how the big press works."

Micah smiled. "It is pretty cool, isn't it?"

"I'd like to see it again some time," Adam said. "I liked the way it sounded and smelled," referring to the strong smell of the ink in the press room.

"Yeah, I like that too," Micah said. "We'll have to go see it again sometime."

Adam smiled and shook Micah's hand.

"I'll be back next week and we'll talk some more," Micah said. "Until then, you get settled in here and make friends with the other kids."

"I'll try," Adam said. "I don't think it'll be a problem making friends with Joanie."

Micah didn't know the names of the other kids, but he nodded and walked to the basement door to let the Daynes know he was leaving. Mr. Dayne appeared at the top of the stairs, led Micah out to his car and when he came back in, invited Adam to come down to the basement to finish the movie they were all watching before dinner.

"How'd it go with your CASA?" Mr. Dayne asked.

"Good," Adam said. "I like Micah a lot."

Chapter Thirty-Six

Adam sat on the bed in his new room. It was just after eight, and Billy was still in the basement watching television as Adam looked around the room he would occupy for the foreseeable future. Even though it had been a whirlwind day, and Adam was really tired, he didn't want to go to bed yet. As he moved the suitcases he unpacked earlier to a corner of the closet, he noticed an envelope poking out from one of the side pockets. The envelope had his name written on the outside, and he recognized the writing as his father's. He quickly pulled open the flap on the envelope, removed the single sheet of typing paper inside and started reading the handwritten note.

Hey buddy,

You're probably settling in to your new place, and I hope the first day has gone well for you. Dave told me as much as he knows about the Daynes, and it sounds like they're really good people who will be there to help you and take care of anything you need until we can be together again.

I want you to know how very sorry I am – for everything. I'm sorry about what happened to your mom, and for the mess I made of my life – and yours – after she died. Mostly, though, I'm sorry for the situation I put you in with Jack and for the mess I've created because of what happened. You've been such a good kid your whole life, and your mom and I have always been so proud of you.

Now, as I watch you grow into the young man you're becoming – so much sooner than you should have to – I see so much of your mom in you. She was so incredibly tough, smart, beautiful and amazing, and watching you reminds me so much of her. Your way with people, how kind and gentle you are, and the courage with which you've handled this whole situation just makes me think of her. I could never have asked for anything more than her love, and the fact that her love produced you – well, it's just the best gift I've ever been given.

I don't know what the next few months or years are going to bring. If all goes well, we'll be together again soon. Or, I might have to go away for a while, but God I hope that's not the case. Because I don't want to miss any of what the next few years have in store for you. I don't want to miss a single minute, because you are such an incredible, strong young man.

During whatever time we're apart, I hope you remember the dad that was there for you before your mom left, and not the one I became during my time with Jack. When this is over, and I hope that's very soon, I'm going to be that dad again – one you can count on all the time and one who will never leave you alone again.

Stay tough, buddy, but never lose all those things that make you who you are – one incredible, brave, compassionate and loving young man. I'm so proud of you, and I'll talk to you just as soon as I can.

Love, Dad

Adam wiped a tear from his eye as he put the letter back into the envelope. Standing up, he walked across to the dresser and placed the envelope at the bottom of the top drawer, underneath all his clothes. Just as he was closing the drawer, he heard footsteps in the hallway, and Billy appeared at the door. Noticing Adam's eyes were a little red and puffy, he walked over and put his hand on Adam's shoulder.

"Want to come down and watch a little TV before bed?" Billy asked. It was by far the nicest thing he had said since Adam's arrival.

Adam choked up a bit as he nodded his head and followed his new foster brother into the hallway and down into the basement.

****

When Micah left the meeting with Adam, all he wanted to do was go home to Kayla and Emma and spend time with them. The brief time he spent with his new CASA child reminded him just how lucky he was with his family situation, but he couldn't help but consider how quickly circumstances could change. While he didn't yet know all the details of the criminal case Adam's father was involved in, it was apparent whatever happened was the result of Adam's dad defending him in some way. Micah had no doubt that, put in a situation where someone had hurt Emma, he would do anything to make it right. He just hoped he would never have to make such a decision.

So, despite the fact he still had some work to do at the office, Micah decided it could wait until Monday and headed north toward his home, rather than south toward the office.

As he pulled his car into the driveway, as if on cue, Emma came running around the corner of the house with a huge smile on her face.

"Daddy!" she yelled, jumping into Micah's arms before he was even fully out of the car.

"Hey there, Rosebud," Micah said, using her nickname as he pulled her close.

Emma gasped a little and said, "Daddy, you're squeezing me tight."

Realizing she was right, Micah eased up and put his face right in front of hers. "I'm just so glad to see you."

Emma giggled, and wiggled her way out of Micah's arms. Back with her feet on the ground, she put her most serious look on her face and crossed her arms across her chest. "Mommy said we're having liver and onions for dinner," Emma said, the smile on her face previously replaced by a frown.

"Mmm, liver and onions," Micah said. "Your favorite."

Emma started shaking her head back and forth. "It's gross, daddy. Really gross."

Micah laughed, knowing full well Kayla never cooked liver and onions and was just playing a game with Emma.

"Well, let me talk to mommy and see if I can get her to reconsider," Micah said, playing along. "What would Princess Emma like for dinner?"

Emma put her hand on her chin and looked to a point in the sky, obviously considering her options. "Chinese noodles!" she yelled a moment later. "We haven't had those in forever!"

Micah nodded. "Well, let me see if I can change mommy's mind while you play."

Emma laughed and ran off to the backyard where, Micah knew, she would go back to the swing set where she spent much of her outside time. Micah grabbed his briefcase from the back seat and made his way to the front door, where Kayla stood while she watched the exchange with Emma.

"Liver and onions, huh?" he said, as Kayla opened the screen door and planted a big kiss on her husband.

"Only the best for my family," she joked, and Micah kissed her back, pulling her tight against him.

"Wow, easy cowboy," Kayla said. "Or I might just have to take you upstairs this second."

Micah smiled. "Well, I guess we better get those Chinese noodles on the way soon, then."

The two made their way to the kitchen, and Micah looked out the window to see Emma swinging back and forth. It amazed him how carefree she always looked when she was swinging and, especially on this day, he wished he could freeze her in that moment forever.

"How was your day?" Kayla asked from behind him.

Micah filled her in briefly about work, but then jumped right into his meeting with Adam, as he knew that was what Kayla wanted to hear about anyways. He told her about how confident Adam seemed, how tough of a kid he was for the way he was handling his situation, but also about the fact that, deep down, Adam seemed lost without his dad. When Kayla asked about Adam's dad, Micah shrugged his shoulders.

"We're really not supposed to get too involved initially in ongoing criminal cases surrounding the circumstance," Micah said. "It's my job to get to know Adam, find out what his home life was like before he needed services, and determine if he would be able to go back with his father once the criminal case is resolved."

Kayla pulled two beers from the refrigerator, opened them and handed one to Micah as she took a long pull from hers. "And what do you think after this first meeting?"

"It's way too early to make a determination, and I really didn't let Adam spend much time talking about his father's case," he answered. "But I get the impression whatever happened was some kind of retaliation for something that involved Adam."

Kayla didn't press for more information, as she knew there were things about the case that either Micah didn't know or couldn't share due to confidentiality issues.

"Anyway, he's in a good foster home, he'll be able to go back to his old school next week, and I think he'll be fine there until the case is resolved."

Micah changed the subject by asking what Kayla and Emma wanted to do over the weekend. Fall had settled in, the leaves were in the height of their change, and Kayla suggested a hike in the park the next afternoon. With a perfect forecast in the high 50s with full sun, Micah couldn't imagine a better way to spend a Saturday.

Late that night, after they had put Emma to bed, Micah was lying in bed with Kayla wrapped up in his left arm and her head against his chest.

"You know, I'm not even fully wrapped up in this new CASA case yet," Micah said, "but I can see how difficult this role is going to be."

"How so?" Kayla asked.

"It's our job to stay impartial, to try to look at each case from all angles," Micah replied, "but all I keep coming back to is an 11-year-old boy who has had his whole world ripped away from him. First his mother dies, then his dad goes crazy for whatever reason, and the next thing he knows he has lost everything he's ever had in his young life. What the hell is wrong with this world?"

Kayla didn't say anything immediately, so Micah continued. "I'm just afraid that every case I get involved in and that every child I work with is just going to remind me of Emma and make me wonder what kind of world she's going to get to grow up in. It's just so different than when we were kids."

Kayla stayed quiet for a moment, but when Micah didn't say anything more, she rolled over so she was looking right into his eyes. "Well, maybe," she said and planted a small kiss on his lips, "you *should* see a little bit of Emma in every child you work with. Maybe that will always remind you what you're fighting for when you do the good things you're going to do to help those children."

"What do you mean?" Micah asked.

"I mean, Mr. Sanders, that every time you help one of these children you make the world a little better for your daughter. Maybe every time you and every other advocate out there helps a child, you change the world for that child so he or she never becomes an abuser or a criminal. Doesn't that make the world better for Emma – and all of us?"

Micah thought about it for a moment, and realized that in those few minutes, Kayla had summed up exactly his reasons for becoming a CASA. "You are one incredible woman," he said, reaching over to turn off the light.

She kissed him in the dark, running her hands through his hair as she did so. "Don't you ever forget it."

Chapter Thirty-Seven

Dave made the call to Barnes late Friday afternoon and left a message with his assistant that he wanted to discuss cutting a deal. Of course, Barnes was not available at the time, and the assistant told him he likely would not be available the rest of the afternoon, but she would pass the message along. Dave had expected as much, but he had hoped for Roger's sake he would at least be able to open the negotiations before the weekend.

As Saturday morning dawned, Dave thought about his client and wondered how Adam's first night in his new house went. He asked DCS if he and Mandy could check in on Adam on occasion, but the supervisor told him it would need to be coordinated with the Daynes and that the recommendation was they gave Adam at least a week to settle in to his new surroundings before paying him a visit.

Roger, in much less comfortable surroundings on the other side of town, was waking up to his regular morning routine, boring as can be but becoming more his current way of life. After a couple hundred situps and pushups, he'd read for a little while until he was led to breakfast to enjoy the weekend "treat" of pancakes, which were nothing like those he was used to throughout his life. Without the ability to drown the three heavy pancakes in as much maple syrup as he liked, Roger swore he'd be chewing on cardboard. Still, the pancakes were a diversion from the daily routine of eggs, oatmeal, eggs, oatmeal that breakfast consisted of the rest of the week.

Roger picked at his breakfast, forcing himself to at least eat something, and didn't realize Sandy, seated across from him as usual, was staring him down.

"You alright, man?" Sandy asked.

Roger didn't even hear the question the first time, but when Sandy asked it again – a little louder – he looked across.

"Oh, yeah," Roger said. "Sorry."

Sandy pressed for more information.

"I'm just wondering how Adam is doing in his new foster home," Roger said. "I couldn't sleep all night, wondering what his first night was like, how he's being treated, how safe he is, and all those kinds of things."

"I'm sure he's just fine," Sandy said, but not convincingly. "You told me what a tough kid he is."

"True," Roger replied, "but he's still just a kid."

Sandy nodded and took a huge bite of pancakes.

"I don't know how you can eat those things," Roger said. "They're awful."

Sandy shrugged. "Like everything else in this place, you get used to them."

Roger didn't even want to think about getting used to them or anything else in the Lands County Jail. For the first time since he entered the jail just over a week ago, he felt depressed and had a hard time looking at anything in a positive light.

****

Adam was waking up Saturday morning after a fitful night of his own. As he spent his first night in his new bed listening to the sounds of Billy breathing and occasionally farting – one of the most awful smells he ever experienced – he thought to himself that he had never shared a room before, and what a blessing that was. Rolling back and forth in the twin bed, Adam occasionally checked the digital display of the alarm clock between them, and the last time he looked at it before finally falling asleep, it was 12:18 a.m. He awakened at 2:40 when Billy left the room, apparently to go to the bathroom, and again for good when Billy slapped him on the side of the head at 7:30 and told him it was time for breakfast. Adam rubbed the sleep from his eyes as he made his way down the hall in his pajamas, and found the rest of the "family" already gathered around the table.

Joanie looked up at him, smiled and said, "Good morning, Adam! You have bedhead." She giggled as Adam took his seat and thanked Mrs. Dayne as she placed a plate of ham and eggs in front of him.

Mr. Dayne looked up from the crossword puzzle he was working and asked Adam how well he slept his first night.

"Fine," Adam lied, and Mr. Dayne looked at him as if he knew it wasn't true. Still, he didn't say anything and went back to his crossword puzzle.

Adam didn't say much during breakfast, just as he hadn't during dinner the night before. Joanie occasionally whispered to Sara, who was her biological sister, but otherwise the table was relatively quiet as they all ate together. The food tasted good, as had dinner, and Adam was glad to see Mrs. Dayne was a pretty good cook.

As they all finished eating, Mrs. Dayne announced to everyone the day's schedule. After they cleaned up the breakfast dishes, they needed to get ready to go to Billy's soccer game at 10, during which the other kids could either watch the game or play in the park where the fields were located. After that, they would go the grocery store before spending the afternoon at home and having pizza for dinner. Sunday morning, Mrs. Dayne explained, they would all go to church, after which they would come home for Sunday dinner. Following dinner, each of the kids had chores to do before sitting down to homework and getting ready for school on Monday.

Adam thought about telling Mrs. Dayne he hadn't gone to church in a long time – since before his mom had gotten sick – but decided to keep that to himself. He also realized he hadn't been to school in almost a month, and he reminded himself to talk to Mrs. Dayne privately about that later. Adam was nervous about the experience of returning to school. He didn't know how much his classmates would know about what happened to him, about his dad being in jail, and about Adam's new living arrangements. He hadn't seen his friends since the day he came home to find Jack waiting for him, and with as much as his life had changed since then, he wasn't sure anyone would still want to be friends with him.

As he took his plate to the kitchen sink, scraping and rinsing it before putting it into the dishwasher, these thoughts ran through his mind and the apprehension he felt began to turn to fear.

What if the kids at school knew what Jack did to him? Would they say anything about it? Surely, if they knew, they would treat him differently. If they weren't mean and didn't tease him about it, which they probably would, they would likely ignore him and talk about him behind his back.

Chapter Thirty-Eight

Micah rarely worked on Saturdays, and he promised Kayla he would go in early, be there for a couple of hours and return home well before noon so they could spend some time with Emma on the weekend. The DCS story, much to Micah's chagrin, was going nowhere fast. Lara Hiller's exploratory committee was obviously window dressing to make the voters and the public feel like they were doing something to combat domestic violence and violent crime.

In a way, Micah was glad for that because the more time he spent with Sandra Bless and Craig Evans at DCS, the more he grew to like them and appreciate the impossible job they did. At the same time, his brief experience as a CASA and the things he learned during his training led him to the conclusion that by the time DCS got involved in a case, it was simply about damage control. The problems these organizations faced were rooted in the much more complex issues of rampant drug availability, lack of education among offenders and cycles of abuse that started generations ago in many of these families.

With a sigh, Micah tried to turn his mind to the work in front of him. He spent some time out of the office the past few days for his meeting with Adam, preceded by a preparatory meeting with his case supervisor. He owed his staff a column for Sunday's paper, and since he barely started it during the week as he should have, he had a lot of work to do in the next couple hours. The blank computer screen in front of him practically screaming at him, Micah set his fingers on his keyboard and began typing.

Action – not reaction – brings the only possibility for change
By Micah Sanders

Tough times call for tough measures. Bad things happen, and the public marches in the streets demanding action. Eye for an eye, tooth for a tooth. We erect memorials for the fallen, pictures from better days, flowers, lit candles, and we hold vigil wondering how something so terrible could happen to good people.

These reactions, these feelings, are perfectly natural. More than that, they're taught to us in our schools, in our religion classes, and in the society in which we live. Mass media imbeds these images in our minds as they happen to other people in other places, and when the tragedy finally hits close to home, we follow the cue and react the same way.

But maybe – just maybe – we need to direct that anger and passion to doing everything we can to prevent the tragedy from happening in the first place. Or, at the very least, try to keep it from ever happening again.

In the wake of a horrible event like the recent Henley murders, it is natural to be outraged, to be incensed, and to want immediate action. It's human nature, after all. Even this newspaper is guilty of joining in, if not igniting, the public outcry when we launched an investigative series before we began the investigation.

Under pressure from the media and the public, Rep. Lara Hiller launched her own committee aimed at taking action, digging into every nook and cranny of the Department of Child Services to see where things went off course. How could they have not acted earlier? How did two calls go unheeded as a sign of things to come?

But here's the thing: we're asking the wrong questions. Let's stop asking why something happened and instead ask what we're going to do to prevent it from happening again. Will sanctioning DCS and taking corrective action against some of its underpaid and overworked employees save the next little boy cowering under his father's anger? Will marching with a figurative pitch fork into the offices of DCS help the next little girl fending for herself while mommy gets high?

Instead of lynching the small number of men and women willing to work way too many hours in a sometimes-hopeless job, let's lift them up. Let's give them hope – and help. Let's show them that instead of creating committees that are going to consider what they did wrong, we're going to recognize what they do right and provide resources that will help them achieve that outcome more often.

The roots of the problems case workers most commonly face – domestic violence, drugs and alcohol – were not created by DCS or the state legislature. Yet, they are the issues on which our subcommittees and task forces need to focus.

There is no easy answer to any of these problems. There's no magic wand anyone can wave that will stop these tragedies from occurring. But there are steps and measures that can be taken to reduce the availability of illegal drugs and weapons. There are ways we can educate victims of abuse now so they do not become abusers someday.

If we start today, right at this moment, it will be years before we see a noticeable difference in terms of actual numbers. And when those efforts save the first child, it won't move the needle in the overall scheme of things. But it will change the world for that child and for all the people he or she is going to influence and touch throughout his or her life. And just like that, we've exponentially made things better for a lot of people.

Do that 10 times, 100 times, 1,000 times, and that needle is starting to move. The tide is starting to turn.

Or, we can throw our hands up in the air, lower our heads, and continue to mourn our dead. The choice is clear, but the way we've always done things is not working. It's time for change in Indianapolis and in Washington, D.C. But the change starts with each of us, and we can't just demand it, we must make it happen.

Most people reading this column are homeowners, are employed, and have family of some kind. Most of you are not clients of DCS and probably never have been. To many of you, these problems may seem like they're in some other state, some other town, or at the very least not in your neighborhood. But that can change in a blink. And the question each of us must ask ourselves when, God forbid, something bad happens is "could we have done something to prevent this?"

The time for action is now and, no, it can't wait another day, another minute or another second. We elect our legislators to listen to us and to do our will for the betterment of society. It's time we make our voices heard and demand they do just that.

Micah finished typing and quickly read through what he wrote. Most of the time when he'd write a column, he'd make numerous changes during the first re-read and a few more the second time through it. This was one of the rare cases, however, he liked the column exactly as he had written it. It was raw, and he knew it would not sit well with some of the elected officials he regularly dealt with, but he felt it conveyed the message he wanted to send. Looking over at the clock, he was surprised to see only an hour had gone by from start to finish. Content with what he had on the page, he hit the enter key to file the story, stood up and walked out of the office to spend the day with his family.

Chapter Thirty-Nine

Adam sat on a bench staring at the soccer field where Billy and 21 other players were about halfway through their game. He wasn't actually watching, as he didn't really feel close to Billy yet but, more than that, he couldn't stand soccer. Adam's dad had exposed him to a lot of different sports growing up, but soccer was his least favorite, mostly because it was a lot of running, you didn't touch the ball much, and goals were so hard to come by that it is normal to have a final score of 0-0. Who plays a sport where a game can end in a scoreless tie?

Joanie and Sara tried their best to get Adam to come over to the playground with them. While Joanie had loved Adam from the start, Sara seemed to be warming up to him slowly. Still, Adam's mind drifted past the soccer field and the playground where his new foster family was engaged, and all he could think about was going back to school on Monday and facing the friends and classmates he hadn't seen in close to a month. He wasn't really scared of going back – in the past couple weeks he found not much scared him anymore – but he was a little apprehensive, as he had been before he met the Daynes.

Adam was surprised, however, when a moment later he found himself lying in the dirt in front of the bench after someone shoved him from behind.

"What's up, Durkin? Where you been?" Adam sat himself up and looked up at his attacker. Standing over him was Eli Collins, a boy from his class who had been known as a bully but had left Adam alone in the past.

Adam wasn't sure what to do, or what to say. "I'm coming back Monday," was all he could think of. Instinct told Adam he needed to stand up while he could. When he did, Eli was standing right in front of him and the two, about the same height, were eye to eye.

"You might want to rethink that," Eli said, a sneer on his face. "Since your dad's in jail and all."

Before he even knew what he was doing, Adam felt his fist contact his classmate's jaw, sending him sprawling to the ground, as surprised as he was hurt. Adam had the feeling like he was outside of his body and looking down at himself standing over the boy he had just punched. Just as it was occurring to him that it was the first time he had ever punched someone, Adam's feet were pounding the ground as he ran away from the soccer field and out of the park. He didn't look back to see if Eli or anyone else was chasing him. In that moment, all he could do was run.

Leaving the park, instead of making a left turn toward his foster home, he made a right and headed down the sidewalk in the opposite direction. His feet moving faster than they ever had before, an avalanche of memories and faces flashed before him. First it was his mom, not the beautiful face from all the pictures he still looked at all the time, but the thin, hollow face he saw right before she said goodbye to him for the last time.

Down the sidewalk and through the outskirts of downtown he continued to run as the dying version of his mom left his mind, only to be replaced by the yellow teeth and ravenous eyes of his rapist uncle, back from the dead and looking for one last chance to haunt his nephew.

When that image cleared, he saw his dad, lying in his bed with a needle in his arm and murmuring. Adam tried to listen to what he said, but it was inaudible at first. He continued to listen as he ran, imploring his dad to tell him he was alright, to tell him what to do. Finally, the words started becoming more clear, and at first he couldn't believe what his father was saying to him, but as he said it over and over the words became obvious. "It's your fault. It's all your fault."

Tears streaming down his cheeks, still dirty from the fall into the dirt after Eli pushed him, and his right hand throbbing from his first-ever punch, Adam left the sidewalk and headed into the woods bordering the road. Even though it hadn't been that long since he cried last, the tears felt like they would never stop flowing, and the road was no longer a safe place to run.

****

Micah, Kayla and Emma were just finishing their burritos at the family's favorite Mexican place when Micah's phone rang. Looking at the caller ID, he saw it Chris Rutherford, his CASA case supervisor.

At first, Micah thought it odd that Rutherford would call him on a Saturday, but then again, he had just started his new case, so there might be some information he needed to pass along.

"Micah," Rutherford said, before Micah could even say hello. "Adam Durkin is missing. He ran away from the park where he was playing with his new foster family. I know you haven't spent much time with him yet, but I thought you'd want to know."

"What can I do to help?" Micah asked, unsure there was anything at all he could do.

"You visited with him for a while yesterday," Rutherford said. "Did he say anything that led you to believe he was thinking of running away or where he might go?"

"No, nothing at all," Micah replied. "If he had, I would have reported it. Did something happen?"

"I don't have all the details yet, but apparently, he punched a classmate of his and ran out of the park. No one knew he left until the classmate showed his parents the bloody nose Adam gave him, and they all started looking for him. It sounds like he had at least a couple minutes' head start."

Micah paused, unsure of what to say next. Rutherford broke the silence.

"Okay, just keep your phone nearby in case we need you for anything. The police and the Daynes are looking everywhere they can think of. I'll let you know when I hear something."

The call disconnected, and Micah filled Kayla in on what Rutherford told him. Since there was nothing else Micah could do at that point, they decided to continue to the zoo with Emma as they had planned.

As they were leaving the restaurant and getting into the car, though, Micah had a thought. "We might have to postpone the zoo," he said. "I think I know where he went."

Pulling out his phone and bringing up his Web browser, Micah typed in a search for the address for Roger

Durkin, and a moment later he had the address plugged into his GPS. They were just 8 minutes away.

****

Crouched in the same corner of his fort he retreated to after Uncle Jack's attack, Adam tried to sit silently as he heard footsteps coming toward him on the path that led from his house. He had only been in the fort for about a half hour, and he couldn't believe anyone would find him that quickly, as the only other person who knew about his hideout was locked up in jail at the moment.

"Adam, are you in there?"

Even though he met him only once a day earlier, Adam recognized the voice as Micah's, and he remembered he mentioned the fort during their conversation. Still, he didn't answer immediately, but a moment later Micah peered through the entry way to the fort. "Can I come in?" he asked.

Adam nodded, appreciating Micah's politeness, but knowing he was coming in whether Adam wanted him to or not.

"Cool fort you have here," Micah said, taking a seat along the adjacent wall about six feet from Adam. "I had one like it when I was a kid, but this is much nicer."

"How'd you find me?" Adam asked, ignoring Micah's compliment.

"There are a lot of people looking for you. When they called me, I couldn't help but think of how much I liked having a place to run away to when I was your age. I remembered you telling me about playing in the fort behind your house."

Adam nodded, but didn't say anything.

"What happened?" Micah asked.

Adam told him about the encounter with his classmate, about what he said about his dad, and how he punched someone for the first time in his life. The next thing he knew he was running away and his feet brought him straight to his fort.

He also told Micah about the images flashing through his mind as he ran. Adam was surprised at how much he was telling someone he barely knew, but he allowed himself to keep going.

"The last image was my dad," Adam said. "Not the good dad I've had most of my life, but the one that was on drugs when things were really bad. He looked at me and told me it was all my fault."

Adam was crying again. Micah had zero experience dealing with this kind of situation, and he paused for a moment before he spoke again.

"What do you think he meant by that?" Micah asked. "What was your fault?"

Adam pulled his hands away from his face, where the tears streaked through dirt and dust. In that moment, he looked so young and helpless, a completely different person from the strong young man Micah met the day before.

Adam cleared his throat before he spoke. "All of it," he finally said. "My mom dying, my dad drinking and doing drugs – even what Uncle Jack did to me."

Micah shook his head but didn't say anything. Deep down, he knew Adam needed to get this out.

"If I had been a better kid," Adam said, "and if I hadn't have put so much stress on my mom, she never would have gotten sick. And if she had never gotten sick, she would have never died. And then my dad would have been happy and not just stuck with me, and he never would have started drinking. And if my mom was still here and he never started drinking, Uncle Jack never would have come into our lives and never would have hurt me. And if none of that happened, my mom and dad would still be here and I would still matter."

Adam was crying loudly now, the sorrow and pain he held back for weeks now pouring forth in front of this person be barely knew. Micah moved closer until he was seated right next to Adam, and instinctively he put his arm around the boy. At first, Micah thought Adam was going to pull away, but after the slightest hesitation he planted his head on Micah's shoulder and let it all out.

Micah let him cry for another minute or two without saying anything, and when the sobs seemed to be dying down, Micah turned Adam so he was facing him. Pulling a tissue from his pocket, he wiped Adam's eyes and cheeks and handed him another tissue.

When he looked like he had composed himself enough, Micah said, "Adam, the way you're feeling is perfectly normal. You've had a lot of terrible things happen to you in the past few years, and it is absolutely normal for victims to blame themselves for the things that happen to them. They somehow feel like they could have – should have – prevented them."

Micah paused for a minute to make sure Adam understood what he was saying. It appeared he did.

"With everything you told me about your dad yesterday – all the great times you've had, the things you've done together, the special moments you've shared – do you really think he feels like any of this is your fault?"

Adam paused for a minute, obviously considering his answer. "But he said it. Dad said it was all my fault."

Micah shook his head. "That wasn't your dad. That was your mind trying to find a way to make sense of all the terrible things that happened. None of this is your fault, Adam. None of it."

Adam was crying again, but softly this time. Whatever final tears he had left were leaving his eyes and drying up.

"What do you say we get out of here, get you cleaned up and take you back to the Daynes' house?" Micah said. "Maybe from there we'll see if we can go visit your dad."

"Can we sit here for just a while more?" Adam asked.

Micah pulled his cell phone from his pocket. "Can I call and let everyone know you're okay?"

Adam nodded, and Micah pulled up his call log, clicking on his most recent contact. When a voice came on the other end of the line, Micah said, "Chris, I have him."

Chapter Forty

Adam's return to the foster home was a nice one. He got a big hug from Joanie followed, surprisingly, by one from Sara as well. Even Billy was nice to him. Mr. and Mrs. Dayne didn't say a word about him running off. She welcomed him with another hug, lasting longer than the ones from the two girls, and Mr. Dayne gave him a pat on the back. Even though he hadn't been gone long at all, it was as if a lot changed during those couple hours.

Everyone thanked Micah, Kayla and Emma for bringing Adam back, and within a few minutes they left and things were returning to normal in the Dayne house. As promised, they had pizza for dinner and Adam was given the honor of selecting the Saturday night movie from their DVD collection. Apparently, this was a weekly ritual and the kids took turns choosing the movie each week.

When Sunday morning came, Adam wore the nicest outfit he had, and the family headed to its weekly church service. As Adam listened to the quiet music playing before the service began, seated between Joanie and Sara, he reflected on the last time he'd been to church. It was right after mom was diagnosed with "the cancer" as he called it, and he remembered seeing tears well up in her eyes several times during the service. For whatever reason, they never went back to church after that day – not while she was alive, and not after she died.

Adam remembered being mad at God for a time after mom died, and he really hadn't given another thought of ever returning to church until Mrs. Dayne told him they'd be going. Now, seated in the row amongst his foster family, he felt a peace settle over him that he really didn't expect. He was still worried for his dad of course, and was very uncertain of his future, but for the first time since all his troubles started, he felt as if everything might be alright.

When the service ended, Adam realized he hadn't paid much attention to anything going on. He had been lost in his own thoughts, but for the first time in a while, they were nice thoughts. And when the family returned home, he and Billy went down in the basement and played some video games as a light rain fell outside. About halfway through a game of video football, Billy kept his eyes on the screen and asked Adam, "How did it feel to punch that jackass?"

Adam didn't answer right away, mostly because he was surprised Billy knew what happened. After a moment, though, he realized the truth was the best option. "Honestly, I don't even really remember doing it. It was just a reflex, I guess."

"That was pretty cool," Billy replied. "He had it coming. Eli's one of the biggest jerks in school."

****

Mr. Dayne woke Adam a little after 6:30 on Monday morning. "Time to get ready to head back to school," he said. The loathing Adam felt all weekend for this moment had passed, and for whatever reason, he wasn't dreading this as much as he thought he would.

When he walked through the doors to the school and made his way to his locker, he was surprised to see he remembered his combination and immediately began settling back into his routine. As he walked into his classroom, the friends he hadn't seen in a month came right up to him, asked how he was and welcomed him back as if nothing had happened. Across the room, Eli Collins, still with a very swollen upper lip, kept his distance and avoided eye contact at all costs. By the end of the day, Adam had felt like he had never left school.

****

Late Monday afternoon, Roger was led into the visitor's room by a guard who told him his lawyer was waiting for him. When he entered, Dave was already seated at the table at which they had sat a half dozen times since Roger's arrival there.

"Sorry, I'm late," Dave said, "but I got held up a bit at Barnes' office."

"How did it go?" Roger asked.

"Well, he didn't accept the deal I sent over, but then again, I didn't expect him to."

"So, did he counter?"

Dave looked at the tablet in front of him, then back up at Roger. "Before we talk about this, I need to tell you about something that happened with Adam over the weekend."

The panic on Roger's face told Dave his friend was bracing for some sort of terrible news. "Oh, it's nothing that bad," Dave said. He went on to tell Dave about Adam's brief hiatus, but that he had been safely returned to the foster home within a couple hours. He also told Roger he had spoken with the caseworker and Micah that morning, and all indications were that Adam had settled in nicely over the weekend and had a good first day back at school.

"So, all in all, he's doing okay?" Roger asked.

"I think he is," Dave replied. "Of course, there will be some bumps along the way, but everything I'm hearing about the Daynes is positive, especially compared to other foster alternatives out there."

Dave could see the relief in Roger's face. "Also, Micah Sanders wants to come in and meet with you this week," Dave said. "That is, if you decide to go ahead and accept the deal we're about to discuss."

"Lay it on me," Roger said.

Dave explained to Roger that, after some negotiation, he and Barnes had come to an agreement Dave felt like he could present to Roger. Under the plea agreement, Roger would plead no contest to the charge of aggravated assault, meaning he was not admitting guilt in the case, although the judge would adjudicate it as guilty. Barnes would recommend to the judge a two-year suspended sentence, with Roger serving six months in county lock-up, assuming good behavior. After that, he would have two additional years of probation, after which the court would consider expunging his record if he had no additional legal issues.

"So, in six months, I'm out of here?" Roger said when his attorney finished explaining. "And no prison?"

"Five and a half months, actually," Dave said. "You'll get credit for the couple weeks you've already served. And you'd serve it right here. Certainly not paradise, but not even close to Fort Wayne."

"But the crime – it's a felony, right? – would be on my record for good," Roger asked.

"It will be on your record for at least the next four years, until they consider expungement. But then again, you probably weren't going back to teaching after all of this anyways."

Roger nodded in agreement. He hadn't really given that any thought, but he knew what his friend was saying was true.

"This is probably a stupid question," Roger asked after a moment. "Can you think of any reason I shouldn't accept this deal?"

Dave had already thought this through. Part of him – a big part – believed Barnes would have a very difficult time getting a jury to convict Roger, once they laid out everything that led up to the attack at Jack's cabin. But at the same time, the trial wouldn't start for at least three months and likely closer to six months, and then they'd be laying Roger at the mercy of a jury decision.

"Roger, I'm not going to tell you there won't be consequences to this," Dave said, "because that would be a lie. After you get out of here, if you slip up in any way during the next four years, the sentence will be unsuspended and you'll serve the rest of those two years plus whatever time is warranted for what puts you back here. And having an aggravated assault on your record will make it very difficult to get hired for anything, get a loan, etcetera."

Roger could tell Dave had more to add, so he stayed quiet.

"But by the same token, there's no guarantee if we go to trial you won't somehow end up with a 20-year prison sentence. While I think that is highly unlikely, stranger things have happened in the criminal justice system. If you take the

317

deal, you'll be back with your boy before summertime. You can sell the cabin, move somewhere nicer than here and start working on some better memories. Put these last few years behind you."

Roger thought for a moment before asking the question, "Is there any scenario where DCS decides I'm not fit to be Adam's guardian?"

"That's why Micah Sanders wants to visit you later this week," Dave said. "My feeling is he has a pretty good understanding of how strong your relationship with Adam is, but he needs to see it for himself. In the next month or so, he'll have to make a placement recommendation to the juvenile magistrate, who will decide what happens with Adam after you finish serving your time."

"His recommendation means that much?" Roger asked. "Isn't he just a volunteer?"

Dave nodded. "He's a well-trained volunteer from an organization that is thought of very highly. His recommendation carries a lot of weight with both DCS and the judge."

Roger thought for only a second more. "Take the deal and set up the meeting with the CASA," he said, feeling the hints of the smile form on his face. Dave smiled back and pushed some paperwork and a pen across for Roger to sign.

"We'll file all of this with the court tomorrow, and barring any unexpected circumstances, the judge should sign off on it in the next day or two," Dave said. "Once that's done, I'll coordinate the meeting with Micah Sanders."

After Roger signed, Dave stuffed the file into his briefcase and stood up to leave. Roger stood, grabbed his friend by the arm and hugged him tightly. "Dave, I can never repay you for what you've done, but I'm going to do everything in my power to try."

Dave could hear his friend was choking back tears and was surprised to see he was doing the same. He looked his college buddy in the eye, nodded his head and walked out of the jail.

****

The week went by much faster for Roger than the previous week. He learned from Dave on Thursday morning the judge accepted the plea agreement and he could begin the countdown to the day he'd get to walk out of the jail – no doubt for the last time of his life – and hopefully hug his son and start their new lives together. Dave had promised to try to arrange a visit from Adam over the upcoming weekend, but first he would meet with Micah Sanders – Adam's CASA – for the first time on Friday morning.

Roger was led to the visitor's room – yet again – and this time was seated before the guards allowed Micah to enter. When he did, Roger stood on the opposite side of the table and extended his hand as he introduced himself to the man who would recommend whether he was fit to take care of his son upon his release. Roger had rehearsed repeatedly what he wanted to say, but as he met Micah for the first time, he forgot everything he practiced and decided it was best just to be honest and be himself.

"How's Adam doing?" Roger asked before Micah was even settled in his chair.

Micah smiled. "He's settling in really nicely. I met with him again yesterday, and I think he's adjusting."

Roger hoped Micah would say something like, "he sure misses you" or "Adam said to say hi," but Micah offered nothing of the sort. Instead, Roger sat quietly and waited for Micah to initiate the meeting.

"So, as you know, it's my job as a Court Appointed Special Advocate, to get to know this case from all sides, learn as much as I can about all the factors involved in the situation and then make a recommendation to the court as to the safest long-term placement for Adam," Micah said. He knew Roger already knew this, but he felt he should make it official. "I've already spoken with Adam several times, have reviewed the files DCS has compiled, and I'll continue to meet with Adam and monitor his progress while he's in foster care."

Roger smiled, more easily than he expected. "I really appreciate that you're there to help watch out for what's best for my son. Through all of this, he's all I'm really worried about. In fact, if it weren't for Adam, I probably would have gone to trial because I really wouldn't care what happened to me."

The comment seemed to sit well with Micah. "He speaks really highly of you," he told Roger, "and he misses you more than I could ever tell you."

Roger smiled at the comment he had been waiting to hear, but at the same time, it hurt, and he fought back a tear. Micah saw this, and looked away to give Roger a chance to compose himself.

"Mr. Sanders…"

"Please, call me Micah."

"Micah," Roger said, "Adam probably told you this, but our life was pretty great until his mom died a few years ago. After that, I really messed up. Drinking, drugs, bringing that monster of a brother-in-law of mine into our lives. I can't deny any of it."

Micah nodded, encouraging Roger to continue.

"But the one constant through all of that was Adam. And when I was too messed up to see it, my little boy grew into a strong young man and stayed by my side, willing me to come back and be the dad I used to. He has been my inspiration, my only real reason for living, since Annie died. I promise you – I absolutely assure you – that when I get out of here in May, nothing will ever again come between me and Adam. I will be the man he wants and needs me to be. I will be the father he deserves."

Micah smiled again, and Roger found himself thankful his son had such a good advocate on his side. The conversation continued between the two men for close to an hour before Micah excused himself and walked out of the room. Before he left, he told Roger that he had some more follow-up work to do, but he thought he'd be ready to make a recommendation on placement in the next two weeks.

Chapter Forty-One

On April 4, 2015, Roger Durkin, with his friend and attorney Dave Carter, walked out of the Lands County Jail for the first time since entering in late September. Before leaving he had one last breakfast with his friend, Sandy, scheduled to be released in just two more weeks. The two promised to get together and have a "real breakfast" on the outside, but deep down both knew that probably would never happen.

As he walked down the stairs and crossed the street to the parking lot, he saw two cars – Dave's Mercedes and an older model Buick SUV. As he crossed the street, one of the back doors to the Buick opened and out climbed Adam. Even though he visited Roger about once a month during his time in jail, Adam looked taller and stronger than at any point during Roger's time inside.

Before he could turn and face his dad, Adam was besieged by Joanie, who threw her arms around his neck and gave him a big kiss on the cheek. "I'm sure going to miss you," she said. "Will you at least come and visit?" Roger couldn't hear what Adam said in return, but he saw him nod his head. Joanie jumped back in the car, and Adam waved to Billy and Sara before moving to the front window, where Mrs. Dayne sat behind the wheel with Mr. Dayne in the passenger seat.

"Thank you both so much for everything," Adam said, and this time, Roger could hear everything. "I consider myself very lucky to have ended up in your house."

Roger couldn't hear the reply from the front seat, but he could see Mrs. Dayne was wiping her eyes as she rolled up the window, put the car in gear and drove out of the parking lot.

When the Buick disappeared, Adam turned and faced his father. He didn't run up to him as Roger had expected. Instead, the two walked to each other, both with dry eyes and hugged, neither wanting to be the first to let the other go. After what seemed like five minutes, Roger whispered in Adam's ear, "It's going to be different this time, buddy."

Adam didn't reply at first, but after a moment, he pulled his head off Roger's shoulder and looked him squarely in the eye. In that moment, Roger saw his son was no longer a little boy. The circumstances of his life over the past few years and the awful situations in which he was placed turned Adam from a starry eyed little boy into a mature and strong beyond his age young man.

"I don't want it to be different," Adam said. "I just want it to be us again."

"Me too, buddy," Roger replied. "Me too."

The End

Acknowledgements

While this is a work of fiction, the basis of this story is very real. All over America, Court Appointed Special Advocates and Guardians Ad Litem work every day to ensure every abused or neglected child is well cared for and placed in the best possible situation. One of the most impactful days of my life was the day I joined the board of Advocates for Children, the CASA agency for Bartholomew, Jennings and Decatur counties in Indiana. There, Therese Miller, the executive director for 26 years at the time of this writing, and her staff work tirelessly to make sure every child in this unfortunate circumstance finds a safe, permanent and loving home as quickly as possible. I can't thank Therese, Rick Scalf, John Nickoll and the other incredible people enough for the work they do and for inspiring this story.

In addition to her professional job, Therese spent several hours with me sharing her experiences, answering questions to fill in the holes for this story. Therese, Advocates for Children – and the many kids you have impacted during your time there – are very lucky to have such a strong, passionate person working to make the world a better place.

To my readers, thank you for taking the time to read this story and learn more about this incredible organization. If you're looking for a way to make a difference in a world that just gets crazier every day, please consider signing up for your local CASA organization. While it is a big commitment, and certainly emotional, trust me when I say there is nothing you can do that would make a bigger difference. There isn't a lot each of us can do to slow the rampant use of drugs and alcohol that leads to so many cases of child abuse, but the biggest difference we can make is changing the world for each child caught up in that web with the hope that someday they will not go the same route with their children.

Another friend who offered some advice and support on the novel was Bryce Wagner, an assistant district attorney for the Bartholomew County prosecutor's office at the time. Bryce walked me through depraved heart after I explained the first 100 pages of the book, and he really helped set the tone for the direction it would take in the second half of the story.

I need to give a special thank you to the people who read and critiqued this story before it went to publication, including my mom and dad. They are responsible for Adam's vacation memories, as they shared so many experiences with me and my two brothers when we were kids, including travel to all 48 continental United States. What an awesome childhood, and what great memories we made as a family. Parents, take your kids on vacation as much as you can. They don't have to be the most expensive trips, and they don't have to be to exotic places, but the time shared together and the memories those times create are priceless.

I want to thank my friend, Robert Campbell, owner of Campbell Creative Group, and designer of the cover of this book. Robert's company produces amazing custom artwork of wildlife, people, and just about anything else – on demand – and his designs are features at zoos, museums, art galleries and attractions around the world. I feel he really captured the essence of Adam and his struggle in the beautiful cover he created.

Special thanks also to my Aunt Pam Rossetti, an avid reader who has critiqued a lot of writing for friends and acquaintances. When I saw her in New Jersey I hadn't yet started the re-write and, frankly, after a year and a half writing and thinking about this story, I was a little tired of it. Her positive review and suggestions helped motivate me to get back on it and finish up.

Thanks go out as well to my friends in Columbus whom I told about the book as I worked on it. All of them have been so supportive, and having that kind of love behind you makes every day better.

Lastly, thanks to my incredible wife, Pam. In addition to her being my primary editor and my everyday reality check, she is my number one fan and my best friend in the world. Since I still worked full time while I was writing this, she sat patiently on the weekend mornings when I had time to write and, for the most part, she kept quiet as the thoughts translated from my mind to the keyboard. I could not have found a better partner in life, and I consider myself very lucky to have her.

Again, to everyone that has read this book, thank you.

February 1, 2017

www.ingramcontent.com/pod-product-compliance
Lightning Source LLC
Chambersburg PA
CBHW070215260626
47160CB00002B/560

* 9 7 8 0 6 9 2 8 4 4 2 4 3 *